UNSUNG : UNSAID.

SYD AND NICK IN ABSENTIA

ROB CHAPMAN

Front cover concept – The author
Front cover design – Cheriton W. Bishop 111
https://www.9thplanetdesign.co.uk

Cover images of Syd Barrett and Nick Drake used with permission

© Estate of Mick Rock
https://www.mickrock.com

© Keith Morris
https://www.keithmorrisphoto.co.uk

My eternal thanks and gratitude to Pati Rock and Sevrin Morris.

Copy editing – Derek Walmsley

Contents

"All my perceptions vanish, the material universe sinks into silence and night – I subsist, however, and cannot help myself subsisting. I am still there with the organic sensations which come to me from the surface and from the interior of my body, with the recollections which my past perceptions have left behind them – nay, with the impression, most positive and full, of the void I have just made about me". Henri Bergson. *Creative Evolution.*

"It is probably true that a man remains for ever unknown to us and that there is in him something irreducible that escapes us. But *practically* I know men and recognise them by their behaviour, by the totality of their deeds, by the consequences caused in life by their presence. Likewise, all those irrational feelings which offer no purchase to analysis. I can define them *practically*, appreciate them *practically*, by gathering together the sum of their consequences in the domain of the intelligence, by seizing and noting all their aspects, by outlining their universe". Albert Camus, *The Myth Of Sisyphus*

"Nothing, as experience, arises as absence of someone or something. No friends, no relationships, no pleasure, no meaning in life, no ideas, no mirth, no money. As applied to parts of the body – no breast, no penis, no good or bad contents – emptiness. The list is in principle, endless. Take anything and imagine its absence." RD Laing, *The Politics Of Experience*

STRANGE MEETING #1

"Could you pass the salt please?"
    "He passes the salt."

The man who was asked to pass the salt did so as requested and in the act of doing so said "He passes the salt" as if complying with a stage instruction, as if he were in a play, which he was anyway.

The man who asked for the salt to be passed spoke in barely a whisper. He had hesitated regarding his choice of words, had in fact deliberated over whether he should utilise words at all. Initially he thought of saying "Would you mind awfully" but decided that was far too formal for both the occasion and the surroundings. Then he considered "If you would be so kind" but this too seemed inappropriate, sarcastic even if he got the tone slightly wrong. Time passed and still he couldn't decide how to ask for the salt. He thought of making some sort of indicative gesture but his body froze at the thought of anything that extravagant. He contemplated moving to the empty table opposite where there was salt, but realised that this would appear terribly rude, and besides, by the time he came to this conclusion a young couple had walked in and sat at the unoccupied space. Eventually, he decided that he was over thinking the entire procedure, that his mind was becoming a jumble of possibilities, none of which he wished to enact and so he took the plunge and in his barely a whisper voice said "Could you pass the salt please?"

He'd rather the man sitting at his table hadn't joined him at all. For the longest time he hadn't. He'd just stood with his plate in the narrow aisle between the seating, still looking up at the menu board as if there was something he'd neglected to ask for. Every now and again he broke off from his stare to peck at his eggs and bacon with the fork he was holding in his right hand. It was a slow, thoughtful motion as if his mind had been elsewhere and he was now startled to find that he held a plate in his hand, and must out of necessity interrupt his contemplation and for the moment at least pursue the act of eating food. At one point he took two measured steps closer to the counter and looked at the cake display. "Do you have elderberry tart?" he asked in a flat, unengaged voice, a sort of drawling, dry-mouthed monotone, well-spoken but devoid of light or shade. The café owner, busy and somewhat bad tempered, merely ignored him and shouted over his shoulder. "Table three. Cold ham and mash." "Do you have elderberry tart?" he repeated, better modulated second time, more sing-song. "Only what's on the board mate," replied the owner, returning to the kitchenette to bark orders at some unseen put upon assistant. It was at this point that the man who spoke initially with the drawling dry-mouthed voice and then the well-modulated voice came and seated himself at the table occupied by the man who spoke in barely a whisper. He sprinkled an indecent amount of salt on his bacon and eggs, placed the salt next to his knife, paused for a moment to stare at the arrangement on his plate and then tucked in with relish. "He tucked in with relish," he said, as if complying with a stage instruction, as if he was an actor in a play, which he was anyway.

The man who spoke in barely a whisper stared hard at his own plate and desperately wished to be elsewhere. There was something unsettling about the whole affair. It wasn't just the peculiar demeanour and the way the bacon and eggs man stood for such a long time in the centre of the small café, it was the way he was dressed, too. In all other aspects but his neckwear he was turned out conventionally a la mode for the time, hippie cool, black velvet jacket, maroon shirt, blue crushed velvet trousers, snakeskin boots, hair straggly and semi-long. Alarmingly though, the whole outfit was offset, unbalanced to the point of sartorial derangement even, by a huge yellow kipper tie. And it wasn't even the kipper tie per se. It was what was embossed upon the tie, a cartoon print of Fred Flintstone, clothed in his trademark leopard skin, arms outstretched in a yabba-dabba-doo gesture of warm embrace. That was the red flag, the warning sign. No matter how hard the barely a whisper man concentrated on his own food, he sensed the presence of Fred Flintstone in such uncomfortable proximity that he could almost feel the caveman's breath. He was only there for a liaison of convenience with his dope dealer, and now he wished he wasn't there at all. Why couldn't his dealer come to Belgravia like he normally did? House calls were always more convenient for the gentry. Choose your poison and nullify in plush surroundings. Sink into opiated dreams. Watch the lilac lava bubble.

They were in the small café on the top floor of the market in

Kensington High Street. The barely a whisper man had agreed to meet his contact here, just this once, a convenient rendezvous point he was assured, arrangements swift, low-key and business-like and all carried out, again he was reassured, under the complicit eye of the owner, who for all his abruptness of demeanour was accommodating and in for a cut. Now the barely a whisper man couldn't remember when the dealer said he would be there. He did say morning, didn't he? Mornings are always quiet, he said. But did he give a specific time? It's not like a drug dealer to be tardy and unpunctual, he rued sardonically. He raked his thoughts for some sense of schedule. Nothing but ennui and existential dread. And now, added to that, the hideously intrusive image of a cartoon Flintstone, barely inches from his averted eyes.

Kensington Market was a three-floor bazaar of fashionable attire and trinkets. Upon entry the senses were assailed by the cheaply cured sheepskin stench of Afghan coats and the heady potency of incense. As the visitor ventured further in, a ramshackle clutter of partitioned stalls revealed themselves in all their finery. Kensington Market sold a range of accessories catering for every micro tribe. There was leather biker wear, army surplus gear, glam Biba satin and tat, Indian print ethnicity, tie dye, hair dye, two tone flares, dungarees, grandad vests, tasselled suede jackets, stack heeled boots, silk scarves, bleached jeans, cheese cloth smocks and maxi skirts. There were candle stalls and jewellery stalls, perfume counters, head shop accessories, tarot readers, pub mirrors, paintings with frames and posters without. Each boutique row or corner alcove was lit in a random patchwork of garish or dim illumination, depending on which part of the premises you were located.

Such was the labyrinthine layout of the market, with its myriad half floors, its ambiguous exit and entry points, and its maze-like mishmash of piecemeal expansion, that it was quite possible to misremember one's route, double back up or down, or stumble across some unexpected three step mezzanine and then get lost completely. Unless the customer had entered with a specific purchase in mind it was best to wander without purpose or designation. To acquire one's wardrobe from an arbitrary selection of stalls was to signify that you belonged to all sartorial tribes and yet to none of them – mix and match montage not yet being the thing, and collaging still largely confined to artists. The audio soundtrack of the premises was cerebral or brash depending on the tastes of the stall holder. Radios played the post-Christmas banalities of the pop charts, seasonal hits that were still hanging around in the Top 30 like so many deflated balloons and unfinished Party Sevens of stale pale ale. The more selective stalls played compilation cassettes, mates' demo tapes or acetates. One stall, in keeping with a certain retro 1920s vibe that was prevalent, played scratchy 78s on a wind-up gramophone. The harshly modulated blare of the Charleston and assorted trad jazz hot-steppers offered a pleasing contrast to the predictable mainstream fare of Radio 1 and Capital Radio. Some stall holders were trying to build an empire, some were biding time till Daddy's trust fund money came through, others were in retreat from obligation to the big bad world of conventional employment. One or two would go on to be pop stars and already were in their heads.

And perched above all of this, through an alcove that one chanced upon as if it were a Narnian forest clearing, was a small café with room for just six tables, three up each side, one of which, middle right, was occupied by a man who spoke in barely a whisper and a man who had chosen to offset his modish garb with a Fred Flintstone kipper tie.

The bacon and eggs man, for his part, gazed at the dishevelled man opposite and thought he looked in negligible health. His pallor was grey, his deep-set olive eyes, when you could see them, seemed permanently narrowed in suspicion. His dark hair was greasy and lank, and he appeared to regard the contents of his plate with an aloofness that verged on disdain. He had asked for the English breakfast and hurried to his seat, thinking perhaps that to hang about by the counter would invite conversation. And now, some while later, the fried bread and shrivelled mushrooms lay untouched and the tomatoes had gone cold. Only the scrambled eggs and baked beans had been given more than passing attention. A residue smear of baked bean sat like badly applied orange lipstick around his mouth. There were crumbs of scrambled egg on the frayed edges of his brown polo neck jumper. Presently he gave up on his food and turned his attention to rolling a cigarette. He took out a beautifully engraved metal tobacco tin from his coat pocket, peeled a wheat straw Rizla from the packet and began shakily crumbling Golden Virginia into the paper. The bacon and eggs guy licked grease from his own upper lip and studied the tin in front of him. Silver gilt. Elegantly decorative latticework and heraldic chevrons flaked and faded by time and use.

Having rolled his cigarette the barely a whisper man attempted to extricate a match from a box of Swan Vestas, but his left hand was shaking so badly that some of the contents spilled on to the table. When a series of matches refused to strike the bacon and eggs man took a blue Zippo lighter from his pocket and sparked up a flame in front of him which the barely a whisper man leaned into gratefully.

"Thank you," he hardly said.

"I like your tobacco tin," said the bacon and eggs man returning to his food. "Did you design it yourself?"

"A friend," said the barely a whisper man drawing nervously on his roll up and, for want of somewhere better to look, staring down at the unfinished contents of his plate.

"Where is Alex?" he thought. "He said morning. It must be 12 by now. Did he say morning?" The fraught situation induced frightened nervous chatter in his head. "I wish this man would just go, and take that frightful tie with him. Will Alex even come to my table if he sees him here? He'll think he's the drug squad. Perhaps he is the drug squad. Must go. I'll go".

He does not go.

"Did your friend go to art college?"
Oh God, he's speaking again. Please shut up. Please go.

He does not go.

Say something. Perhaps if I just say something it will be sufficient to placate him and he'll eat up and leave. He's nearly finished his food. He seems to have a ravenous appetite. Surely, he'll leave.

"Yes," said the barely a whisper man presently. "Epsom."

"Nice silverwork. I went to Camberwell," said the bacon and eggs man.

Now look what you've done. Goodness me. You've started a conversation. We might be here all day now. Is that what you want? I'll go. To the car. And wait there. Then come back. And he'll be gone. But then I might miss Alex. I'm trapped. Never again. This is unendurable agony. I'm trapped. I have to converse. It would seem rude not to.

"I took English," he muttered, as if to himself, an involuntary impulse. "Fitzwilliam."

"I was in Cambridge," said the bacon and eggs man. "Not the University. I mean I just grew up there. School. And then some college."

This uneasy discourse, with its halting proximity to conversation, was shattered by the café owner coming round and noisily clearing plates and cutlery from the newly vacated table opposite.

"I gave up," said the bacon and eggs man presently.

Barely a whisper man looked at him blankly. The bacon and eggs man's eyes registered for the first time. Deep dark holes. Brown flecked with emerald green. Traumatised gaze. Imprints of frozen fear branded onto dilated pupils. It occurred to him for the first time that the man might not be from the drug squad after all. Not with those eyes. There are only so many ways of going native. This man presented perhaps a different, more familiar kind of damage.

"College I mean. My art studies. I gave up my studies."

"Yes, so did I."

Oh, listen to me now. We're virtually the best of friends. Getting on like a house on fire. A veritable cabal of drop-outs. Where is Alex?

The café owner went behind his counter and selected a cassette tape. *Astral Weeks* by Van Morrison. Momentarily soothed by the interweaving countermelodies, the barely a whisper man relaxed a little. Nevertheless, his stiffened body language continued to discourage unwelcome dialogue. Head bowed, his hands made prayer shapes, clasped tightly as if he was in religious contemplation, which in a way he was. He stared at his roll up.

"Do you like this music?"

Oh God, he's talking to me again. Say something. Then go. Just go. Forget Alex. Just go.

"Yes," he said, softly, "very much. Do you?"

"I prefer something with a jumpy beat," said the bacon and eggs man, wiping rapidly at his chin with a paper towel as if trying to erase all memory of food.

Just at that moment, having made his rounds on the lower floors and carrying enough folding money to warrant further questioning at the station, Alex walked in. He glanced briefly at the barely a whisper man, a subtle acknowledgement, be with you presently, dealer's prerogative. Seating himself at the recently vacated table opposite, he rummaged in a bag and took out a plain white LP and a clutch of eight-track cartridges. "Got you the new Dylan bootleg and some decent sounds for your car, Carl," he said to the owner who came out to greet him. "Machine's bust," said Carl. "What can I get you?"

At this point the bacon and eggs man jumped up suddenly from his seat and asked the owner "Do you have a water closet?" "The toilet's through there," said Carl, unphased and used to dealing with a regular array of eccentrics on a daily basis.

"Nice tie man," said Alex.

"Thank you. I'm collecting the set," said bacon and eggs man, stopping to contemplate his purchase. "I got it from a tourist shop. The one near Harrods. They do all the cartoon ones."

"Up for the day are you man?" said Alex. "Touristing?"

"Oh no," said the bacon and eggs man. "I've just moved to Chelsea. Not fully though."

"Well anyway, nice tie all the same," said Alex.

"Thank you," said the bacon and egg man, reverting to his dry mouth monotone. "It's nothing to walk home about though."

"Through there. The toilet," reiterated Carl impatiently.

"Strange guy," said Alex as bacon and eggs man headed for the lavatory.

"At least he bought something. It's the ones who sit there all day that annoy me. I've got a business to run. I don't put music on half the time. It only encourages them. They only sit there and listen to it if I do that. It's not the fucking Biba roof garden. Do you want a cup of tea?"

All this said in earshot of the customers.

"Yeah I've got time for a quick Lapsang," said Alex.

"None of your foreign muck. I've only got English tea," said Carl. "English tea from India." He discharged the phrase with something resembling half a smile and went off to locate the blue jar of Lapsang Souchong that he put aside for discerning customers.

Alex went over and joined barely a whisper guy at the table and dipped quickly into an inside coat pocket for goods that he, too, put aside for discerning customers. "Got you some nice Temple Balls, Nicky," he said. With the transaction swiftly completed and five pound notes passed nervously under the table, he got up to resume his place with Carl.

Nicky took this as his opportunity to get up and leave but as he did so Carl emerged from the back with a hot cup of china tea and reminded him politely that he still hadn't paid yet.

"Oh, I'm...."
"That's okay mate. Tea and the English. 45p."

Nicky flushed red at his indiscretion and fumbled for change. Realising that he had just given the last of his funds to Alex for a wrap of Temple Balls, he scratched nervously at his pocket linings for any evidence of coins. "I think I might have some loose change in my car," he heard himself starting to say, but this merely compounded his panic and humiliation. Just then, bacon and eggs man came back from the toilet and walked up to the counter again. "I hear the elderberry tart here is excellent," he said. "Only what's on the menu," said Carl, having the measure of him by now and suspecting this may all be an elaborate put on. "In that case I'll have one of your excellent Brook Bonds," he said. "45p mate," Carl said to Nicky, going into the back to make more tea.

Nicky, flustered and rigid with fear, looked in vain for Alex to help him, out but Alex was now occupied at another table deep in conversation about Dylan bootlegs. "Let me get this," said bacon and eggs man kindly.

"Oh I couldn't possibly allow..."
Bacon and eggs man placed a pound note on the counter and said "Would you like more tea?"

Feeling it would be awfully rude to refuse an offer from a charitable man who had just helped him out of an awkward mess Nicky acquiesced. Carl came out with teas and placed them down on the counter. "I'll just get your change, mate," he said agreeably. "Oh no, you must keep the change," said the bacon and eggs man, sounding somewhat affronted.

The two men went and sat back at their table and settled into a mutually appreciated hush, agreeable habitués of each other's silence. They slowly sipped their tea and assumed the kind of disposition which suggested that introversion came easily to both of them, and that what had gone before was more than enough interaction for one day. It was lunchtime by now and stall holders drifted in from downstairs, filling the café. A Dutch woman came over from an adjacent table with an unlit roll up and in a confident baritone asked, "I'm sorry. I want to smoke but I have no fire." Bacon and eggs man smiled warmly at this and offered her his Zippo lighter. Nicky smiled too at the broken English. It reminded him of more carefree and sociable times, not long past, in France. Trying to brush up on his second language and stumbling gamely through many a harmless verbal faux pas.

Carl put on some Doors. Head music for the lunchtime clientele. The candle shop holder and the biker ware stall holder nodded reverentially as Jim Morrison laid bare his Oedipal complex and his habit of waking before dawn. The music unfurled in a hazy drone and lay its healing hands on the denizens of the Kensington Market café. 12 minutes passed. Agreeable vibrations rippled from table to table. Calm settled on one and all and there was an exquisite quietness about the room. The music having reached its climax, there was a brief reverential pause in all conversation. It was the bacon and eggs man who broke the silence. "All that effort to produce something that tedious," he muttered. "I mean imagine making it to the end of that and thinking you've learned anything."

With that, he got up and walked towards the exit. Nicky watched the curious loping bounce of his retreating gait, a heel walker like his friend Lucy. A parodic flounce almost. He pondered what the bacon and eggs man had said, this man he initially thought a perfect fool, then drug squad, then mad, then generous. He was still thinking about it when he reached his car, parked in a square just off the High Street behind the market. "You can use my allocated space while I'm away," his friend Luke had said. "Just square it with the lodge warden." But Nicky hadn't done that. Too much complicated conversation to negotiate. He took the parking ticket from behind the windscreen wiper, carefully folded it, put it with the others in the glove compartment of his Austin 1300, and made his escape from London. Once he was free from the clutches of the city his route took him up the A40 through the Colne Valley and the Chilterns and on into the gently undulating countryside of Oxfordshire. The fuel gauge pointed perilously close to red, every fourth field lay fallow and the rolling hills sat barren and stark against blue grey clouds that threatened snow. He thought once more about the peculiar man in the frightful Fred Flintstone tie. What a peculiar man, he thought. And such a frightful tie.

The bacon and eggs man loped purposefully up Kensington High Street towards Knightsbridge. At the Albert Memorial he cornered neatly into Hyde Park, rounded the Serpentine and made for Speakers' Corner. The park was sparsely attended and a harsh wind cut up rough. Winter's personae played out their allocated parts in all their starkness; the trees, bare and unbudded, bent rheumatically in the easterly gusts. He took the underpass beneath the traffic and emerged on the south side of Oxford Street. People scurried, suitably attired against the elements, in and out of shops. Inadequately dressed and buffeted by the breeze, he hurried towards the Charing Cross Road. At a certain intersection point, it might have been by Bond Street station, it might have been at Regent Street, a half-familiar voice called out to him. "Where are you going?" It might have been David O'List and the answer might have been "To the other side of London. I must hurry." It might have been Noel Redding and the answer might have been "I left the city of Manchester five weeks ago precisely." It might have been Roy Harper and the answer might have been "Further than you could possibly imagine." It might have been a BBC radio producer and the answer might have been a cold stare and silence. All these were possible and remain so. The options change slightly in every retelling. London too is a character that thinks it's in a play and is anyway. It is dress rehearsal, scenery, cast and crew. It is afternoon matinee, bit-part player, moving backdrop and best supporting actor up for nominations.

When he reached the Charing Cross Road the man who ate bacon and eggs and had paid for a distressed stranger's meal walked into Top Gear in Denmark Street. He gazed for some time at the array of guitars on the wall and presently asked the young assistant if he might try the Gibson SG Junior, no not that one, the one with the extra pickup. Holding the Gibson as if it were a stranger to him, he plucked indiscriminately at the unamplified strings. "It's not what I'm used to," he said softly and put it aside. Then he asked the young assistant if he might play the Sunburst Strat without the tremolo arm. He carefully tuned top and bottom E but none of the other strings and strummed hesitantly. "The strings are somewhat slack," he said as if to himself. A young long-haired guy who was purchasing a fuzz pedal turned around to look at him inquisitively. When he picked up a third guitar, a Telecaster Deluxe, and plugged it into a small practice amp, the store manager murmured to his young assistant. "He'll want this one. You watch. It's always the third one." A brief burst of Bo Diddley shuffle beat rang around the shop, followed by a sudden atonal cluster of chords that followed no regular pattern of progression. The playing concluded with a few bars of open-string strumming, calm, harp-like in the spread of its caress. Then he walked up to the counter with the guitar. The store manager and his young assistant exchanged knowing glances. "It's

260 quid that one," said the store manager. "There's a second hand one in the rack there for 195 if you're interested," added the young assistant. "Same model. Only came in last week." The man who had chosen the third guitar lay it flat on the counter and said nothing. "Just be a moment," said the store manager going into a back room and picking up a phone. "Bryan, it's Jim here at Top Gear. Yeah, I've got Syd in again... not for a while no. He's picked up a Telecaster and I'm pretty sure he'll... no, not for a few weeks. Not since before Christmas... has he? I didn't know that. Shall I... okay I'll stick it on the account then. It's 260. I'll tell him then... yeah, thanks mate... no, it's quiet. Kipper season, you know how it is after Christmas. Business stinks. Yeah, of course. No, you get the other call. No, that's okay. Yeah. I'll talk to you soon man. Yeah of course. Take it easy. You too. Bye."

Back at Kensington Market, the café had emptied out leaving a less stressed Carl and the entrepreneurial Alex to shoot the breeze about under-the-counter Dylan recordings. "One day when they come to write the histories of these times they'll have to talk to the drug dealers and the bootleggers," said Alex. "You'll get a very one-sided story otherwise."

LIKE FATHER LIKE MUM

Consider these two young men. Regard them in every aspect. Compare and contrast their differences and similarities. Study their deportment and disposition, the manifestations of their strengths and frailties. The one bounces on his toes, spring-heeled as he walks, nervous urgency in his stride, full pelt, fast sprinter. The other, taller, hunches into himself, shuffling gait, crouch steps set against the world, stoops to touch the flowers that bend.

Both are the products of comfortable upper middle class background and breeding. Impeccable manners. Inherited traits. Well-spoken and spoken of. Nick, a colonial child, Burma born and fled, and lately in flight from his birthright. Syd, from East Anglian flat land stock. Black earth, chalk hills, the sedge and dredge of the Fens. His late father Max, an eminent pathologist and part of a golden generation of medical students in the 1920s and 30s. Nick's father Rodney, the son of a Harley Street physician, trained as a construction engineer. Posting to Rangoon. Met his future wife out there, Molly, the second daughter of the Province's Deputy Commissioner. Doing the dashing debonair shall we dance duet with the shy girl. Returned in 1951 to a post-war rationed Britain.

Imported Nanny in residence. One of the family. Residing in a comfy spacious pile called Far Leys. Shakespeare terrain. The literary pastoral and an Arden both mythical and actual. Grand piano in the sitting room. Expansive gardens. Languid strolls across the mole-hilled croquet green of a vast lawn, spread on a gentle incline down to a meandering plashy brook. Well-tended beds and borders. Privet-walled privacy and shade. Weathered stone. Distant hills.

The Barretts' Cambridge town house is a little less grand but no less luxurious in its way. Substantial reception hall. Cloakroom. Study. Range-warmed kitchen leading to a garden room. Bedrooms you can spread out in. Galleried landings you can hang a row of paintings on, ride a tricycle along. Dank dark cellar and attic eaves full of cobwebbed mystery. A third of an acre to play in outside, patio and pond. Syd's late father, when not scurrying to his study to concern himself with the latest scientific papers on morbid anatomy and histology, used to be a keen amateur botanist and ornithologist. He had his own key to the Botanical Gardens across the road. Max was also a member of the Cambridge Philharmonic Society, a chorister, and an accomplished pianist. A dab hand at watercolours, too.

Both homes display strong maternal bonds. Syd and Nick are both close to their sisters. Syd's younger sibling Rosemary (Roe) will train as a nurse. There they are on the beach as children. Little boy Roger, not yet Syd, holding a protective parasol. Padding through wet sand. Nick's older sister Gabrielle (Gay or sometimes Birdy) beckoned up to London and the lure of the bright lights. RADA trained. Entre into 'that world'. Films and plays. Mother Molly is an able pianist and poet. Sings in a wistful breathy voice of how things come and go. Syd's mother, Win, a charitable big-hearted accommodating woman, runs the local Girl Guides troop and the house is frequently full of bustle, bonhomie and organised kitchen chaos, particularly when the girls are earning their cookery badge. Hills Road Cambridge like Far Leys, Tanworth-In-Arden is open house for a wide circle of friends and colleagues. Elevated conversation. Tinkling tea cups. Sing-song soirees around the baby grand. The Barrett household takes in lodgers, mostly females from Homerton Ladies College, but also a future notable or two. Everyone is very well connected and very well informed. Intelligence is a birthright not readily abused.

The upper middle class had undergone considerable change throughout the first half of the 20th century but some of the reassuringly dependable rituals remained intact. A certain easy ambience prevailed. Deck chairs on the terrace. Luncheon parties and drinks on the lawn. Chin-chin. Any relative hardship or temporary dip in fortunes is soon smoothed over and put down to jolly bad luck. Ingenuity usually triumphs over adversity. British pluck travels well. When it comes to talented offsprings there is an absence of scrutiny or judgement, only encouragement and subtle steerage. Excellence thrives in such circumstances. Quirks (in modest proportion) are abided, idiosyncrasies endured. The heedless and the flighty are permissible within reason. Unpleasantness is generally avoided. Tolerance is boundless, both tolerance as kindness and tolerance as a regime, a benign smothering and stultifying. One might grow maladjusted within the confines of such material security. Wealth and privilege can prove insufficient safeguards when talent turns to something more troubled. Out there, the world can be harsh and unforgiving.

These are secure lives and lifestyles that resonate with love, literature and music. And yet. And yet. Each man is slowly coming adrift from his moorings. It becomes harder to ward off the dark fog that settles. Both are drawn increasingly towards hermitic solitude. From late 1972 Syd is chiefly domiciled in London. Rarely going home. Ostensibly engaged in a music career that is currently on hold and has lapsed into languor and lethargy. Social contact is dwindling to chance encounters and avoidance. Intimacy is scant, no girlfriends, no bandmates, nothing ventured. Nick meanwhile pursues a sporadic erratic shuttle service between Tanworth-in-Arden and London and sometimes points beyond. Taking off in his car, driven by who knows what impulse, dead of night or early morn, destination unknown. Rarely accounting for his motives or whereabouts. The great mystery with Syd is what does he do all day, how does he fill those uncreative hours? The mystery with Nick is where does he flee to and who does he know? And do any of those he knows know any of the others he knows? Under normal circumstances the only people who live willingly like this are terrorist cells.

Boys once. Ordinarily mortal before the cloak of charisma was donned and the crown of thorns betrothed. Nick excelling at track and field at Marlborough. Captain of the first XV at rugby. Photos of a well-groomed, straight-backed smart young man in his uniform. There he is in the Cadet Force band, second row from the left, second from the back, carrying his saxophone with measured military precision. Syd a keen scout, tents pegged and pitched in the beech woods, summer vacation campfires and sing-songs in coastal inlets. Sailing on the Norfolk Broads. Knowledgeable about tacking, headwinds and valve pumps. Swallows and Amazons world. Describes Dean Moriarty from *On The Road* in a letter to his girlfriend as 'a mad big head'. Intelligent, resourceful and quick-witted but not intellectually gifted. Regular kid. Those same letters are full of the gushy argot typical of a love-struck 16 year old. Approving references to Joyce Grenfell and Charlie Drake in among the day in the life minutiae. Nick is similarly unelevated in his youth. Kept a sweet little diary log of songs liked and loathed. 'My Gramophone Records' ranked and rated. Sarcastic ripostes and arm's length approvals. A callow and earnest universe where twee love songs are considered "soppy" or even worse "soppy and utterly silly". Where "not all that bad" passes as praise. Expresses a schoolboy liking for Nero and the Gladiators at a time when all bands have names like that. His letters home during his first term at university spill the same aura-free admissions. Thinking of joining the classical guitar society. Seemingly disappointed that there doesn't seem to be a college karate club. Had to be coaxed into Cambridge with letters to and from the right people. The old school tie. The privilege gift. Bright but lazy. Reticent to the point of dull in class. Not what you would call natural Uni material. Not exactly a willing recipient of all that is laid out before him despite the obligatory right word in the right ear. Not what you'd call ungrateful, either, but aesthetically compromised you might say when music not books is the lure. Writes home to complain that English students are nauseous. Mother writes back telling him what a proper little snob he has become. Mothers know. Mothers always know.

After periods of promise, potential and studious application (Syd's as an artist not a musician) both men's labours come to fruition during an intensely concentrated phase of fulfilment. That period when the seeds and slow growth bud and flourish with abundant colour. When all the hours spent meditative, focussed and locked in suddenly click, and some unseen godly hand throws open the doors of perception so that the world can be gazed upon as if for the first time at the dawn of creation. For Nick, the blues and folk apprenticeship, all those modal discoveries, all that unconventional tuning and retuning, all that endless meticulous refinement, it all comes good when the inner voice begins to chime in harmony with the outer expression. Language and lexicon in accord. Strong hands. Nimble fingers. An outpouring of unassertive mystery from a beguiled and beguiling mind. Everything settles into configurations of entrancement. The prophets they conspire in a cryptic alphabet.

Nick's songs are full of courteous detachment. Bursts of crystalline clarity recede to a vanishing point of impenetrable vagueness. Not commercial. Stevie Wonder is commercial. Cat Stevens is commercial. Chart songs are full of specific generalities. They disclose the whereabouts of their treasure. They seek to be clear and inclusive. Nick's songs embody a rare magic, but they conceal as much as they reveal. He is incapable of a banal simile or greetings card sentiment. His psyche can only tolerate so much clarity. The truths are spilled sparingly. Too much daylight fades the enchantment.

Syd the painter has up till now mastered the art of passable pastiche and is still in pursuit of his own singularity. Sleight of hand will only carry you so far in cool school. Musically he can fashion similarly passable forgeries. Soon he will be seduced by the flicker of the light show, captivated by the blare of the beat. Treats his

Telecaster like a canvas and coats it in thick aggregates of impasto, layers it in delicacy and gossamer-light slide notes. Pedal and echo effects are spattered and daubed into infinite abstract possibilities. In one intense six month period from the autumn of 1966 to the early spring of 1967 he writes the entire body of work that will make him a pop star. Simple minimal lyrics, fairy tale bounce, wistful lilt. Everything shines. And then all at once he becomes a toiler. It was never a toil before but here comes the itinerary chore. The image trap and the crass habitat. Questionable commitments. Beer rooms. Shirt and tie guys. The spontaneity is curtailed, the conceptual frivolity frowned upon, the improv diminished. Do it the same. Do it again. Suddenly the muse no longer beckons fulfilment. The road ahead is paved with obligation and stress. Fretwork fraying. Strings snapping. Vision dims to Transit van dashboard horizons. Distant glimmers of dead zones.

At some point both men merge into spirit and myth. Cohabitating each other's souls. Synchronizing a muse, an outlook, an inlook. Syd sailing down to the depths of the Northern Line. Warm displaced air rush of an oncoming train. Gazing at the shoe shine. Meeting no one's eye. Nick stumbling fumbling on through impulse, grasping at pie in the sky. The innocent abroad in See Emily Play is simultaneously the waylaid ingenue Betty who waterside wafts through the stillness on her way to greet the River Man. The Syd who retreats to a sad town tavern and ignores the raucous clamour of the clowns outside is the Nick who sits in a station bar and travels far in sin. They only see what they choose to see. They eliminate all other options. Everything that went before is empty essence, vapour trails, uncertain brush strokes, broken notes.

Stop the town square clocks. Pause the plot. Freeze frame and sepia tint the picture. In some parallel world, in some alternative reality, myriad possibilities play out indefinitely and the imagination is free to do its own bidding. The life of the mind is endlessly embedded with criss-cross patterns. Footfall has many destinations. Paths that still may cross. Perils that might be avoided. Speculative scenarios that may yet prove fruitful. One of these things in preference to. Some of these things instead.

IN CONCERT

Queen Elizabeth Hall Sunday July 25th 1971

John Martyn
Bronco
Nick Drake and band

On a simmering hot Sunday evening a congregation of the hip and the knowing discarded their Afghans and furs, put on their coolest cheesecloth and diaphanous dresses, and shimmied and shimmered along the banks of the Thames to witness something a bit special.

Billed as An Evening of Island Delights the main purpose of the concert (and this was very much a concert not a gig, with gold leaf-embossed programmes handed out in the foyer) was to showcase the beguiling talents of singer-songwriter Nick Drake, whose most recent album *Bryter Layter* sold impressively, but not in sufficient numbers to set the LP charts alight. The support acts from the growing Island roster were also more than able. In fact, I would like to have heard a great deal more from John Martyn, whose ability to marry an agreeably mischievous stage demeanour with some exquisitely crafted songs went down well with the early arrivals. Performing solo without partner Beverley (although she did put in an appearance later in the evening) Martyn's set mostly drew on selections from their two albums *Stormbringer* and *Road To Ruin*. There were also a couple of enticing new songs from an as-yet unnamed forthcoming album, *Head And Heart* and *Bless The Weather*. Both bode well for the future. Martyn encored with a playful rendition of 'Singin' In The Rain' (yes that one!) and went down very warmly indeed.

This most pleasing of opening sets was followed by Bronco's heady mixture of soporific harmonising and laid-back boogie. Can you be laid back while boogying? Bronco managed it. And in the heat of this sultry July evening there was no other way to boogie but languidly. In Jess Roden they have a convincing front man with a strong lead voice and some very attractive country-tinged compositions. He was ably assisted by an accomplished rhythm section and this fine band get better and better each time I see them.

The line-up on John Martyn's *Road To Ruin* album basically comprised the same unit that backed Nick Drake during his set, i.e. a smattering of Fairports, Dave Pegg, Dave Mattacks and Richard Thompson, augmented by Chris Wood of Traffic (piano and organ), Ray Warleigh (alto sax and flute), Dudu Pukwana (tenor and soprano sax), Lynn Dobson (flute) and Rebop Kwaku Baah (congas).

Things kicked off nimbly with 'Hazey Jane II' from the recent LP. Drake himself is a most unassuming front man but for the most part looked completely at ease, stood centre stage surrounded by his all-star line-up. After the nifty opener and the 12-bar bluesy 'Man In A Shed' things settled into something more mellow and mellifluous. A seamless song suite consisting of 'One Of These Things First', 'At The Chime Of A City Clock' and 'Poor Boy' was jazzy and soulful, the later considerably enhanced by the presence of PP Arnold, Madeline Bell, Doris Troy and, yes, Beverley Martyn on backing vocals. Such is the deceptively muscular strength of Drake's guitar work that you find yourself hearing the orchestral augmentations that colourise the *Bryter Layter* album even when a string section is nowhere to be seen. This harmonic strength was amply illustrated when Drake sat down alone to perform 'River Man', arguably the finest thing he has written to date. Sans Harry Robinson's album arrangement it was still a beguiling dreamboat of a song, meandering its way into the hearts of the enraptured audience. You could have heard a pin drop.

The first half eased down with 'The Thoughts Of Mary Jane' and 'Saturday Sun' and the palatial Queen Elizabeth Hall suddenly assumed the intimacy of a St Tropez beachside bar. If the concert had ended there I'm sure many in the audience would have gone away happy and fulfilled, but there were further 'Island Delights' to come in the second half of the programme. 'Cello Suite' the programme tantalisingly promised us. What this entailed was a series of extended extemporisations of material from Drake's *Five Leaves Left* album, augmented by arranger Robert Kirby and a 'broken consort' string and wind section consisting of two cellists, oboe, flute, lute, recorder and violin. The suite commenced with a long, hypnotic intro which turned the introduction to Drake's 'Cello Song' into a protracted drone poem, the song itself appearing almost as an afterthought about halfway through. The 'Cello Song' section wound down with a bit more string and flute raga before the ensemble performed an unannounced song I wasn't familiar with but which I think was called 'Princess Of The Sand'.

The consort players then performed the andante section of Bach's *Brandenburg Concerto No. 4* before segueing seamlessly into Drake's 'Way To Blue'. There was a charming moment before this commenced when the shy and slightly stiff Drake stepped forward to apologise for a misprint in the programme which suggested that the andante was from the *Brandenburg Concerto No. 3*. "And there isn't an andante section in number three so don't go looking... and I'm pretty sure you wouldn't anyway," said Drake before dissolving in giggles. It was a lovely moment where the Queen Elizabeth Hall was suddenly transformed into a school recital, and it was a joy to look up and see the Island Records bigwigs in the box seats beaming away like proud parents. The juxtaposition of the Bach with 'Way To Blue' perfectly illustrated Drake's neat classical touches and drew attention to their similarities of orchestral textures. It was a bold move and revealed just how much depth and resonance there is to Drake's music. Something similar was in evidence when the string and wind section played the 'Antiquae Pavan' and the 'Tristes Pavan' from John Dowland's *Lachrimae* before everyone launched into a brisk version of Drake's 'Day Is Done'. It was a little too muscular and up-tempo for my liking and some of that song's sonorous grace was lost in translation, but everyone on stage seemed to be enjoying themselves enormously.

As with the Bach I assume the intention was to establish lines of influence and lineage between the different forms of music. It does however raise an interesting question about how Drake presents his music to the wider public. Does he go out on tour as an augmented folkie with back-up band, classical musicians, et al, or just keep it simple and play solo? He's clearly a cut above the average singer-songwriter but one does wonder how well such a concert would play in a less sophisticated environment. It will be interesting to see how this section goes down should Drake take the set out on the road.

After 'Day Is Done' there was another beautifully arranged song called 'Time Of No Reply', which appears on neither of the Island albums and augers well for further riches to come. The show ended with a lengthy jam session based around 'Three Hours' from *Five Leaves Left*. It started off promisingly but became a bit of a meandering free-for-all after a while and a few audience members began departing for late night trains and buses. There was an odd moment midway through the jam where Drake drifted off stage, seemingly bored or dispirited by proceedings. He came back on to take applause at the end but gave a most reluctant bow and his body language suggested that he would almost rather be anywhere than in the limelight. It was like watching the host want to leave his own party. He rallied sufficiently enough to strap on an electric guitar for the encore, another new song called 'Parasite', which took things into a much heavier direction and hinted at a darker, more foreboding direction in Drake's lyrics. The incessantly plangent rhythm was like the tolling of a bell and suggested that there are hidden depths to his already considerable talent that are yet to be unleashed. Perhaps we shall discover more on the next LP. Drake goes electric? We'll have to wait and see.

There were muted calls for a second encore but once a roadie came on stage and began removing Rebop's congas we took that as our cue to leave. Something of an anti-climax to what had been a hugely enjoyable and at times mesmerising musical journey.

I do hope Nick Drake's music will reach a wider audience than it does at present. The hall, it has to be said, was only three quarters full and several of the music industry's most notorious liggers and freeloaders seemed to adjourn to the bar with undue haste during the orchestral section in the second half. Their loss, not Nick Drake's, who after this performance can only go from strength to strength.

Anthony Bradwell, *Melody Maker* July 31st 1971

TO SEE SUCH CRAFT

Depending on the vagaries of weather, Syd either turned left or right when he departed his top floor apartment at the Chelsea Cloisters hotel. Left took him up Sloane Avenue and past the gilded palaces of Bromptonia towards South Kensington or Knightsbridge. Right took him down past the mansion blocks and the Marlborough junior school. On this particular morning there was a keen north wind scything through the streets so Syd chased the hastening clouds down to the Kings Road where he turned right again. He asked for "Camel filter brand" in the newsagents and a woman in a mink stole paused to give him a wary look as she bought her Black Russian Sobranies. Syd lingered in the shop doorway to light a cigarette and then carried on towards Fulham. At World's End he stopped to look in the windows of what he called The Rocker Shop. The boutique sold backdated styles to teddy boys and girls, retro kids who preferred the 1950s cut. Drainpipes, drapes, creepers and crepes.

Syd brought his painterly eye to the ever-evolving collage of the Rocker Shop window display, took in the geometry of the thing. It had once been easy for him to reimagine the early rock and rollers as cubists. Form with a backbeat. Movements complementing the vocabulary of the art. Distortions drawn from the source. Cool jerks. The shape up. Shoulder moulded triangulations tapering to pin thin legs. Reverse pyramids pirouetting on an apex. Primal gyrations. Angular arms and hip thrusts. Knock-kneed Eddie Cochrans on Rapier guitars. Hunched energy. Parody of primates. Flick knife quiff and grin. Spray of hair oil. Whiff of grease. He'd never cared much for the music other than as apprenticeship material, chords to learn on his instrument, but oh the look and oh the shapes. He'd worn his hair like that at the County School before the beat groups brought in fringes and the French cut. Street scenes he saw as a kid proved formative. East Anglian bikers. Ton up boys on a burn up. Sidewalk catwalk models mooching outside the caffs. You didn't need to go to the galleries. That was a living canvas right there. All action broken down into Picasso and Braque molecules. Museums were for the money guys and the mausoleum-eyed. The pavements were where the interaction was. Kinetic life force energy. Montage blurs of sneers, pouts and poses. Bloated imported autos. Buicks and Chevrolets. Hyper real. Reflective sheen. It all fed in. Musical notation and newspaper cuttings glued and pasted. Touch of drag and drip. Drive-in hamburger joints. Splash ads. Jukebox lights. Bit of splatter to signify the spats. Just a hint within the haziness of the thing, no more than that. Don't obsess over the detail. No need to finesse. Sometimes an outline is enough.

As Syd stood looking in the window day-dreaming old paint dreams the owner came out. A fairground barker parody of what a boutique owner should look like. Curly red hair. Stiffened quiff doing a boomerang in the breeze. Comical, really. Syd suppressed a grin. "You won't always need that uniform," he felt like saying.

Different uniforms are available. The styles they come and go. The owner, flushed in the face, like he'd just enjoyed a blowjob, smiled knowingly at Syd. Then he glanced warily over the road at the traffic warden working his way along the morning delivery vans, stopping periodically to point out the nuisance value of static traffic to an irate driver, occasionally issuing a ticket. The fairground barker saw traffic wardens as bastions of mediocrity and oppression. He had a long list of shibboleths and traffic wardens were on it. "Bit parky this morning," he shouted. Bit of an air gasp gurgle in his laugh, like a baby just come off the bottle. "Bit parky, eh?" he repeated to Syd with another knowing smirk. There was the one brief moment of stand-off. The two men staring at each other. Neither of them aware that there was any more history to come up this less fashionable end of the Kings Road. Down came Syd's own shop shutters. Face a blank to ward off unwelcomed intimacy. "Please yourself," said the fairground barker going back in to finger the float in his till. Once inside the shop, he perched himself on a precarious stool and waited for the museum trade to resume, the flow of retro kids who would inflate the day's takings, forever hoping some sparky boys and girls might walk in and kickstart something new. He knew they were out there somewhere. Still 15.

Syd incautiously crossed the road, causing a Knowledge Boy to swerve and lose his place on his clipboard. The wind picked up. A man looked assertively at his wristwatch as he passed close by. His arm curled aggressively as he did so, flexing a fist. The bulldog he was walking enacted the same posture, mirroring his master, cocking a canine front paw and marking out its own anger territory in menacing dog paces. A few yards further up the road it stopped to squat and shit but its owner impatiently yanked the leash and forced it on.

Syd would often head for the Fulham Road with the intention of enjoying a solitary half in The Queen's Elm before too many famous faces drifted in. Or he might stop off at The Markham Arms and avoid all eye contact with the showbiz nobility, but after walking for about 20 minutes he dismissed both options and decided instead to visit his music publishers. Retracing his steps, he walked back up the Kings Road, up Sloane Avenue, through South Kensington and on towards Knightsbridge. He imagined himself as a Knowledge Boy on a rich route. Reaching Harrods, he stopped to browse for a bit, then walked on across Hyde Park. From here, he headed up the Edgware Road and Marylebone Road to Lisson Street where Lupus Music had its office. His publishers had just taken possession of a brand new sofa to replace the battered old horse-haired thing that had sat in the main office for as long as he had been a client. Syd liked to go and sit there and while away a morning. The staff always seemed pleased to see him, and although conversation could be halting once the initial pleasantries had been exchanged, the Italian coffee was nice and always on the brew.

"Are you fully moved in to the Cloisters yet?" asked Clara, as she typed away at a binding contract.

"Months ago," said Syd, distractedly leafing through the pages of an old *Melody Maker*.

"Only..."

Clara thought of how much trouble it has been to get Syd into

TO SEE SUCH CRAFT

Chelsea Cloisters. How there had been complaints from his previous domicile concerning unpaid room service bills. First, she had managed to convince him to ship his considerable accumulation of guitars over to Chelsea and eventually, after much subtle persuasion and a forceful edict from Bryan the boss on high that the room service bills had to cease, Syd took up tenancy on the ninth floor.

"How does it compare with the Penta. Is it homely?"

"It faces north," said Syd. "It doesn't get much sun."

"Oh, I'm sorry about that. Would you like me to arrange a move to a different room?"

"No. It's fine," said Syd. "The vista is good".

And that's how it would go. A little inconsequential chat. A regular coffee top-up, until at some point either just before or during lunchtime, Syd would slip away to negotiate the rest of his day. Sometimes there would be an abrupt "must be going now" (Clara was rarely given any indication of the intentions implied in that "must".) More often than not, she would return from the toilet or swilling out cups in the kitchenette to find Syd gone, until the next time he vaguely drifted in then out again.

"Oh, before you go Syd... Duggie dropped by. He left these."

"Oh."

"Yes, he said he's popped up to the Cloisters a couple of times but there was nobody in."

Clara handed Syd a bulging brown parcel.

"He said there are still some canvases of yours up there. In your old room. Shall I arrange for them to be picked up?"

Syd was still studying with some bemusement the package in his hand.

"I'm sorry, some..."

"A few of your paintings I presume."

"Tell him to keep them," Syd said absently. "Whitewash them and use them again. Might as well."

He headed towards the door, still staring at the parcel, like it might contain wires and a timer.

"Bryan would love to see if there's anything you can do with those," said Clara hopefully.

"He's in Berkshire for the week playing polo, but he should be back in town on Friday. I'll tell him you picked up the words."

The words. Oh yes, the words.

In truth Syd had left them at Duggie's intentionally. They had become an unwanted burden. Dead weight and mental debris. With the sun brightening a little he walked back to Hyde Park, sat on a bench and gave the contents of the package a cursory peek. A few pages became dislodged from the untethered bundle and blew away in the breeze. He left them to their eddying.

When he got back to his room he threw the parcel on the bed, made a cup of tea, turned on the telly and watched a school's programme called *Words And Pictures*. After a bit the pull of curiosity got to him and he emptied the papers onto his eiderdown. Some were bound with clips, others were stapled. There were loose leaf sheaves and pages torn from sketch pads. There were neatly typed sheets, and parchments of scented blue velour covered in left slanting scribbly black ink, there were strips torn into cut up columns, and fragments gone faded with sunlight and age. There was stuff written specifically for his band and lines penned in idle rumination, lines that might one day turn into verses, verses that might embrace the possibility of song. At first he cast a dispassionate eye over the random accumulation, leafing through the pages as if they were someone else's work. As time passed he grew more curious to see who he might once have been.

Beechwood
Across the chalk path
Into the wildwood
Between the tall trees
Into the beechwood

All through the dawn light
The daisy'd meadow
The morning shadow
Cast by the Beechwood

Can I drive up to your door
Can I take you places
Not like it was before
Doesn't need to be a reason

Across the chalk path
Into the wildwood
Between the tall trees
Into the beechwood

All through the dawn light
The daisy'd meadow
The morning shadow
Cast by the Beechwood

Watch the world turn on its side
Laughter echoes in the rafters
And I'm not sad like I was before
Not like I was before

LIVING ALONE
Living alone I get stoned
Gotta find something else that's new
All alone/I get stoned
Get me out of this room

Now I must be clear/had a girl that kept me from the dark end
days/But I never seem to see her anymore

Living alone I get stoned
Gotta find something else that's new
All alone/I get stoned
Get me out of this room

And I don't like the distance
Miss my pictures on the wall
What I said to you is hard to recall
And who knows what I really thought
Living sometimes in the afterthoughts
Living my life in the afterthoughts

WORDS #2
Crochety Terpsichore citadel copper roundelay impudent synthetic
sand old goad prefect defect pervert sherbert adverb ailment reason
easel silk scattered florin adhesive six listen alive-o ampersand
landscape reseal slip grip rinse nether neither clover armoury
discount motion notion porch porcelain madrigal nylon rayon
fridge raga pesticide bracelet glove oven uniform scissors octagon
building scatter lucid signage dreaming oak detour able label sulphur
viridian meridian propulsion sill still parcel battlement lectern end

Poetry Broth #1
The cloud body holster
Like heaving sheets/in every
Seaside were twirled for
The sake of my health
Aaah! To the earth
Meek earth
I sat on the shelf a
Silken sun shed
Withering like poison oaks

Poetry Broth #2
Winter is as a rule sleeping
For its ice cream dragon lingers
To float on snow turbines
The smiles were meeker when
The lost fire brigade had its oceans

He came across an early version of 'Swan Lee' that he had

initially called 'S/Laing' in which he adapted the trochee form of Longfellow's *The Song Of Hiawatha* and lifted lines directly from the epic poem. This he had abandoned when close to completion, preferring to start anew and fashion his own passable forgery in a less regular metre.

S/Laing

A sky red with sunrise gave life to the marshes
Met with eyes that shone radiantly
A wind got up in the rustling branches
Canyons ran deep from the sand to the sea

Fiercely the purple clouds of sunlight
Flecked the shadows and spread serene
Blessed enchanted with magical virtue
Fed to the starlight the young man's dream

Birds hopped and sang in their shining plumage
Above the tree tops they circled and soared
The rain fell in glittering rods of silver
The earth shook with tumult and the ocean roared

The great war eagle sat on crags high above him
From the margin of meadows came a force unseen
Fanned the air with a whirlwind that spun him in circles
He fled to the far lands in garments green

(Two verses at this point had been made indecipherable by a turpentine spillage)

So in time he watched them gather the harvest
The maize was ripened and made ready to eat
The women and maidens stripped husks with their labour
A fire was lit and they prepared for the feast

At the end of his journey the boy ventured homeward
Past reedy islands and warriors brave
The fires gleaming scarlet the ravens above him
From the cool clearing waters he returned their wave

On another set of stapled pages he found a series of lyrics illustrated with intricately detailed drawings of fairy tale characters. Some of these had been borrowed or adapted from children's books remembered from infancy, others were pure inventions of his own imagination. The first of these, 'The Hop About', he had written as a round, annotated with numbered instructions for entry points for the descant singers. These numbers did not conform to a regular pattern, the idea being that the song would gradually become incomprehensible once multiple voices were singing.

The Hop About
To pudding pocket lane we go
Up at the first up at the first
The table is set for such a scene (1)
We merrily to and froe
Set your teacups down
Hip hurrah dip hurrah
Up and down the lane we go (2)
The bells will tell us when it freezes or blows

Merrily to and froe

We skim along we go out for an airing (3)
Snip and snap snitch and snatch
The wind will blow us fast along
We hop about and go

Cat at the cream pot the cake is burning
Fox in the morning bake and brew
Let yourself through let yourself through
If it takes a day then it's okay
To pudding pocket we go

Join the dots and shed the leaves (4)
Ducks in a row at the rifle range
Figurines and china tea
To pocket and locket land we go (5)
Arrows flashing as far as we go
Hip hurrah dip hurrah (6)
All the bell horses four for a penny
Needles and sand slung in a bag
Swing was over four leaves and clover
Up at the first we go

Written around the same time as 'Scream Thy Last Scream', he
remembered showing 'The Hop About' to Andrew in the office who
murmured approval and to Roger in the studio who said nothing
and carried on trying to tune his bass guitar. On the back of the
sheet was another song from the same creative spree. An older song

he'd carried around in his head for ages, directly inspired by an old girlfriend. He thought it might make a good single.

Penny Belter
Draws the dots and spreads the leaves
Under the eiderdown under the eaves
Won't be back for several years
Penny Belter

Behind the curtain duck down
Get to the ground with a frown
Behind the curtain bob down
Go to ground

Hand burns hot and jump bucket drop
Skipping and hopscotch and lolly pop
Ice cream van chiming hurry your lunch
Penny Belter

The sun if it's shining we're never afraid
Several fat hens and a chamber maid
Piggy he piggy he was the game that we played
Penny Belter

Behind the curtain duck down
Get on the ground with a frown
Behind the curtain bob down
Go to ground

Cat by the fireside bird in a cage

Combing your hair down with grace and a gaze
Clutching a keepsake just to save face
Penny Belter

Baby bouquet and it's three and away
Jump with surprise at the end of the day
Drop her a curtesy and thoughts go astray
Penny Belter

All those songs he never dared show them, fearing lack of interest, sensing disapproval. So many more like this. Indicating other ways the group could have gone. Multiple options that were made available to them in studio storerooms. Keys to so many cupboards that could have facilitated such strange and wonderous ensembles. Melodies augmented with spinet, clavichord and celeste. Simbalom interludes. Calliopes on a forever-go-round. Barrel organs and player pianos fed through echorec. Orchestras of wheezing ocarinas, bellows, hurdy-gurdys, wind chimes, whistles, bells and Sally Army soldiers. EMI sound effects EPs. Ballet dream scores for wound down metronomes and wind-up toys. All that opportunity passed up. A little too offbeat for the public the moneymen said. Better left in the head. Always better in the head. Stuff he put aside for a solo LP and then Joe lost the demo tape. He remembered all this as he read on. It pained him. Dark shadows cast.

Dance Over
With your golden purse and your holiday shoes
Gown of silk and sews a fine seam
Lips rouger/eye peeper
Gotta keep her/yeah

Dance over to me lucy lee
Powder your face and fix your wig
Caper and crow on a hazel twig
Put ribbons in your hair/yeah

All the while/all the while
The wind outside blows shrill (x2)

Little lucy cut her foot/all ashamed now/not to blame now
Travelled east/travelled west/she's come home now/
Lawn swings in her garden/yeah

All the while/all the while
The wind outside blows shrill (x2)

The remainder of the package consisted of a large bundle of miscellaneous loose leaf pages, shuffled and reshuffled into endless permutations. Flicking through them, he could no longer tell which songs were which or where one lyric began and another ended. Everything seemed to run into one long ream of free verse without clarity or cohesion, and yet all the unsorted unsense still made sense of a sort to him. All those pop songs started, dismantled, discarded. All that endeavour that required so little effort, just a quick and nimble brain, work that rarely seemed like work at all. Here it all was in torrents of wordage, an unmediated cascade of image and babble. Monuments to a convulsive creative energy. Chunks hewn from some grander design that lay forever beyond the symmetry of feasible architecture.

UNSUNG:UNSAID.

Yeah yeah yeah seeking you/Calling out in dream drowsy
Send my flowers far for you
Driving myself to a standstill
My mind on its way/wind lifted/blink into life in
the quiet night/sent her away
Weave her a song in silence today

You fill me with love in your room
In the fade dappled light
In the sadness
Don't you feel me love you
In hedge nests/through crevice cracks/ledge
To sedge/idle nooks and sad looks/rooks caw
In a line/it's fine/lie in bed all the time

I came looking for the sky in your candletown
Tread meadow to the way you are
Getting around in your candletown
Silver and satin to be nearer by far

I came looking for the sky in your candletown
moon bump the night now
Getting around in your candletown
Sable and lace to be nearer by far

Came looking for love in your candletown
Eye spy you fragrant/crab apple craving
Cowslip meadow and catkins wavy
Charmed on the heath/daisy gazing

TO SEE SUCH CRAFT

There they go the snow birds
There they glow in ice cracked clusters
Feather lined limbs shiver tremble
Warm winds in spring ring the toll bells
The best way for marigolds to grow/you can tell

With your rainbow rings and the smell of your hair
Listen I know
Capering sand and sea shells/to dwell there/I go
With your rainbow rings and the smell of your hair
Fresh thatch/key latch
Swept away on the gleam of the sea
We gaze in dreams/our noonday
To go there again some day
Warm wind/casts you in/heard you sing
By and by in the breezes
Even the flowers in my garden/turned
To wave at you when you'd gone.

Away we go/to the graces
Roman candles/aglow
Green scorch glimmer eyes
Swing twisting wind twisting
Sky peels of thunder eyes
Earth pearl the dew-side
Flap awnings/The roar from an outside

High worn wall/the cattle
Driftwood beach fire and scatter that

UNSUNG:UNSAID.

Feel the ground and the world turn around and away
See you sway/spread of the night stars
Walk on in silence and spaces

Spread your wide eyes cast in tears/
she came into sight bright blue
And that had become her movement in time
Second time/it's fine/
Move through the evening/in rain pattern maze
You were the light/you were best in the light/
We were both through all walls flying fast
Came to keep/said in sleep
Split open my mind to find the you that I like at least
Spring dappled ground glossy bright
Birds go to roosting/chattered all night

Tipping my life to the skyline
Safe and sound and waves below
Sand and softs of the shoreline
Rock spawn crags pebbles
You could walk around/we could walk around
Should you wish to
If you care to
I'm breathing the life/the air
That you choose
Should you want to/Should you wish to

All the shiny seas
Shingle to spit

footprints to move through your dream days

Wind in chimney corners
soot tumbles and toast we glow
Telling the merry tales we know
Sing Wassel the laurel adorned
A tiny tassel of song/we learned long ago
Into the greenwood go/Go the rushes o/arc of the birch beech
over/o
Praise sung peel of the bells/
Wind blows over the chalk heath/o
Over/o

The trees that hid the spire ahead
Birds in their high top cradle
Smoke stubble haze/places to play
hay in harvest dust in days
hide and seek
embers and eaves
your laugh and your give-away sneeze
barn seed and hessian
sat on sacks
laughter to rafters
Spoke in the echoes you please

Watching a shoal in muddy clearing
Scurry and flurry/senses still/
The thrill/
In the oldest light at the water's edge

Harbour boats bobbin
Nearness of you/
No one else near but you
Brought you all the way to see/
The seaweed and starfish
Brought you all the way here to see
the shoreline that spills the wreck

The girl in the cavern dress
Walked her wilderness
The girl in the cavern dress
Drip dry/to impress
With her wildness to send
She needed no friends
Was her own trend

The girl in the cavern dress
wandered over and said
Would you be so inclined to be more like me
I said I'd consider her request

Oh oh I shape
I got more than you
I got someone new
Somebody else not you
Cast the spell that divides me from you
Oh oh I shape
Betrays in your eyes honesty lies
And every wish I wished for you

TO SEE SUCH CRAFT

Unfold a path well-trod to you
Untold a tale that ended in you

Oh oh I shape
Apple eye/taut strings/violin
tense serenade
Robed in your ruby red coat
I count the freckles on you

Oh oh I shape
dancehall daubed in melody song
Necklace and pearl gem diamonds for you
And now she's turned out so very new
She would have done anyhow

Rain spatter patterns
Peach bloom blossom penny royal
Pretty hair in a curl
Content in her world

Maybe the world where you're looking
Heading to where you will find
I saw you walk on the ceiling
I was following close behind
I was falling down in the evening
Glad fields in the nearness of now
Feeling so gone in the rain
Spiral bow of the branches again
Can I call out to you in the lane?
Will you even remember my name?

Hide and go the glow worms
Fairy dust glisten and dales far away
blossom burst of you/a smile
Light as a lily skated day
Dead leaves flax embers
Hasten away
Screech owl flitter/scatter
Through darkness to day

I remember your whispers/orchard fruited sweep of the dry land
Bay wreath foxtail and teasel
Rose scented tendrils
lichen and larkspur
out in the dark with the mousing owls/away she flies to the black
skies

Finally, he came to the last plain A4 sheet. On it nine neatly typed lines of an unfinished song.

MEDDLESOME MADDY

Meddlesome Maddy sang her sharps as flats
Put pins in her hair and some in her hat
Who knew what she thought about this and that
She had blue stark eyes and a wild cat

I take the trouble to call/I hear
her dance her way down the hall
I saw her again in the market square
I see her most times she goes there

TO SEE SUCH CRAFT

Meddlesome Maddy gave the glad eye

Grown dizzy faint after endless pages of word swirl Syd put the sheets down, lit a cigarette and went and stared out of the window for quite some while.

57

GRAND GO THE YEARS

Dear Joe,

I understand from Andrea in the office that you are in America at the moment and might be away for a while but I'm sending this anyway while thoughts are fresh. I hope you will afford it the courtesy of your attention when you return.

I've been giving some consideration to what I should do next. Not exactly agonising but thinking very carefully about how I present myself on the next record, assuming there is to be one! As *Bryter Layter* failed set the world alight I think I might step away from my own compositions for a while and attempt an LP of other people's endeavours. I don't necessarily wish to return to the kind of material I first played when I was learning the guitar. I'd hope to do something more adventurous that that. And while interpretation of other people's songs might not appear to be my forte I thought it might be fun to spend some time working on fresh arrangements for the songs I have come up with so far. (See list below.) When you return from America perhaps you can tell me if this a good idea or merely a frivolous one. It might be just a passing impulse, I don't know, but perhaps something impulsive might be just what I need just now. The truth is, I'm not entirely sure what people want or expect of me. Does the record company view me in the sensitive troubadour mould with a folio of earnest witterings that need to be sugared up to be made palatable? Or is there perhaps scope for me to branch out and display a side of myself that people haven't really seen yet? I would love to hear your thoughts. Be as honest as you wish.

The songs I've come up with so far are as follows.

I Think It's Gonna Rain Today. I love Randy Newman's first LP as you know. I think Robert could really do something with a fresh arrangement of this song, and we could, I'm sure, come up a suitable treatment. Randy Newman has a dry throwaway quality to his delivery of songs but it would be nice to sing it straight. My style of singing might suit it.

Ghost Story. When we worked together on 'Northern Sky' and 'Fly' John Cale gave me a copy of his solo record, *Vintage Violence*. I was quite taken aback by this song which seems to stand out from the rest of the compositions on the LP. It's somewhat unsettling and contains some very odd imagery. The Fairports would be great as accompaniment, should they be happy to participate. Or Traffic. Are Traffic still functioning? I understand Steve Winwood has been very ill. Is Chris Wood still around? I would envisage him playing the organ part on this.

Marig Ar Pollanton. I've never really explored Celtic music, not even when I was busy learning to play every new discovery that came my way. I'm far more versed in traditional folk, blues and jazz. Somebody gave me this Alan Stivell LP recently. It's called *Reflets* (or *Reflections*) and I'm very taken with it. The singing is in the Breton language but I thought I might either play it as an instrumental or even attempt to write a fresh lyric. There is some beautiful harp playing on it. Do you know any harpists? I would love to use the instrument at some point. Does John Cale play the harp, do you know?

Auntie Aviator. I love this song so much and the words mean a lot to me. I'd very much like it if Beverley sang it with me, perhaps on the chorus, or alternate verses. I don't know if John will mind, or if he is at all possessive about the material on *Stormbringer* and *Road To Ruin* but as he has now ventured upon his own road to ruin (I mean solo career) hopefully he won't object too much. If he does object I will of course think of another song to put in its place.

White Summer. I don't know if you are familiar with this instrumental. It's by The Yardbirds before they became Led Zeppelin. I've worked out a different tuning for what would be an improvisation on the basic structure. If you don't know it, the Yardbirds version is very Arabic sounding, but it never really takes off for me. I think I can make a decent fist of it. Anyway, I've been tinkering with it and it's sounding very good.

Maybe The People Would Be The Times (Or Between Clark And Hilldale). I'd love to attempt something from *Forever Changes*. When we were recording *Bryter Layter* I thought of this. It crossed my mind that it's somewhat similar to 'Hazey Jane'. A very Spanish style arrangement. The lyrics have a certain lilt and I'm intrigued by the way the lines run into each other. It has a name doesn't it, that device but I've forgotten what it is. I'd love to sing this with the Hazey Fairports. It would be good to work on something brisk and up tempo.

Loneliness. I went with my mother to see John Betjeman speak at Stratford and he read this poem. After the reading, believe it or not, Mother charmed him into giving her his handwritten copy. It is I believe unpublished as yet. It's somewhat gloomy. One thinks of Betjeman as light and jovial in his verse, often downright comical but he can be very acerbic too ("come friendly bombs") and there is some very gloomy imagery in this. I actually heard an arrangement in my head as he read it. I don't know if there are copyright concerns here. If there are I shall drop the idea immediately of course. I don't know if the great man himself is amenable to this sort of thing. I probably should have asked him but shyness intruded at the crucial moment. Perhaps someone on your publishing side of things could make enquiries on my behalf.

When I Look In Your Eyes. My parents are very fond of this song and have two versions at home. One is by Jack Jones – the crooner not the trade union leader. The other is by Tony Bennett from an album called *Something*. The Bennett version is a particular favourite of Mother's. It's a Leslie Bricusse composition. Quite a jazzy arrangement and I'm very taken with it. I like the moods it evokes. A sort of mournful yearning. One could be quite playful with it as long as we avoid the dreaded crooning. (I cringe at the thought.)

It's funny, listening to the song a few weeks ago I did wonder if the melody had a subconscious influence on 'Day Is Done'. It's similar to some of our arrangements on the two LPs. This didn't become apparent to me until recently – which makes me wonder how often this sort of thing happens. We all take on things unconsciously of course. It's very intriguing - to me anyway. I don't suppose Bob Dylan sits up all night worrying about such matters.

How Wild The Wind Blows. This is a song Mother wrote and has been known to perform at the piano when the mood takes her. I think she would quite like to have been a Parisian chanteuse in another life, or something involving Palm Court Orchestras and Tea Dances perhaps. At any rate this is a more than passable effort with an interesting lyric. It's short but quite meaningful.

Blues Run The Game. If I'm going to delve back into my old stuff and do anything from the carefree busking summer of three years ago (it already seems longer somehow) then it probably ought to be this one. Or a Bert Jansch perhaps.

Beginnings. This is from the Chicago LP that came out a little while ago but I heard Astrud Gilberto's version on an LP called *Holiday* and instantly fell in love with her arrangement. It's quite busy and again like the Love track it has an up-beat tempo, up-beat by my slothful standards anyway.

Birdie Told Me. I don't really know what to make of the Bee Gees. Some of their songs are a complete drag and quite an endurance to listen to. They seem to write the dreariest kind of ballad but they do have a great sense of melody. They sound like the Beatles sometimes, there's an element of that on this one which sounds like a bit of a steal from 'In My Life' but I love the simplicity of this and it reminds me of my sister who's up in town making a film at the moment. This is just a sneaky little thing for her to enjoy really, a sort of family in-joke for all the encouragement she continues to give me as I plug away, getting nowhere.

Time Of The Season. I should love to do a Zombies song. Either this or their hit, 'She's Not There'. I don't know if this track came out in England. I understand it's been a hit in America though. I love the singer's voice. I feel quite at home with that kind of unforced singing. I hear a gospel choir in my head when I listen to 'Time Of The Season', a bit like the Rolling Stones on 'You Can't Always Get What You Want'. This might be the best idea I've ever had or utterly the worst.

I've thought of one or two other songs but I'm still undecided as yet. Perhaps something by Bridget St John from her *Songs For The Gentleman* LP. I love Ron Geesin's arrangements on that record and should like to collaborate with him one day. And possibly a song by François Hardy of course, by way of compensation.

As a title I thought perhaps *Grand Go The Years*, which is a line from a poem I read, or if that seems too grand (!) something simpler like *Snap Shots* or *Close Ups*, or *Pin Ups*. No not *Pin Ups*, cross that out. Silly idea.

Anyway, no doubt I shall bore you with more about this

impulsive scheme of mine when you return from the USA. Until then please excuse the haste and untidiness of my scrawl. In order to address this shortcoming I'm thinking of doing the Pitman script class. The adverts look so appealing on the tube.

Nick.

CANTABRIGIANS

Playground chatter. Fifth form theatrics. Dress rehearsal for all the physical exhibitionists in their health and efficiency get up. PE kit duffel bag fust and plimsoll sweat. The breeze whiff of testosterone, blended with disdain. The weekly ritual of sniffing out the weakest in the pack. Easily located. Just stay quiet and hope it passes, either that or soak it up, sap.

Projectile mockery and self-mockery to keep warm. Flexing and joshing, shivering and stamping feet as everyone awaits the shrill peep of a Gamesmaster's whistle on an overcast March afternoon. The majority trot off with as much enthusiasm as they can muster. Double period last thing on Tuesdays. Off around the well-trod route and back again. Runners ranked according to ability and desire. The front ones set off as if they are still enacting the Rome Olympics. The median average main group shuffle off the premises with the middle management compliance that awaits them soon enough. At the back, last through the gates, the slackers, the smokers, the rejects, the oddballs and the impaired. Once out of sight some of them, those who can barely be bothered to break into a begrudging shuffle, will head for the Spinney, a favoured nicotine refuelling point. Here they will huddle in cliques, cup hands around lit woodbines, cough violently and emit stringy trails of beige white spit. The more enterprising will take a short cut through the avenue and adjourn to an empty house. Parents out working, none the wiser. Once out of school they stroll with the carefree abandon of those who will be leaving in a few short months. They take a dim view of running. As with the Norfolk four-course rotation, algebra and quadratic equations, they are determined never to put these questionable acquisitions to the test ever again.

Only one 15 year old boy among that fifth form gaggle deviates entirely from the group. As soon as they have crossed Hills Road, heading for the Cherry Hinton hinterlands, he peels off left, and jogs back to his house 50 yards away. He takes a key from under the front door mat, lets himself in and bounds upstairs to his bedroom.

"Is that you Roger?" comes a voice from the kitchen.
"Yes, Mother," he shouts from halfway up the stairs. "I forgot something."

He goes into his mess of a room where an easel stands prominent and a half-finished watercolour awaits completion. He pulls up a chair and goes to his work. A blue brush sky dab here. An emerald green flicker of reed bed there. He reaches under his bed for a red and white pack of Gold Leaf cigarettes, opens a window, strikes a Swan Vesta, inhales deeply and contemplates his work in progress. Every now and again he casts a wary eye on the street outside, waiting for the runners to return.

A stack of LP records sits under the window sill. An acoustic guitar is propped against the wall by the bedroom door. A poster from last year's Young Contemporaries exhibition at the RBA has come unstuck in one corner on the wall above his bed. From downstairs he can hear the sound of the wireless in the kitchen. Sidney Sax and his Music Brings you Melodies for Mid-Afternoon. Syd the painter taps a strict tempo foot in time with the Light Programme big band blare. He glances at his own stack of records and wonders if he has time to drown out Sidney Sax with one of his own selections.

Syd too is an incomplete canvas at this point, still awaiting the application of subtle shading. Colour him Monk or Miles shaped. The hip Beat options. More than likely, colour him as a callow apprentice, betraying a passion for Dusty, the singer with the Springfields. Or better still cloak him in some echo-spooked instrumental caught in the crossfade late one night on Radio Luxembourg. The signal drift from the Grand Duchy is the one they all still chase at this time, before the Beatles, before the offshore pirates, before the blam pow of chemical readjustment. Pop lives lived in the nocturnal ethersphere. DJs Tony Hall. Don Moss. Pete Murray. Jimmy Savile's Teen and Twenty Disc Club. Oh, the innocent pre-twist and shout excitement of it all.

Absorbed as he was, Syd didn't notice the first of the runners returning on the last leg of their journey. A surging sprint from one of the leading group and victory would be within their ambitious grasp. Looking up he noticed the main pack ambling back and quickly made a burst for the door. On the landing the opposite bedroom door opened and the lodger, Gillian from the Ladies College, offered Syd a broad toothy smile and made as if to begin a conversation.

"Must dash," said Syd apologetically and shot off down the stairs.

Win was in the hall sorting through a stack of her late husband's medical books. "What had you forgotten?" she asked absently as she separated P for Pathology from P for Physiology. "The reed beds," shouted Syd as he headed for the front door. "They need to bend in the breeze a little more."

It's lunchtime a few weeks later. Indoor break as it's pouring with rain. An air of boredom and practised indolence prevails. Teenagers jaded and lugubrious beyond their years. Idiosyncrasy and annoyance manifest themselves in all their myriad forms. Folded paper is tested for aerodynamic efficiency. A boy methodically runs a fingernail up and down the indentations of a slide rule. "Doesn't it sound like the speedway bikes on *Grandstand*?" he suggests weirdly. Another has taken the chalk-encrusted board rubber and is patting rectangular patterns in a precise line across the middle of the blackboard. Two acne-scarred prodigies are hunched over a ruby lacquered travel chessboard pondering the permutations of their next six moves. Rotund Simon loudly breaks wind to the evident sulphuric distress of those in close proximity. Someone is cribbing a classmate's maths homework in exchange for a teacake from the tuck shop. Two gayly raincoated girls from the Perse School go scurry-laughing along Hills Road heading towards town. Misted windows are rigorously elbow rubbed. Implausible suggestions are offered as to the Perse girls' motives and sexual availability. Their impressive deportment and the confidence of their leggy stride is evaluated. Erotic desire is expressed in bravado grunts. In the far corner by the store cupboard a boy has erected a wall of science textbooks, behind which he is making notes for the forthcoming school debating society meeting. The motion is "This house would prefer the contents of the school library to those of a sack dress" which he is going to rigorously oppose, making it clear in fairly graphic terms that he very much prefers the contents of a sack dress to the library.

At this point a more senior sixth form Roger enters the room, resplendent in Second World War fighter pilot headgear. Nobody regards him with anything more than polite curiosity as he scans the room looking for other School Cadet Force recruits. In another corner Syd and a clutch of classmates are strumming a repetitive sequence of major chords on acoustic guitars and attempting to finesse the fenland backwater blues. At this stage, owning the guitars is the coolest thing they do with them. Nailing those chords is an earnest and worthwhile endeavour to them and a fag to those who don't much see the point of devoting an entire break time to tedious minstrelsy.

The older Roger makes for the guitar group and begins to address one of their number in tones commiserate with those of a disaffected and slightly superior prefect. "Taylor," he says. Forenames are verboten in school. Formality is all, even among friends, but especially among Cadet Force members. "Taylor, you specimen," he elaborates as he reaches the table. "Rifle club's cancelled." "I know," says Taylor, reluctant to break off from the Chuck Berry riff he is now attempting. "Yes, I know you know," says the older Roger, gazing with furrowed disdain at the boy who has now completed his chalk dust mosaic on the blackboard. "Was there anything else then?" says Taylor, breaking off wearily from his GDCDC and resting his hands on the upper body of his Kay Acoustic. "Yes," comes a slow deliberate voice from deep within the fighter pilot carapace. "I believe you know where the key to the munitions store might be located."

"No, not the actual key," says Taylor warily. "Although we did make a mould copy in metalwork and it sort of works if you jiggle it about a bit." By now the entire guitar quartet has abandoned its break time strum and is listening intently for clues as to where this conversation might be going. The exchange is made all the more intriguing by the fact that the older Roger keeps the fighter pilot headgear in place for the duration, goggles and all, save for loosening a strap slightly where it is rubbing his chin.

"Only, I'm rather keen to get in there," he elaborates. "Can't it wait till Cadets?" offers Taylor. "Ah, well that's it you see. I've been ejected from the Cadet Force for my political sympathies." "Do conches have a political party now then?" calls out a smart alec from the doorway. The older Roger affects not to have heard this slur upon his affiliations and persists with his questions about the availability of the forged key. "I'll show you where we keep it," says Taylor. "It will have to wait till after double English though." "Can't wait," says the senior boy impatiently. "I have private study all afternoon. Show me now."

"What's the rush?"

"I need access to artillery, Stens, bazookas, that kind of thing. I believe there's a Kalashnikov in there, too."

"You'll never be able to assemble the bazooka. We've tried."

"I'm prepared to try harder."

And off they went. Taylor finally browbeaten into compliance by the older boy. The older boy looking like he should be standing on some windswept tarmac in blood red twilight. Lined up in readiness by a row of warbirds. Engines running. The smell of burning fuel. Night mission. Thumbs up. Chocks away.

Mirthful and full of focussed mischief, Syd was up for the prank. He was curious to see what might transpire from this scheme that involved secretly forged keys and the promise of access to military grade weaponry. Nothing did transpire of course. Things rarely did. Just another impulsive bout of unfulfilled malicious intent from a feverish mind. The older Roger was close to completing his A-levels and would be off soon. They all would, all Syd's friends in the upper sixth, who accommodated him willingly for his wit and charm. Syd would be off too. A most reluctant scholar anyway. Nothing but a brace of O-levels to show for all those ticks in a register. Eagerly heading for the Tech to do his art foundation. He's already left in his head.

The dispersal of his older peers didn't bother him unduly. Everything was still ahead. Tomorrow didn't exist. Teatime didn't exist. He lived in the moment even then and rarely gave any consideration to how things might play out. Displaying a devil-may-care disregard for consequences, he wished merely for a world that ran on random and, with a little willing, mostly it did. Life did his bidding. Life was carefree and untrammelled. The only thing he cared deeply about was his art. The next sketch. The next primed canvas. The next idea. The one after that.

In a crowded corridor on the way to English, Syd overheard a passing teacher ask Andrew from the upper sixth why he was wearing a black armband on his school jacket.

"Has someone in your family died?" suggested the mortar-boarded master with due solemnity.

"No sir, Ray Charles has been busted again."

The previous November, Charles had been arrested in a hotel room in Indiana and charged with possession of heroin and marijuana. It was the first time Syd had heard the word "busted". He made a note of the argot. He magpied all the time. A guitar beat here. A brush stroke there. Fashion tips from the *Elle* and *Mademoiselle* magazines left by the previous lodger. The one before Gillian. The French girl who sat in her room all evening smoking, listening to Georges Brassens and Edith Piaf records, rarely venturing out. Tight black sweater. Lipsticked lips. Fantasy images of her in that room. Syd imagining the walls away and wishing himself into her arms and into her rented bed like something out of the songs.

Those last few months of school captivity were an utter chore and a bore. Much more fun to be hanging round the pubs he couldn't drink in yet and the clubs he was already sneaking into and the park playground where he first locked eyes with the Dairy Box girl. Someone else to fixate on. A girl who laughed eagerly and not just at his jokes. Laughed at the absurdity of things. A girl amenable to his advances. Sketching her in caricature. The way she crossed her legs. Pretty bow of that mouth. Candy floss coloured hairband. Hint of a dimple. Faded freckles. Alive eyes. Such alive-o eyes. Pupils widening in surprise. Alert to his bold suggestions.

IF YOU COULD BE A SHADOW

[transcription of Philips cassette tape letter found among Nick's personal affects. Date and intended recipient unknown]

Hello my good fellow. I hope you don't mind me communicating with you via the medium of audio cassette. It might seem bizarre but I feel that it enables me to order my thoughts much more succinctly than if I were rambling in your presence. I was just thinking about how often I used to do this with Father's Ferrograph tape recorder, which remains in fairly robust condition I have to say [laughs] and is still wheeled out on occasions. We used to record on it all the time. Gay would use it when she was rehearsing for her plays and as you might remember I would record songs on it from time to time.

Oh, speaking of which, I recently found a reel with several old recordings on it. I barely recognised it as me but there I am keening away, singing about my true love's eyes and all the pretty momas and good time gals. I mean, it is me obviously but when one hears oneself singing some of those songs now about that train leaving the "deepo". [laughs] The tape had a, well I suppose you would say, a terribly low-fidelity quality to it, due I suppose to the poor acoustics of that summer house, which for all its undoubted benefits was never intended to be a recording studio. Or perhaps the tape has deteriorated, I don't know. Some of the recordings we do have in storage have oxidized awfully. But it gave it a kind of patina if you know what I mean. I find it hard to explain but it had the quality of some of those old recordings that blues singers made when you hear those really old records. Sort of timeworn I suppose. And I did start wondering if that's part of the charm. No not charm. That's not the right word. [lengthy pause] Anyway, I don't know what the right word is but perhaps that's what we hear as much as anything else when we listen to those old blues records. We hear the ancient. And it's only about three years ago, my recording I mean, the one I found, but I've already, mentally at any rate consigned it to history. Or perhaps I'm just embarrassed by it. Embarrassment is so often the first option when one hears one's earliest endeavours.

There seems, I suppose now, when one finds one's style, or begins to, there is something faintly absurd in someone of my breeding, for want of a better word, singing blues songs where suffering is involved, and the experiences of those original artists would not be one's own experience, because of one's upbringing obviously. The very idea of me assuming the mantle of a blues man. I somehow doubt if Blind Lemon Jefferson was ever called upon to make up a fourth at bridge. [laughs] The lack of impoverishment does handicap one enormously. I remember a friend of Father's saying that he didn't like Frank Sinatra singing about toting that bale because what would he know about that? And he's American Italian. Sinatra I mean, not the friend of my father. Who is from

Basingstoke. [laughs] But you see what I'm driving at I hope. On that midnight train, once it leaves the deepo. One thinks of it all as an apprenticeship. Goodness know what it was an apprenticeship for though. A preparation for failing perhaps. [sardonic laugh]

One feels so fraudulent replacing the words of an old blues song about a bordello with my meanderings. Or dressing the chords of "summertime and the living is easy" with my own words. They are such simple structures to learn though. The appropriate idiom is another matter, of course. It's all learning I suppose. [sigh] In the end. I realised from listening through the tape that one of my compositions, 'Blossom', borrowed something from 'Freight Train'. Do you remember that song? [sings "Freight train, freight train, down the track..."] It's fascinating what one absorbs unconsciously. That's part of the magic in a way. If you can call it that. One has to be careful of course otherwise you find yourself unintentionally cribbing, I don't know, something the Beatles wrote ages ago, or something you've been listening to a lot. It's easy enough to do.

At the time of course, you learn whatever comes your way, and the words I suppose are a useful device, with which [considered pause, audible drag on cigarette] but I think I learned far more about tuning and different techniques from those old records than I did from singing about, or from the viewpoint of, one of those old Delta blues men. Whatever viewpoint that was. It's a devilishly hard thing to pin down anyway, what the blues is and where it comes from. And the few things I've read, or tried reading, other than the sleeve notes on LP records I mean, it all seems to... I... there's a lot of contradiction and disagreement. As with most things.

Can you imagine all these scholars hard at work trying to find the source of the blues? Which is a fool's errand if ever there was one. A fool's errand for fool's gold. I read one musical theory which said that the ten-beat vocal phrase followed by a six-beat instrumental phrase comes from a Wesley Methodist hymn. So that would make the father of the blues some slave plantation owner in, I don't know, the 18th century or something, which is absurd when you think about it isn't it? Anyway, this is all far too academic and somewhat boring I feel, so I won't bore you any more with that.

What else is there? Let's see. Oh yes, before I forget. I'm thinking of taking a computer course. This is partly Father's suggestion. What I know about the world of computers could be written on the head of a pin. But it seems like it might turn into an agreeable option should the music career run up against the buffers. More trains you see. [laughs] Anyway, I'll be sure to keep you up to speed with my progress in the world of computing and I'm equally sure you'll be fascinated when I tell you all my news. I think I have to find something else to do now because music is... not giving me the sense of fulfillment that I hoped it would.

I've been wracking my brain trying to work out what has gone wrong. One could go mad analysing where certain things strike a chord with the public ear and others don't. I suppose there's a lack of resolve in my lyrics. If I can put it like that. I'm becoming increasingly aware of that. And failure, and probably disenchantment too. Let's see. What have I left out? [laughs] I listen to songs now, other people's songs or the odd thing one hears on the radio and it's all "it's up to you the people" and "we've got to get it all together". For heaven's sake. All these perfectly foolish slogans. I used to believe in all that myself once, but no longer alas. To be frank, I'm not sure what I believe in any more.

Don't laugh but I've also given some thought to working in the music industry, not as a musician. Perhaps something else. Some other aspect. I don't know. Perhaps I could write songs for other people on a commission. Or go into artistic development, something like that. Telling bands that they're better than they are and raising their expectations while getting paid. I'm getting very cynical as you can tell. Do you know John Cale? He played on my LP. He told me that he was in Artist and Repertoire for a short while. In America mostly. Discovering bands. I suppose you get to travel.

[tape paused here]

[resumes] I've just made myself a coffee and I was famished so I had some cheese and crackers. I was thinking, relating to what I said a few minutes ago about those crackly old blues recordings on primitive equipment, well actually it probably wasn't, it was probably really up to date equipment at the time, but the thing about the patina, the coating. If you could find a way of applying that to modern recordings say, so that the new sounded old, and my records could be made to sound like my old rehearsal tapes or remnants from another age. Anyway, one has such faraway thoughts and dreams. I'm terribly inattentive and unfocussed of late. I can't remember when I last finished a book for instance. Or a song. I have all these fragments lying around. In search of a chorus or a chord. Or a flourish. A flash of inspiration. Do you know what I mean? And

it's constantly evolving isn't it? Or at least it should be, otherwise one would just fossilize or go to seed. I do need... I'm in dire need of some divine inspiration to get me out of this rut.

I think in the future I might wish to rid myself of all the adornments. In the music I mean. Well here too in the here and now if I'm to be honest. I feel that I'm beginning to live like a Trappist monk. And it's not altogether unappealing. That way of life. Perhaps a vow of silence would be in order. Who knows? And would anyone notice anyway? I need to change something, that's for sure. Who's to hear me now I wonder? Who is listening? I feel that there is a... what's the word... something I can rely on in my music, well in my technique at any rate that I'm still trying to catch up with. In my emotional outlook I mean. Perhaps I never will. I feel like I'm doomed to flounder in its wake so to speak. Or perhaps I'm talking nonsense. As always. Again, I feel that... you see, this is why the monastery life would suit me. Just take away all the everyday befuddlement and padding and one wonders what's left... what you're left with when you've finished stripping it all away... all the layers... the soul perhaps... is that what you're left with?

It must appear that I'm terribly self-absorbed. I don't mean to be. The lateness of the hour lends itself to this kind of pondering, there's a kind of clarity of thought when it's so quiet outside, and, there... there was an owl hooting just now. I don't know if the tape picked that up. Probably in the beech tree. It's such a sultry night. I hope it is where you are. The weather hasn't been so good here but I have to say it's really put on a show the last few days. I would compose a poetic ode if I was given to such extravagance. Or had the necessary talent.

Perhaps one should try and write a form of poetry that... words that just exist in the ether, like vapour. Or liquid. I don't know what I'm talking about. It's the heat getting to me. I have such trouble sleeping. Thoughts like this keep me occupied... preoccupied... I feel it's the only kind of intimacy I understand. These pure abstract ideas. If one could just eliminate one's sense of self... the burden of it all... of expectation... and the pointless demands one makes of one's self... like the eastern mystics, rid the self of ego and striving, return to nothing. If you could just be a shadow. Go about your life like that... assume some other shape... no earthly body to carry about. Lugging all your troubles and burdens everywhere. Perhaps that's what the blues singers were trying to do, eliminate their suffering, casting it off into a shadow... I don't know. There must be some way of transforming... of transcending oneself, one's soul.

There's a wondrous scent rising up from the garden. I really wish you could smell it. It must be the honeysuckle or perhaps the night-scented stock. There's such a pretty arrangement of them below the window, mother sewed them in spirals. A bat flew in through the open window late the other night, and then flew out again. A visitation.

I will end there. I hope to see you again soon. It may not seem like it but I do miss talking to you. I should come and visit you. Perhaps I'll just take off and drive down there some time. It's been too long hasn't it?

[tape ends]

BLOW UP

Syd had two recurring dreams. In the first and most frequent he stood before a grand circular mosaic. Sometimes it assumed the form of a multicoloured window mounted in the nave of a church. At other times it hovered gravity-free without support. As is the way with dreams the mosaic was both see through and opaque. That is to say the mosaic pieces were simultaneously small tiles of non-permeable stone and yet let through filtered light as would stained glass. Sometimes in the dream they were solid entities, polished and gleaming, at other times they had a gel-like consistency, squidgy to the touch.

In the dream Syd would gaze in awestruck contemplation at the mosaic. He would admire its compositional geometry, the harmonic ratio and proportion of colour and shape. When back-lit by the sun a radiant prism of flickering spectrum shades would play across his face, giving him a translucent pallor, and making sparkling jewels of his eyes. He would try to hold onto this precious moment in his dream, hardly daring to breathe, lucidly awake to the realisation that things could change at any moment. He knew that if he consciously tried to assert control over the structure then the moment of splendour would pass and perhaps never return.

Sometimes the mosaic would fold in the wind, shapeshift, become malleable. But if he reached out to touch or attempt to manipulate it in any way the thing would shrink to a dot, or simply hurtle away into space with an audible whoosh. At other times his intense concentration would cause the mosaic to shatter into tiny pieces which would sparkle in the air, then drift slowly to the ground like glitter rain. Syd would sink to his knees, become receptive to these adjustments and alter his perception accordingly. This ritual was usually enacted in a mood of benign passivity, as if he was at peace with the new dispersal and merely admiring the patterns freshly formed. On other occasions he would grow distraught, paw at the ground, blood oozing from beneath blackened fingernails as he tried to restore the configuration and make it perfect again. In time this would usually be the way the dream ended and he came to dread its inevitably and the night terrors it would invariably induce.

In the other dream Syd would attempt to make his own paper and ink. Firstly, there would be the slow methodical treating of leaf pulp and coal dust or fragments of cloth. These would be slowly blended by some unknown alchemical formula into useable parchment. Alternately he might strip bark from a tree and peel it thinly into segments. An inquisitive venture into a woodland copse might yield up to four or five pages from each torn strip. At other times he tried writing on bound pages of lettuce or rhubarb leaf with ink of his own making. He would brew a concoction of vinegar and tube paint, whip it into a fine paste of useable consistency and then, dipping a calligraphy pen into the mixture, attempt to etch a legible script. Sometimes if he pressed too hard his writing seeped through the layers superimposing a faint trace of hieroglyph onto the porous pages below. These patterns would forge a syntax known only to him, a dream lexicon of runic etchings and archaic fonts beyond human comprehension and untranslatable when he awoke. At times, if the ink was laced with too much acidity, the pages would emit a thin hiss of steam and ignite into tongues of flame. In the dreams he would sometimes be able to manipulate the level of combustibility, making legible blaze shapes that would lick and weave into plaited tendrils in accordance with his conjured commands. New literary works would emerge from these endeavours, reams of lyrical prose that were the match of any opiated fever dream that spilled from Coleridge or De Quincy. These visionary moments were rare, though. Mostly the flames gave off an acrid odour like scorched asphalt or burning tyres. These would leave him with a sharp metallic taste in the back of his throat and he would awaken bolt upright to find he was in the middle of a coughing fit.

On his more mended days the dreams made him want to go back to his painting, urged him to pick up again where he had left off, to try and recapture something that lay dormant waiting to be reactivated. Mostly, though, they were a source of anguish, a painful unwelcome reminder of an aesthetic paralysis that had all but consumed him in recent months.

Occasionally he was haunted by his inactivity and would remember a time, not so long ago, when it wasn't like this. The willing art student who had found his vocation. Who left his North London house full of architectural ad-dabs early and went south of the river to Camberwell where he eagerly absorbed himself in the application, the apprenticeship, the vision thing, carrying about him a painter's gaze, all seeing at all times, full in the eye vibrant. The way the light catches the gleam of silver shore mud on the Thames, rain wetted primroses dotted among woodland moss, the soft brown downy underside of a moth or leaf, the memory shimmer of heat haze in foreign climes, those distant mountain blocks that looked like gold bars molten in the sun. He enjoyed the canvas caressing smear of a palette knife. He was alert to the texture of woodgrain and the way a subject takes the brush. Splintering form and figuration into abstraction at the beckoning of an impulse. (As in music as in art. But art first, art long before, way before.)

He only intended to pause the art because he got better at the music, found fresh new ways to apply the theory of one to the practice of the other, but now just a few years later the entire creative life seemed to be on pause. Suspended animation. No more fizzing lines of overlap, emotions muffled and muted, no spontaneous joy or quickening pulse. Forsaking depth for flatness. In the end, all was flatness. In art. In voice. In wordless breaths and avoidance.

He thought back to the portfolio he had to show in order to get into the Camberwell School of Art. Scattered untidily about the floor by a reputation-shredding tutor who had little time for surly rebels, who thought nothing of walking all over your work, or giving each piece the dubious benefit of his ruthlessly analytical mind. That English mutter and shrug. The grudgeful load-bearing murmur that was meant to convey "not a complete idiot then". Gazing down at his endeavours in that interview room as if they were the works of someone else who was auditioning to be the him that was now auditioning, and not minding at all that the tutor was trampling all over his earnest efforts and his showcase daubs which now looked a little shallow in the daylight of a different room. He was happy then to play the part of an unjudgmental self who himself didn't care about being judged. The work itself, the craft skill was its own validation. He should have known from that moment that he wasn't cut out for this, the participatory bit, interaction, negotiation, gallery life, the exhibition cage. Framed and restricted. Permanent pigment.

And yet. And yet. He loved the busy industry of the place when he first got there. The rigour and ritual. The studio intimacy. The air thick with the smell of French cigarettes and turpentine. Robert, the recently installed Head of School, sensed upon arrival that the place had no lack of imagination, too much precious sensibility and not enough intellectual ordering. And so he set about his task, instilling a sense of perceptual rigour in his young charges. Told them to ignore that whole Euston Road School style that the college had built its post-war reputation on and was still everywhere then. Got them thinking tougher. That's where it was at, not imitating the concerns and techniques of the previous generation. All that dot and carry, plumb line and proportion. "Just bring a tape measure next time dear," said Maggi, the most extravagant of that year's intake to a bemused Syd, when a tutor attempted to promote the old agenda. "I think it's a branch of tailoring."

Robert cast out the drizzle and demob dreariness of the 1950s. Get them critiquing. That was his thing. Get them questioning the relationship between seeing and painting. Give them systematic exercises to shake them up. Get them to look closer, get them to explore the micro-tonal gradations of grey that lurk between black and white. Limit the palette to yellow ochre, black and vermillion. Set a vase and a bowl of fruit before them and tell them not to copy Cezanne. Do the same with some old bus tickets, music scores and an empty wine bottle and tell them not to look at it like Picasso or Schwitters would look at it. Borrow a spectrometer from the printing department down the corridor. Separate white light from the spectrum and absorb new methods of perception. Syd found all this mind-blowing and life-changing.

That first year at Camberwell passed in a whirl of fresh ideas and ever-changing colour fields. Robert made it clear that he had little time for charismatic tutors who developed the cult of personality, who bred a coterie of devoted uncritical charges, who all painted in a given style, i.e. the style suggested by the charismatic tutor. This pleased Syd immensely. The only direction he ever needed was directions to the store cupboard where the oils and brushes were, and he too had little time for overbearing tuition. He also found Robert extremely sympathetic when he approached him about dropping his studies at a time when the music was starting to look lucrative. He agonised for ages before seeking permission to take a sabbatical and pause his apprenticeship. In his own youth Robert had crossed paths with Pablo Picasso, Jean Cocteau, Marcel Duchamp, Serge Diaghilev and André Gide. He called Benjamin Britton "Ben", Bertolt Brecht "Bert", TS Eliot "Tom" and WH Auden, who he knew intimately, "Wystan". His expansive circle of friends spread from the more amenable members of the Bloomsbury Set to everyone who was anyone in the world of theatre. He knew people who had converted to transcendentalism and followed Shri

Maya Baba in the 1920s. He and his partner Rupert took Baba to the cinema where the Master greatly enjoyed Laurel and Hardy films. The fluctuating temperament and temptations of youth were only too familiar with him and he gazed across his desk at this beautiful young student with the blazing eyes and advised Syd to take a year out and see how it goes. "You can always come back," Robert said to the polite and inwardly torn young man, who was now possibly for the first and only time seeking career guidance. The office was still. The day was clear and bright. Robert exuded an air of calmness and come-what-may. The first of the autumn leaves were falling from the trees outside the west facing window.

Syd still had that interview portfolio back at home, in Cambridge. Down in the cellar probably. Gathering dust. He tried to remember what was in it. The keenest of his efforts. Plant life studies, fungi and fauna in abundance, butterflies stripped to their exoskeleton, moths sketched from pin board exhibits. Very little life drawing, save for some workaday juvenilia drawn from the common stock of schoolboy surrealism, phantasmagorical faces, skull-like masques and such like. Aside from this there was minimal engagement with human form. A few incomplete anatomical studies. Hardly any portraiture, and even then, only frontal and flat, no sidelong profiles or crowd scenes of people going about their day. More than one of his girlfriends had been willing to pose for him, undressed if he wanted. He never once wanted. For all its accommodation of new techniques and textures his work frequently reverted to an old-fashioned liking for uncritiqued representations of nature, much of it informed by his local East Anglian landscape. "That will pass," said his Camberwell interviewer dismissively. "I prefer these," the tutor murmured when he saw the abstracts. A dizzying skid, a smear evaporating at the edges. Scratched out bleachy skies, thick pigment coarsened with sand, the tactile application of it. Canvases dumped outside the back door or down the Hills Road garden, left to the elements and allowed to weather. Fissures and imperfections corroding their way into the grain. He would work that up into a theory of sorts, given time. The application of avant-garde procedure to outmoded materials. The nursery rhyme bounce filtered through the feedback squall.

At art school he was told that as a painter you only have permission to be yourself. Be methodical and always be questioning your painterly instincts. Learn to know when the unmediated innocence of impulse is deceiving you. The trick is to avoid received technique. Symbiosis of muscle and touch, sense and sensation, that's where it's at. That and the initial surface joy before the idea is absorbed into mannerism, before the paint soaks in. Hang onto that. That's the very beginning and end of creation right there. To finger sculpt structure from void. There's the magic. Paint fog but don't do Monet fog. It's been done. Get your own. There are infinite gradations of blue-grey to choose from. Forge your own blurry imprint. Develop your own lexicon of smudge. Internalise the light-absorbing fenlands. The way the landscape sucks the daylight down from the big sky. The weather memory of dusk in unlit drawing rooms and dead flowers in a table vase a long time ago. Etiolated petals. Grease-softened stems in dank water, curlicued by harsh scissoring. Brushes in a big green Tate & Lyle treacle tin. College lectures about non-Euclidian space and depth, random symmetry, reverse perspective. Slide show presentations on how to apply the multi-evocative. Weighty principles half-grasped by inattentive undergraduates who assumed that learning comes from application not text books and were eager to get back to their artisan undertakings. All learning nodded through and never discussed in the canteen. Table talk was for ready gossip and glances. Checking out who was wearing the latest what and who Maggi would allow to sit at high table.

Going out into the late afternoon Camberwell sun and waiting for the number 12 bus on Peckham Road. Walking about a London made shabby by bombs and demolition dust. A glint and a gleam on the Thames. Driftwood bumping the shoreline. Barges heading off eastwards up the estuary out to open sea. Horizon clouds gathering. Cobalt blue to gun metal grey. The old boy at the bus stop who insisted on telling Syd about the dray lorries and totters carts and how the streets used to be full of rich manure for the gardens. Syd smiled indulgingly at the old timer's obsession with shit-paved streets and told him about Cambridge city centre, about the cows that grazed on the Fen Causeway meadowland with traffic passing and the ducks that waddled about the busy market square. "At the art college are you?" said the old timer. "You should go and paint the old canal before they fill it in." He never did.

That was then. Barely a beginning. And it precipitated a slow decline. Laboured time spent on increasingly negligible progression, just the slow sludge and slap of pigment going on. He rued his ability to talk himself out of his calling and all because momentarily he thought his destiny lay elsewhere, in the blare and the beat of pop song. Without the incentive and discipline of art school the work decayed. Scrape off. Begin again. Then again. In the end don't even bother doing that. After a while each incomplete canvas becomes a confirmation of limitations. Why not forsake all that? Abandon the project entirely in order to ward off a growing sense of failure. Ditch it all and do nothing. In the end there is only negation. Tubes unsqueezed and easels unattended. Rituals abandoned, the learning rejected, the impulse fled. Erasure and oblivion. These were now the preferred options. The ultimate anti-gesture. The perfect auto-destructive art was to do no art at all.

Back in now time Syd went into a newsagent and bought a copy of *Private Eye*. Latest Princess Margaret and Roddy sightings. Cartoon of rag and bone man shouting "any obsolescent material!" Very droll. Syd still liked droll. He remembered that time Snowden came to the college. Some of the students even combed their hair. Syd thought that preposterous. Long time ago. Going to all the exhibitions. Frank Auerbach coming in to give guest lectures. Lucky generation. Never had it so good. Adequate student grant. Took it all for granted.

Syd went into another newsagent and bought a copy of *Time Out* and 20 Kensitas for the coupons he would never cash in. He wandered across town to an exhibition at the Notting Hill Community Centre entitled Writing On The Wall: A Photographic Documentation Of London Urban Graffiti. He liked the sound of that. London as ever-present character and cast. Another walk on part in his daily dérive. Discordant jazz was playing as he entered the community centre. Piano and drum duets. Frenetic flurries of blue notes. His capacity for loud sound had diminished of late. He had once aspired to that kind of intensity but too many things had got in the way. Too many through routes turned to cul-de-sacs. It was the same with the grand narratives of acid. Too much ersatz cheapens the voyage. Once you get into something. He had a yearning for small scale now. Photos framed and mounted. Less sensory bombardment. All surface. Less to assimilate.

He studied a scroll that ran the length of a wall. The photo, taken on a hot July day in 1970, showed the brick wall outside the fire station at Euston. In off-white emulsion drips it declared:

The Tygers of Wrath Are Wiser Than the Horses of Instruction

Another photo of a whitewashed wall. It hides an overgrown locked garden in Ladbroke Grove. In black on white it says "This used to be ours. Give us the keys."

Syd's eyes glide to a hilltop city view. A backdrop of heat haze. Dockland cranes in the distance. In the foreground, two smartly dressed middle-aged men lean against rusted iron railings, expressions fixed, waiting for the camera flash. Behind the railings a squatted building is daubed in rebel script. No justice, no peace, off the pigs, it says on the heavily fortified door.

Syd pauses to dig the symmetry, the straight guys and the message, the joy of juxtaposition, the effortless next-to-ness of it all.

Syd stands next to a shot of an electricity sub-station behind some rusted railway tracks. Weeds thrusting up between rotted wooden sleepers. He reads an accompanying caption. "Loop Line: Waste Ground". A patch of scrub and gorse. The shell of a former bonded stores in the background. On a wall beside the sub-station it says "KICK OUT THE JAMS MOTHERFUCKERS". Stencil etched.

Syd crosses the small hall to look at the opposite wall. A gathering gaggle of W11 heads nudge each other. Word has got around. Look who it is. You remember Syd. The card reads "Fulham Palace Road. 1971". The graffiti says "Free Oz". Another dusty hot day. Three schoolchildren, one black girl, one black boy, one white boy, aged eight, maybe nine, are walking into shot, stage right.

Syd scrutinised a polaroid. Taken from the front seat of the top deck of a bus through smeary steamed-up glass. And through the glass an approaching road bridge. And on the road bridge bricks it said "Vietcong Vietcong". No, not said, sang, sang like a song. Vietcong. Vietcong.

Syd puzzled over an inscription he didn't understand. Taken on the walkway between two platforms of a disused railway station, closed after the Beeching cuts. A photonegative of some ghost line gone for some time now. It read:

? Did Cane really kill Able
? What about the harf nevre been told

Syd studied another inscription. Uncaptioned. A field of freshly harvested wheat, haystack monuments, a thin strip of Essex hedgerow, a dome of deep blue sky. Three quarters of the photo was sky. In the foreground, a corrugated barn reddened with rust. "No To Stanstead" painted on its roof.

Syd narrowed his eyes at a photo of a filthy black day. A rain lashed road. A low sided lorry passes in a blur, its tail light glow directs the gaze towards an archway wall. White emulsion illuminated in premature winter twilight. The verdict is "Hanratty is Innocent". It looks like a rushed effort. The name neatly scripted, the judgement follows in a hasty scrawl. The slogan questions the certainty of justice. Lay-by crimes. A man hanged. The white writing shines against a dark foreboding sky.

Syd glanced across the gallery at a well-dressed couple. The woman myopically studying a caption. A photo taken in the Hyde Park underpass next to Speakers' Corner in 1972. On scrubbed white tiles in bold red lettering it said "Lesbian Nation". "Do you suppose that was a term of solidarity or abuse?" Syd heard the man murmur. "I don't know," the woman said, as if to herself, "I don't know."

The Community Hall fills up a little, not substantially, but enough to make Syd feel uncomfortable. The group who had recognised him becomes a swelling throng. Word travels fast on the Vietgrove grapevine. A freak lingers in close proximity as if he is about to make an approach. Syd thought that one of the gathering looked familiar but he couldn't place her.

He became increasingly wary of the swelling crowd. His mood shifted. Suddenly the photos didn't look small scale at all. They looked like surveillance and intrusion. Cautionary tales blown up big. Perhaps too big. And far too overloaded with polemic for his liking. Syd fled the room.

Later that night he watched Michelangelo Antonioni's *Blow-Up* on TV. It seemed only appropriate that *Blow-Up* was on. He remembered going to the launch with Lucy Lea and the smart set. All of them surging on strong acid. Watching it again, alone, high up on the ninth floor reminded him once more of those days. He still loved the way Antonioni laid his paper trail, then turned on the wind machine and blew all the clues away. He loved the way that the film pursued the enigmatic and elusive. He loved the way Antonioni used the big screen to tamper with circumstance, to alter and enlarge, until the varnish coating cracks and flakes, revealing the chasm between the world assumed and the world unknown. The way Syd saw it, which of late was alone, the curtains shut, the heating on way too high, *Blow-Up* ultimately revealed nothing, nothing apart from what the actors and the onlookers chose to see, nothing apart from the associations one chooses to make. Antonioni the auteur, the illusionist, the visionary. The camera simultaneously obscuring and unmasking, a now-you-see-me paradox. Evidence recited in riddles. The further you go, the more you explore, the less there is to see.

Sitting there alone on the ninth floor, Syd reacquainted himself with the film's arcane vocabulary, the Metrocolor, the rain on the roofs, the Elizabethan psychedelic London, the bolted-on references to birds and queers and junk. Syd absorbed the Method dossing, the minds wide open, the high rises going up, the brand new garbage (even the litter looked like props), the audio hum, the loaded silence, the empty people, the sinister park, the undressed dolly girls, the icy seductions, the frozen then. Thomas the photographer cranking up the metaphor machine and click-clicking away. Every click a conjuring trick, a chimera, mything up the real. Click. The illusion. Click-click. Illusion layered upon illusion. Life as a negative. A dark room fix.

Blow-Up still spoke to him. It took him back to what he had often thought long before he ever saw the film. There is only the game, and the game is only as real as you want it to be. *Blow-Up* was simply a confirmation.

But mostly it reminded him of that night with Lucy Lea. The bit they liked best. The bit they mimicked when they got home from the premiere, still glaze eyed and glowing, coasting on their acid. The dope scene. The bit where David Hemmings puts on a jazz record and Vanessa Redgrave starts sofa jerking to the hep Hammond beat. Hemmings tells her to dance behind the beat. She isn't dancing properly. She isn't wigging out properly. She isn't smoking properly. Syd and Lucy found that hilarious. That idea of a proper hep way of doing things in Antonioni's idealised portrayal of Hepsville. Which when it came down to it was no less real or unreal than anyone else's depiction of the dayglo patented unreality of swinging London, whatever or wherever that was. Syd and Lucy Lea loved the dancing bit. They used to act it out all the time.

ANOTHER STRANGE MEETING

"I say. Would you mind awfully..."

Right hand raised in hope, with one foot on the pavement and another in the road, Nick looked like one of those *Vogue* photo shoot models snapped in hailing-a-taxi mode. Less well attired, obviously, unless dishevelled was now de rigueur. And arguably it was, dressing down having long since displaced dressing up as the dominant look. Brown, beige and faun dictated the drabscape. Palette daubs of dreariness and fag ash scurried by as Nick stood rooted to the spot, his broken-down Sunbeam Rapier festooned in parking tickets and facing the wrong way up a one-way street.

"I don't suppose you could..."

Passers-by hurried to be anywhere rather than here offering help in the pelting rain to a tall, hunched and slumped stranger who would also rather be anywhere else but here, helplessly stranded in the aimlessly busy London bustle.

This is the reality that Nick barely hints at in his city frieze.

A street-lined tapestry of dullness and drift. A tableau of everyday quiet sufferance and despair. All the junior clericals clutching luncheon vouchers and a first edition of the *Evening Standard* with the better paid Sits Vac jobs optimistically biro-circled. All the Matthew and Son filers and clock card punchers. The sweatshop immigrants hidden behind walls that haven't seen a lick of paint since the Luftwaffe. The Dickensian remnants who inhabit alleyways like skeletal apparitions. The labourers who gaze blank-eyed from upper floor loading hatches as the world below goes about its purposelessness. The Eleanor Rigbys who glance wistfully across the office and gossip sparingly, who window shop after work and go home alone to metered lodgings, to the one-bar glow, a takeaway and a secondhand paperback off the station stall. They dream themselves into a well-thumbed world of carefree women called Bunty and caddish men who cut a dash. This is an unromanticised Poor Boy London glimpsed from grease-coated caffs by an ever-shifting population of slow tea sippers and quick serve egg and bacon bolters. The weather delivers little but overcast skies and a taunting peepshow of sun that lingers teasingly behind cloud partitions of variegated grey. Late winter seems to drag on till late spring and the kerb stones are the colour of gravy.

This is a city segmented by building work and rubble, fenced off, leased out and ID stamped in Conrad Ritblat signs on slanting blue partitions. Bill posters will be prosecuted. Bills posted regardless. Wrestling promotions. Strip clubs. Variety nights. Van Morrison at the Hammersmith Odeon. Mervyn Conn presents the annual Easter Country Music Festival at the Empire Pool, Wembley. Alvin Stardust tour. Bill Hayley tour. Cleo Laine tour. This week at Ronnie Scott's.

Bright lights beckon in a hastily assembled bricolage of the glued and pasted. Last week's transient thrill nights already defaced and faded. Tattered and torn itineraries from previous promotions peek through like strata from a bygone slap and dash era.

Nick gave another hopeful twist of the ignition key. Nothing. He opened the driver's side door and attempted to push with his right hand and steer with the other but the task defeated him. "Need any help mate?" said someone finally. He turned around to see a taxi driver leaning out of his cab. Consumed by indecision, he stared at his vehicle and then slowly back at the cabbie.

"Only make your mind up. I've got a fare down here."

"Do you have jump leads?" asked Nick as the man approached him.

"Nah, sorry mate. Get in. We'll see if we can push start it."

Nick got in as instructed. "Stick it in neutral guvnor. You have got it in neutral, haven't you?"

Yes, Nick had it in neutral. Neutral was his natural setting of late.

"You need to get off this road, mate. You'll get nicked. Din't you see the arrars?"

Nick din't see the arrars. Already knew he wanted to get off this road, guvnor. Didn't want to get nicked. Not with what he had in his pockets. Just needed jump leads. To restore the battery. ECT for the car's brain. Car depressed. Engine damp. Mechanism silted. The weather soaks in on days like these. April showers and roof slate skies.

He tried the ignition again. Nothing but a feeble splutter. "Try it again." The car was shoved along a few feet. Again nothing. Nick steered absent-mindedly into the kerb, his shoulders slumped in defeat. "Hideous piece of junk," he thought to himself. "Should never have bought it. Should have listened to Dad."

He looked in the rear-view mirror and there was somebody else there alongside the taxi driver. Shoulder to the boot. Making a strenuous effort to get the thing moving again. Dressed in pop star clothes. Red velvet shirt and black velvet jacket, purple brushed velvet trousers, snakeskin boots that had seen better days. Long dark hair in dank tangles. Jet stone startled eyes. The car gave an involuntary seizure and almost sparked into life. "Nearly had it that time," said the cabbie hopefully. The man who was dressed like a pop star stopped pushing, stood up to his full height and bent his back a few times. He began to ask the taxi driver about The Knowledge and how he might sign up for it.

A white van behind the taxi beeped impatiently and the cab driver returned to his vehicle. "I'd call the AA mate. Have you got membership?"

"I've really no idea," said Nick with a despondent sigh. The cab driver shook his head and muttered something about bloody students. He thought Nick was a bloody student. And the other man, the man who offered to shove and wanted to know more about The Knowledge, he thought he was a bloody fruit and nut case. Streets are full of them. His job had taught him that much.

The man in the pop star clothes wiped a hand across his brow and watched the cabbie get back into his vehicle. Yes, that might be the life he thought, driving around, taking people to where they wanted to be, those who knew anyway. Good to have a purpose. He seemed a little lost now that the cabbie had departed. Just stood there, wondering how the day might develop from this point onwards.

"Do you drive?" asked Nick. "Only if you get in I thought I might..."

"Not lately," said the man in the pop star clothes. "I gave my car to Micky Finn." Nick assumed this might be some kind of argot. Cockney slang perhaps. "It was parked in the road," the helpful stranger added absently, but not particularly helpfully. Nick glanced at him, still vacant and far away, and wondered like the taxi driver if he was in full possession of his faculties. Something in his demeanour suggested otherwise. He did not pursue the thought.

Leaving the solicitous stranger to his musings and his Micky Finn argot, Nick rummaged around in an untidy glove compartment. In among the detritus he found the Sunbeam Rapier log book, cover page torn off and missing. Pencilled on the first page was a series of phone numbers, one of which he assumed to be his AA membership. Searching his pockets for spare change he found none, and so glancing at the helpful stranger who was still there, lost in contemplation, he ventured to ask if he might have a spare 2p for the phone box across the road.

"I have three," said the other man brightly. "Glad to be of assistance."

After protracted and painful negotiation with the numbers at his disposal, Nick first managed to phone a London friend by accident who asked eagerly where Nick might be calling from and invited him round. Deciding that Swiss Cottage was too far to contemplate either by walking or by public transport, Nick put the phone down with an apologetic mumble. He then called the RAC by accident and put the phone down again, this time without mumbled apology. After several stressful minutes, during which he thought about reversing charges and seeing if his parents were at home and might help him out, it dawned on him that his membership was with the RAC not the AA and that's why the number was on the log book. He phoned again and was assured that a helpful representative would be with him within the hour, "depending on the traffic."

Seeing that the helpful stranger was still standing there, Nick assumed that he was awaiting repayment. "Let me go into that café and change a pound note," he gestured towards an adjacent premises. Receiving only a blank look he began to explain his reasoning. "Yes, let us adjourn to a café," said the stranger suddenly as if jump started into conversation. They walked.

I can watch the car and wait for the RAC man, reasoned Nick, although he had little desire to sit and attempt chit-chat with the maladjusted man in the snakeskin boots that had seen better days, and yet had despite his bedraggled bearing loaned him 6p.

"Let us repair to a café, you could say," said the lender as they walked. Nick winced at the weak pun. Relatively unversed as he was in the ways of suffering fools, this one would do for the moment, he thought. Could probably tolerate worse and indeed have done.

Nick tried to order two teas but struggled to make himself heard above the hissing of the urn and the sizzle of frying food. "Two teas," shouted the man in pop star clothes just as the urn stopped hissing. His alarmingly strident voice startled an old man sitting by the door, who missed his sip and dribbled lukewarm soup down his chin.

They took their teas and sat down to watch London go by. Just two more anonymities in a city of such. Two more hazy outlines glimpsed from the road. You wouldn't have given them a second glance. They blended in effortlessly with the clientele, the daily flotsam. The businessmen, the bookies and barrow boys. The poplin-bloused check out girls and the meter maids who were martyrs to their corns. The restless, the uprooted and the eternally moved on. The people seeking little but comfort and temporary respite. The ones usually left undisturbed in library reading rooms and the more tolerant museums.

"Do you have far to go?" asked the 6p lender. "In the car."
"Unfortunately, yes," Nick replied without elaboration.
They sipped their teas and stared out of the window.
A radio played piercing trebly pop tunes from a high shelf. Off channel sibilance filled the café. S-seasons In The Sssun by Terry Jacks. Remember Me Thisss Way by Gary Glitter.
"Do you work in town?" enquired the friendly stranger.
"No," said Nick. Again, without elaboration.
"Well in a way yes," he said eventually. "I was doing some recording. I mean I was meant to, but..." his voice trailed away. Two Soho working girls came in and ordered expressos. They smiled at the two young men by the window. The radio played "The Cat Crept

In" by Mud.

"Music, you mean?"

"I'm sorry."

"You said you were doing some recording."

"Yes," Nick muttered. "I make records. That's the idea anyway."

"I used to be in the group," said the inquisitive stranger in a faraway tone.

Nick shot him a puzzled look. Sat there in his crumpled pop star clothes. "Used to be in the group." THE group. What group, pray? Just another sad story in the city of unfulfilled ambition he supposed. Pubs he guessed. The groups who play in pubs. Chalkboard on the wall outside. Wednesday nights. Support slot. Hired PA. No wages. Glad to have turned his back on that. No heart for the slog. Slip away.

"What do you play?" asked the friendly stranger. "In your group."

"It's just me," said Nick. "Just me and a guitar."

Every utterance was torn from him reluctantly. He had a habit of sounding like he was trying to erase the sentence the moment it left his lips.

"Three," he said, almost despite himself. "I made three. I might as well have made none."

The radio played the 12 o'clock news followed by He's Misstra Know It All by Ssstevie Wonder.

The friendly stranger cocked an ear. "I heard a song on the radio this morning that said love has many faces. How many faces do you suppose it has?"

"None," said Nick. "I don't think it has any faces at all."

The 6p money lender smiled sardonically at this. To anyone else it would have been a conversation stopper.

"Do you perform your own songs?" he asked eventually after several slow methodical sips of tea.

"I don't perform at all," muttered Nick, bringing his own cup to his lips and warding off further enquiries.

One of the working girls came over and asked for a light. The 6p money lender took out a Zippo and obliged. "I don't suppose you young boys are looking for company, are you?" said the working girl as she leaned in with her cigarette. Generous cleavage. The intoxicatingly sweet scent of the provocatively perfumed. "Only I live just round the corner." Three floors up. Pink flowery writing on a white card by the buzzer. "Swedish model" it reads. Push bell and walk up narrow stairs. Speak to the Madame first. Pay and go in.

"No thanks," said the Zippo lighter man, turning away and gazing out of the window. The working girl lingered for a moment, then sensing something in these two young vacant lots that went way deeper than indifference, returned to her table. You'd get more joy out of the guy over there gumming his way toothlessly through his pie and mash, she thought. He would love to be able to stretch to an affordable fuck. Or perhaps the nervous young man with the Dobells record bag who has just wandered in out of the rain. Make eyes at him when he's ordered and sat down. Make him blush. Not him though. Not the one pretending to study the racing pages. I remember him. Proper kinky bastard he was.

All this random interaction in one lunchtime café. An everyday *Threepenny Opera*. Not a single twitch of it would ever find its way into one of Nick's 'Poor Boy' cityscapes. Sixth form dorm stuff. Intangible yearnings. Rarefied sensitivity filter. No over-perfumed tarts in those reckonings. How long is this RAC man going to be, he thought, glancing with mounting agitation out of the window. The working girls sat sullenly, legs crossed, smoking. The radio played an endlessss ssstream of irritating ads.

The nervous young guy with the Dobells bag paid for his tea and made to walk over to a table adjacent to the window. Something in the demeanour of broken-down car guy and Zippo lighter guy seemed to make him change his mind. It was as if both men were throwing up an invisible force field of bad energy around them. He went and sat by the door instead.

"Here, let me pay my debt," Nick offered as if suddenly remembering his manners. "The 6p for the phone calls."

"There's really no need," smiled the helpful stranger without averting his gaze from the window. "Then let me get you another tea," said Nick.

"Yes, another tea would be very nice."

"Sorry, I am so terribly rude," said Nick. "I don't even know your name."

"The sugar bowl is empty," said the stranger.

"It's okay, I don't take sugar," said Nick.

"Neither do I," said Syd.

Nick went to the counter and returned with two teas which

he placed at the table with the grace of a head waiter. The working girls applied lipstick, uncrossed their legs and got up to go. "See you girls," said the owner wiping crockery. "Be lucky." "See you Alf," said the one who hadn't asked for the light. Neither of them Swedish like it said on the door.

Nick and Syd sipped their hot teas in silence. The rain came on heavier. "Did I leave an umbrella here?" asked a bedraggled voice from the doorway.

"I can't write," said Syd suddenly, as if to himself.

Nick looked at him sympathetically. He detected a weary air of regret in the utterance. An assumption of struggle was implied and then trailed away. Demo tapes sent and never answered no doubt, thought Nick. He has that look. It's the look of spurned opportunities. You see it on the Kings Road and the Soho alleyways all the time. In and out of the drinking holes. Languidly sozzled and ashen. Costumed in the latest apparel. It's all about the breaks. The clothes aren't enough. The clothes are never enough. He looked at Syd, still costumed in the finery, faded a little, in need of dry cleaning perhaps, but still clinging to his skin like a reminder of what he could have been.

"We started off doing other people's songs," said Syd.

"Yes, we all did," Nick smiled weakly, rekindling his own memory. There was a brief flicker of empathy between them that lasted no more than a few seconds.

"And it was fun," said Syd. "At first I mean. When you start out knowing nothing but are willing to learn."

"What songs did you use to do?" asked Nick.

"Oh, you know," said Syd. "The usual."

He stopped for a moment and then changed tack. "It's not difficult though is it? Anyone can write songs I suppose. They're everywhere."

Nick put his elbows on the table, clasped his hands and leaned forward, intrigued. He didn't find it easy at all, not anymore, but he wasn't about to offer that hostage to fortune and certainly not to a stranger who, for all his bluster had probably never written a song in his life.

"It seems to me that you should just be able to make up songs from found... I mean all the words have been used anyway so... my friend Kevin had a song that went *everything you can think of has been sung*" and that's how..."

"Your friend Kevin sounds wise," said Nick.

"Yes. He reads lots. Well he did. I don't know... I haven't seen him for a while."

"Are you still making records?" asked Syd, eager to shift the emphasis.

"Yes. I'm supposed to be. I'm not obligated though. It's something I inflict upon myself. There's a sense of if I fail... I'm torn between stopping completely and toiling on up the hill until I get it right."

Nick felt suddenly very tired. And a long way from home. Even halting conversation had exhausted him. He couldn't remember the last time he'd endured a stranger's company for this long and talked with such relative coherence, too. A familiar fog began to settle in his mind. The streets seemed to darken in daylight and not just because of the rain. It was a while before he came back. When he did he noticed that his companion's eyes were full of foreboding.

"It's that chap again, the one who keeps following me everywhere," said Syd, glancing anxiously towards the door. No sooner had he uttered the words than a short stocky man walked in, probably in his late twenties, denim jacket and jeans, thinning hair, puffy face, pasty white complexion. "It's you, isn't it?" he said, digging about in the holdall he was carrying. "I couldn't believe it. I was just walking past and it was you." He took a magazine from the bag and began waving it about excitedly.

"I'm afraid that you are grievously deceived," said Syd, looking away towards the window, beyond the window, beyond the world.

The intruder smiled through crinkled and moistened eyes. "It's you on the cover this week. Haven't you seen it?" He pointed again at the magazine. Inky black *NME*. April 13th issue. "World's snazziest rock weekly" strapline below the famous red title block box. Headlines promising Steely Dan and Man tours. A full-page photo of a musician with windblown hair looking down into the lens. And under that it says, "Syd. Whatever happened to the cosmic dream?"

"I'm sorry, look. I've asked you before. Please leave me alone," pleaded Syd. But his pursuer saw nothing of normal flesh and blood before him, only an idol, an icon, a vacuum in his life he could fill with worship. And now, here he was in this café, the cosmic dream himself, immortalised on the cover of the *NME*.

The cosmic dream got up hastily and made towards the door. "It was very nice to meet you Nick, and good luck with the songs," he said. Nick looked at the music magazine on the table and again at the man heading rapidly for the exit and out into the lunchtime rain. Until this moment he had assumed Syd to be just another failed audition from a long, long line of unsuccessful applicants. Nothing in his manner had given any hint of a successful past.

The fan stood there breathless, not knowing what to do now that his mythical Syd had fled. He looked like he was about to cry. "Are you a friend of his?" he asked, desperately hoping for the magic of secondary association.

At that moment a blue RAC service van pulled up across the road. A uniformed man got out and walked towards a badly parked Sunbeam Rapier. "I really must be going," said Nick, just another passing stranger in a city full of passing strangers.

THREE HOURS FROM LONDON

Nick started the car and headed off once more into the secretive realms of his compartmentalised life. He liked to drive. It was the most unconventional of anti-stress mechanisms, being on the road, surrounded by haulage wagons and flash Jags and rust buckets and open top jalopies. Surface spray smearing the windscreen. Wipers barely adequate. Tail lights of the vehicle in front twinkling. Guiding him on. Pre-motorway blue Bartholomew's route maps of negligible value tucked away in the glove compartment. Signposts frequently blocked by high sided trucks with whip crack flapping tarpaulin. Missing a turn off and continuing onwards anyway. The car steering him. Busking it. A road and B road therapy easing the pain. Any road would do. All routes lead somewhere eventually.

But to where?

Oliver (or was it Ambrose?) sent him a recently published book called *Zen And The Art of Motorcycle Maintenance*. He didn't get on with it at all. In fact, he found it immensely disagreeable. If the aim had been to get him to empathise with the author's open road philosophy then it failed spectacularly. In fact, the book sent him into a tailspin of depression that only getting behind the wheel could assuage.

There might once have been a time, not so long ago, when the book's beatific outlook chimed with his own exploratory yearnings, but not now. Not now he had less rough edges to chip away at. Life laid bare found little sustenance in cracker barrel truths and homilies. Had he retained a shade more of his youthful naivety he might have nodded with empathy each time he encountered a paragraph that echoed his own experience. But all that stuff about the travelling being better than the arriving and the serenity that lay at the heart of everything. Honestly! What serenity? There was little evidence of serenity anywhere. Why lie about it or offer false hope through spurious cant? The French would never fall for any of that flimsy bullshit, he thought. More backbone to their tracts. Spines that don't grow creased and lined. Glue that doesn't dry and unbind. It all reminded him of those confessional singer-songwriters he was sometimes lumped in with – if anyone thought of lumping him in at all – with their earnest epistles. Nominally singular but accumulatively doctrinaire in their coarse lay preacher pieties. Conflicts resolved by encountering a comely maiden. Strident certainties about the scheme of things. Political issues reduced to placard platitudes. The thought that anyone felt that he was part of all that brought on surging waves of nausea.

And as for that chapter where the author likened a car journey to being compartmentalised and cut off. And the assertion that what you see from your windows is just more TV, whereas a motorbike rids you of the filmic frame and puts you at one with nature. What nonsense. Just on a practical level he knew this was unpalatable. He remembered that one time he accepted a pillion passenger ride on the back of a Triumph 650 up to London with a friend who was "going that way". The pouring rain ran in rivulets down the borrowed oilskins that were meant to keep him dry. Water seeped in at the waistband. When they stopped at a quaint mock Tudor teahouse en route, the proprietor refused to let them in because they were drenched. When he reached his destination, Nick was so chilled and cramped from the journey that Simon (or was it Nigel?) had to administer his newly acquired reiki training to get his bladder and kidneys working again before they could all get down to the weekend's serious business of smoking Thai grass and listening to Miles Davis and Tim Buckley records.

Never mind being in contact with the awesome totality of nature. At least in a car you could stay warm and dry. Even have a kip in a layby should tiredness overwhelm you. And besides, he liked it all framed like that. The cinematography of it. The countryside as a gallery sequence of still lifes. A line of electricity pylons left side. Farmhouse and cattle sheds to the right. High cloud battlements ahead. Rolling hills receding in the rear-view mirror. This was all immensely preferable to flies and dust in the face and hailstones that might blind you and make you fatally overshoot a bend. A car cocooned you. Sheltered you. You could pause the journey and enjoy hot food in a transport caff without getting snooty stares. No heavy helmet or protective layers that made you sweat. If the stop off was too busy or loud he would take a polystyrene mug of tea out to his car and watch people come and go. There was something splendidly democratic about the great British truck stop. The anonymity of all those people he would never see again. The one-off encounters. The lorry drivers. The commercial travellers. The caravans and transit vans. Everyone in transit. Just passing through. A Bourbon chocolate biscuit and a quick smoke from his stash and on his way again.

But to where?

Although he wasn't a fan of science fiction Nick sometimes liked to imagine that he was driving through some tear in the fabric of the spacetime continuum. Parallel earthing into his grandfather's world in the 1920s. Seat high up and a blanket on the lap in some frightfully modern vehicle. Sounding the horn and frightening the sheep and shire horses. Chancing upon a country pageant in the springtime. Stopping to watch. Maypole ribbons a rainbow lattice. Skirts all a-swirl. Tea with a nip of brandy from the hip flask. A stiffening wind shivering the blossom from the trees. Crank the handle then off again, up dirt roads and onto deserted highways. Back to the daydreams. Back and forward in time. The ghost tread of his vintage vehicle merging with the smooth tarmacadam of a newly built motorway. His modern Sunbeam Rapier ripping through the decades and eliciting a gasp of disbelief from some old toiler in the fields. The faithful farm hand, Nick called him Joshua (sometimes Samuel), believes he has seen a fancily transported alien from another dimension. He tells the other old boys down the pub about what he glimpsed and they all pat him good-naturedly on the back and tell him of course he did. The landlord stands him a drink for the literary flourish and flare of his tale. You should write that down and send it in, the landlady tells him.

He would spend entire journeys preoccupied with this fantasy. On along the empty 1920s roads. Then the 30s. Then the 40s. A spectral dial next to the speedometer measuring the decades and the landscape's rapid erosion. The fantasy tended to peter out when he reached the 1950s. Too close. Too familiar. Traditions still cloying and clingy. Customs weaved into the fabric. Itchy shorts. Bound and gagged by uniform and uniformity. Free will only negotiable up to a point. I am a product of societal forces, he thought. I contain colonial multitudes and all the monographed baggage of privilege. This bothered him endlessly.

Pause the headlong rush. Take time to decelerate and observe the finer, more intricate and multilayered details of these societal forces. Shake it all up in a kaleidoscopic swirl of century dust. See how the dance of the ages syncopates its quick step and marries its restless energies to the dizzying dazzling pulse beat of progress. Observe the wrecked splendour of those grand abandoned merchants houses that would in time be converted to rooms for bedsitters to dream or go bad in. All those City chairmen and stockbrokers fled to greenbelt pastures. House keepers, parlour maids, cooks and gardeners economised to the below stairs minimum or dispensed with completely. Country piles reduced to crumbling rack and leaky ruin. These same palatial remnants willingly thrillingly accommodate the Bloomsburys, the Noel Cowards and Ivor Novellos. They play host to the late night shrill and the camp. The nouveau-riche of Hollywood and the Hamptons intermarry into old money. The stuffy relics and the vibrantly new learn to coexist in that peculiarly British way.

Tradition and modernism rub shoulders. Aspirants and

slummers. Bolsheviks and bloodline nationalists. The practising heterosexuals and the fragrant lovers who dare not speak their game. The faded grandeur of shabby genteel takes on a new lease. Starchy plus fours press against flimsy flapper dresses in the ballroom. Oak panelled antiquity bears witness to contemporary indiscretion (which is very much like the old indiscretion). Entrance halls and banqueting suites are lined with the country sports haul, culled, bagged, stuffed and mounted. These vulgar carnivore trophies are regarded with disdain by the back to the landers, the ascetics and the faddishly vegetarian. A way of life once rendered in Landseer stags and Stubbsian thoroughbreds goes geometric, goes garishly electrically bright and bold.

Time collages everyone and everything. The gene pool of privilege becomes muddy. Propriety is maintained in the face of conspicuous decadence and debauchery. Gazes are averted from peculiarity and peccadillo. The shrill thrill of nocturnal nude bathing. The incorrigible uncle who tiptoes along the creaky landing late at night. The candle-lit liaisons that will be indiscernible by breakfast. Blind eyes turn. Mum's the word. And matron. And nanny. In place of the old order comes a newly minted upper middle intelligentsia. More amenable to foreign thought and food. A contemporary haute bohème. A freshly dressed avant-garde. Out of all this activity, forged between two world wars, emerge the permissive possibilities that give birth to the 1960s. Time waves ripple back and forth across the decades. The past gifts the seeds of nascent possibility to the future. The present acknowledges its bequest. The 1920s and 60s are similar in so many ways. Pock-marked with ancestry that refused a title but somehow manages to limp along with limited means.

The unbroken retinue of old Harrovians gone wrong. The double barrels holed by circumstance. The decades breed familiar vanities. Similar bright young things. Identical denials of political realities with their look-no-strings trust funds. Alexander Plunket inherits £5000 on his 21st birthday which allows him to co-finance the Bazaar boutique of his partner Mary Quant. Plunket is the nephew of David Plunket Greene, one of the dashing debonair dandies immortalised by Evelyn Waugh. Similar connectivity is everywhere, spawning innovation and greasing the wheels with cultural and fiscal capital. The same familial guidance makes it entirely feasible for the Who to be managed by the son of Constant Lambert, for Ronan O'Rahilly, the Chelsea based grandson of an Easter Uprising Irish rebel, to keep Radio Caroline afloat with the shareholder pin money of Cadogan Square dowagers, for the scion of a colonial trade fortune and royal decree to launch Island Records, and for one of his artists to be driving to the Berkshire country pile of John Lennon, who is absent in America and has left his young personal assistants and their coterie of aristocratically connected friends in charge of his estate.

Nick wanders the south west wing of those hallowed halls with Tobias (or was it Tabatha?) in hushed reverential silence. Gold records on the walls. Shiny showbiz baubles. Dew softened mossy lawns. Endless spread of lush mansion acres. Stables, garages, gatehouse and guest cottages. Everyone outside on warm midsummer nights. The lakeside all lit up. Peals of laughter and tinkling champagne flutes and the nearest neighbour a mile away. Nick slips away from the revelry and goes inside to play those four perfect bars of 'Pink Moon' piano over and over again on Lennon's white baby grand, a mantra balm to soothe his soul. Yoko's Perspex art pieces are scattered about the room. He enjoys these precious solitary moments, curator of his own private exhibition. Soon enough he slips away again onto the open road. Back into the dream swirl of his imagination. Autopiloting down winding Suffolk lanes to Mildenhall to see John his producer. Avoiding Cambridge and the seat of his unlearning. Musing ruefully about how, had he locked into more orthodox thought lines, he could have amounted to a scholar of sorts. Leather patches on elbows. Library stepladder for the high shelves. A more convivial habitat for his airy detachment, perhaps. The occasional obligatory hour at the chalk face and then back to the sanctity of early Anglo Saxon and ancient volumes. He shuddered at the thought and banished the what if.

To where else?

To Witchseason. To a lobby full of newspapers and pop periodicals and warmth and coffee. To a reassuring smile from Andrea. A daily paper perused and then back to the non-conversational retreat. I half-read the news today, oh boy. There were few intrusions in the office. He liked it there. No one bothered you. He sometimes liked to go and sit there and while away a morning. They always seemed pleased to see him and although chit-chat could be forced and halting once the initial pleasantries had been exchanged, the Italian coffee was nice and always on the brew. How's it going Nick? A mumbled "Fine." And that would be the extent of it. The minimum of inconsequential detail. A regular coffee top-up, until at some point just before lunchtime Nick would slip away to negotiate the rest of his day. Sometimes there would be an imprecise or abrupt "must be going now" (although Andrea was rarely given any indication of the intentions implied in that "must".) More often than not she would return from the toilet or swilling out cups in the kitchenette to find Nick gone, until the next time he vaguely drifted in then out again.

And then where?

To the rolling South Downs and the sea air of Sussex to see Brian in Eastbourne or John and Beverley in Hastings. Never staying long. Barely a whisper. Bedroll and blanket in the spare room. Self-contained. Everyone a stranger, a threat, until they're not. Because he was so self-absorbed and solipsistic it would never have occurred to him that the young woman hurrying to the post office to buy a stamp was Shirley Collins who could have told him all about the folkways and the blues itinerants and her travels across America to coax singers out of backwood shacks for the price of a beer. Nor would it have occurred to him that the old chap gathering rosehips by the roadside was Bob Copper who could have taught him all about the oral tradition and the homespun harmonies that don't show up in the sheet music, and about how the seasons unfold in song and so much more, all for the price of a little help lifting a heavy wicker basket full of hedgerow harvest into the boot of his car.

One night in a rare coincidence of temperaments, he and John found themselves high on cognac and common accord. They agreed that what they did wasn't folk music. John by assertion, Nick by nodded acceptance. "What we do Nicky," John slurred, "whatever it is it isn't folk with a capital F. It's more metaphysical." There was rambling talk of woodland whispers and murmuring winds and traditions come undone. Of a currency altogether more ethereal. Songs that float in less solid air. The dark art spell of the sorcery wand. Melodies that dwell among fleeting shadows and flickering silhouettes. Beverley went to wake Nick with tea the following morning and found an unslept bed and a car gone from the drive.

Too sophisticated and urbane for the muck-spreading joys and deprivations of the countryside. Too broken and bruised for the ear-shredding cacophony of the city. Displaced and out of his water wherever he was. Storm tossed and untethered. Homeless even at home. Yearning for something resembling emotional anchorage, for a sense of place that couldn't be found anywhere. All along perhaps, in flight from himself. And so, on to the next distantly lit destination. A series of aloof wanderings and abrupt departures. That passage from Lord Byron: "The Lakers who whine about nature because they live in Cumberland. The Cockney School who are enthusiastical for the country because they live in London." A quote he'd encountered and disregarded with an amused shrug at Fitzwilliam. Now it was beginning to make sense.

All those places you visit. In time you come to realise there is a reason they are called old haunts. They are full of the haunted. Ghostly remnants of better days and games once played. A life at ease with itself. An assured eloquence and stature now reduced to startled stutters and broken bearing.

Driving back to his familiar patch of homeland. Safe shire seat. A sea of blue rosettes on election day. Tidy strips of manicured fields.

Showpiece gardens prettified by topiary and fortified by high hedge barricades. Mazes, follies, ha-has and kissing gates maintained by hired helps and dailies. An England made of manners and certainties and harvest festivals. Anglers on private permit lakes. Keep out.

When he got home, Nick went to the newsagents and bought a copy of *Melody Maker*. Father Rodney recorded this in his diary. On the front cover was a photo of Kevin Ayers, John Cale, Brian Eno and Nico, advertising their forthcoming June 1st appearance at the Rainbow Theatre. Ayers described the gig as "having a family feeling" and Nick pondered momentarily what life might have been like had he maintained contact with John Cale and become part of this family feeling. He mused on what direction his career might have taken had he written a song or two for Nico. He suspected that Kevin might be the person Syd had referred to, the one who read deeply and thought everything that could be thought of had been done.

He flicked on through the news pages. Graham Bond, possessed by all-consuming forces, had thrown himself under a tube train at Finsbury Park Station. Jon Hiseman in tribute had called it "a failure of the social services". Alan Stivell was playing Birmingham Town Hall the following Friday and Nick wondered if he could pluck up the energy and motivation to purchase a ticket. He reflected on the fact that Steeleye Span had sold out two nights at the Royal Albert Hall. The meteoric rise was duly noted. The Raver in his regular *Melody Maker* column remarked on how not that long ago they used to draw a small crowd "at the Cork & Bludgeon off the Keel Haul Road, Harlesden". Further on in the paper Nick read a review of their live performance at the Free Trade Hall in Manchester and was surprised to see that their set now incorporated a glammed up mummers' play, complete with fancy dress spacemen and vicars.

In the singles column he read scathingly sardonic reviews of new releases by The Original London Cast of The Rocky Horror Picture Show ("The Fugs did all this about a decade ago"), Roxy Music's Andy Mackay ("inconsequential fare for sure") and Bryan Ferry's cover of 'A Hard Rain's A-Gonna Fall' ("does the contours of the song scant justice.") Of Paul Simon's recent orchestral re-recording of 'The Sound Of Silence' the reviewer remarked "all meaning is lost amidst a big ballad production" and concluded accusingly "you have become a star at the expense of your identity". Nick had some sympathy with this final sentiment and momentarily felt vindicated in his decision never to obligate himself to trial by music press.

A large promotional advert from Bradley Records for an album called Clocks by Paul Brett boldly stated "includes the hit single Soho Jack" and bemoaned the fact that "the music world hasn't caught up with Brett yet." That's just what Island said about me in that full-page ad for Pink Moon, he thought ruefully. He couldn't recall ever hearing the supposed hit single 'Soho Jack' on the radio or seeing it on any pop chart. More record company hype and PR bluster. The usual tale of pretty promises and heightened expectations to be followed no doubt by the crushing come down denouement when the 'product' didn't sell. Nick imagined this Brett chap towing the line, touring the college circuit, third on the bill to some hard rock act, and for what? And when you see what they have been.

In the back of the paper he became engrossed in an interview with Alan Stivell. Stivell commenced by complaining about the local Breton farmers who had torn up the hedgerows and left the topsoil at the mercy of the north west winds that blew in off the Atlantic. Nick had witnessed a similar phenomenon in his own part of Warwickshire as the agricultural landscape began to change from small patchwork strips of field to something more uniform and large scale. He wondered too if the elm trees had started dying in northern France like they were in England. He thought about driving down to Brittany to meet Stivell. He quite fancied negotiating those twisting narrow lanes and feeling the full force of those Atlantic winds on his skin. Perhaps sitting by a roaring log fire in the evening and jamming a little with the Breton harp player. No words would be necessary. They could commune entirely through the medium of music. He filed the thought away for another day.

He read on, marvelling at Stivell's focussed articulacy, envying the lucidity with which the harpist outlined his musical philosophy, and about how aware he was of his musical lineage. He admired his positive outlook, the way he was fighting for his place in the margins, indeed justifying those very margins not as a precious dwelling for rarefied cliques but as a creative space where identity might thrive. Stivell credited the audience with intelligence and quietly suggested that kindred spirits always find each other where the circumstances are favourable. Nick willed himself to believe that this was so and tried to convince himself that everything would turn out all right for him too if he, too, just hung on in there.

Flicking on through the pages he was sardonically amused

to read in the introduction to an interview with Arthur Lee that the Love founder member, floundering of late, was shrugging off comparisons with what the journalist referred to as "zombie unproductive curios like Syd Barrett and Skip Spence."

At the back of the mag he found the usual gig ads. Among the folk listings he saw all those familiar names he'd once rubbed shoulders with, shared a small cramped stage with or watched from the wings with one eye on the hat being passed round and one eye on the exit. Clive Palmer, Vin Garbutt, Mike Absalom, Martin Carthy, Dave and Toni Arthur, and countless others, all of them still doing it, still putting petrol in the tank and searching the post-performance streets for a late night lock-in or curry house. Traffic were headlining The Rainbow. Michael Chapman was on at The Roundhouse. Julie Felix with Danny Thompson and band were playing the New London Theatre in Drury Lane.

After a while all this information began to make his head spin. Everyone from Horslips to Ornette Coleman was out there blowing the notes, being busy, trying, failing, reaching, innovating, enduring, never thinking of putting it all aside or squandering the gifts they were granted. It made him feel a complete failure and a fraud. He tossed the paper across the room and went downstairs to see if there was any cereal in the kitchen cupboard. Finding the shelves bare he went outside and sat on the garden bench to have a smoke. The night air was sultry and still. The moon scythed to a sliver. He gazed up at the vast cosmic vacancy of the stars and thought how brittle the universe seemed. He felt as if the entire canopy of the sky could come crashing down at any moment.

SOME CHIME, SOME CHING

Syd clambered into the attic rafters. Stale air ensnared up there, a thick unfiltered film of it, hanging with the bats and cobwebs. He surveyed the excess clutter of family accumulation. Ration cards, gasmasks, luggage trunks and hat boxes. Bashed and battered suitcases scented with the vintage fust of post-war boarding houses, the kippered carriages of steam locomotives and demob-happy waiting rooms. Wedding invites and blue ribboned RSVPs. A vanity set locked forever because someone lost the little pink key and no one could bring themselves to force it open. Broken toys and Brooke Bond booklets full of warships and wild flowers. Childhood volumes. *The Little Blue Jug. The Little Grey Men. Piggly Plays Truant. Palgrave's Golden Treasury. Junior Laurel & Gold* anthologies. An old play fortress coated in a stippled grainy wash of green. Portcullis, drawbridge and detachable moat still intact, rusted nails sticking up through the battlements. Bundles of his and his sibling's school exercise and college text books. A set of auction-purchased watercolour prints that father had meant to frame and mount but never got around to it. A box of brittle Shellac 78s, some cracked and split. All the stuff that migrates upwards to a darkened loft space, cast off but never cast out because everything retains its sentimental resonance and its shared memories.

Downstairs he could hear his father playing piano in the drawing room, less frequently than he used to, now that he was getting ill, but just as fluent.

Syd peered deep into the doll's house darkness. Shadowy recesses where the light never goes. Dwelling there among the numinous and the unilluminated. What else comes to life in that secret inner world? Where else would the inanimate be animated but up there in the belfry air of the attic?

There was this kid at school called Noel Spicer. Syd sometimes used to hang out with him. His father Lionel Spicer, like many of his generation, was a backroom boffin, building wireless crystal sets from the diagrams in *Junior Scientist*, making rudimentary light boxes that served little practical purpose but gave off a glow. Syd and Noel used to go to his father's garden shed to smoke and leaf furtively through a hidden stack of *Spick & Span* glamour magazines from the 1950s. Blank eyed busty women posing artlessly topless in artists' lofts and backroom studios or in some secluded sand dune corner of a windswept goosepimply beach. Mostly, though, Syd liked to go to Noel's shed because that's where his father kept his collection of automata and old shop dummies. It was the best museum he knew. Even when Noel was called in for his tea, Syd would stay there, gazing in awe, inventing stories for the liquid-eyed mannequins and diamond-rouged masques. A world of cogs and whirs. A mouse runs round and round a rotating mechanical disc. See mouse scamper. Silly mouse. Princess gazes out in despair from her locked tower. Full of thwarted love and infinite loneliness. Stupid bloody princess. Boo-hoo. What is the point of all that pomp and regality when all you can do all day is sit at your loom and be full of gloom? Daft girl. Giddy girl. Paint her morbid. Daub her in thoughts. Who is this mystery girl? And how did she come to be there? Invent her a personality. All the King's horses come clattering across the cobbled yard below. She won't look up from her darning and dreaming. Lonely in her tower. Wish she had wings. Give her wings and let her soar away. She waves sadly at her face with a clockwork fan and waits for a prince that will never come. Give her some detail. Make her fan a sequined one.

Marvel at the exquisite precision of tiny trill birds made audible by penny whistle metal breath. A grinder's monkey bares its teeth but doesn't chatter. Animals of no fixed species wear a groove into the ground with their mechanised pawing. Clockwork toys leave no imprint. The fox will never catch the hens. Woodworm has more life than this. Some of these animals don't even look like animals. They are the bolted together sum of Lionel Spicer's spare parts. They remind Syd of the painted phantasmagoria on the fairground hoardings when Thurston's comes to the Common every summer. (He broke into Thurston's yard once, where all the rides go to hibernate during the winter months. Walked among the ghost fayre exhibits. More animated imaginings.)

Look at all these things. Listen to their lonely choreography. Coil sprung shrill bells emit a tinny echo from a clock tower. Who could be hiding up there? Exiled. Gazing out across a deserted city vista.

A hurdy-gurdy turns. Woodland creatures conjured into life. Scuttle among makeshift undergrowth fashioned from crepe paper triangles and bramble wire. Moorish stone breakers and church makers. Blackamoor princes with their caskets of hidden treasure. Have they come for the princess? Will she hear them call her name? Will they sing their sad brooding threnodies? Turn the handle and make them dance. Tumblers and jugglers. Harlequin and Columbine. Unfurling cobras and earth brown charmers. A model of a model making a model in a workshop full of models. The inner life endlessly mirrored.

Syd's whole stop-start thing. The stasis and momentum. It all begins here in this phantasmagorical world of motionless play dolls and wind-up toys. All that time spent in attics and sheds. The memory odour of stale perfume. Syd, the boy child, is dream time narrator and becomes part of the narrative. Narnia wardrobes. Slip right in and feel the fine powered snow beneath the shoeless feet.

Ideally, he would have liked a room like this, full of mechanicals and automata. That would have been grand. Places to go where this stuff makes a different kind of sense.

"Why explain? Explanations are for those grown disenchanted by magic." The man on the TV programme said that. It went in.

A compulsive doodler and drawer, Syd stuffed entire sketch pads and exercise books with inventive wordplay and cartoon characters. His letters to girlfriends (which were frequent and expansive) possess a devilishly mischievous wit that skitters off the paper, sometimes literally so. (Ballpoint sketch of man hanging from bottom edge of page. His legs continue to dangle helpless on the other side. Man hanging by his fingernails from window ledge. Caption reads "thank you for your support".) The cast of characters is sizeable and ever changing, a crackpot ensemble of eccentrics and mishaps that in another life would have earned him a career as an animator or children's author. They included:

Jack Glow & Beatrix (charcoal-shaded bulb-shaped man with sinister illuminated smile, hand in hand with Fairy Girl with gossamer wings. Speech bubble caption above her head says "I'm Beatrix. I just potter about.")

Mister Currant Egg (drawing of electrified egg man in chequered trousers and John Bull waistcoat with potato tuber antennae shock hair standing on end.)

Ken Odd (buck-toothed man with ladders for legs and invalid crutch arms, single strand of electrified hair in the shape of a question mark, ping pong ball stuck on a stalk on forehead. Knitted T-shirt with big K emblem.)

Rice Mandy (egg timer figure on a pock-marked crispy grain of breakfast cereal, blond bobbed hair in bunches, tight busty sweater, Bic-shaded blue tights, her wet-look lips blow bouquet kisses of heart shaped flowers.)

Sniffles and Snuffles (Two germs. Identical twins. Drawing of flies avoiding them and heading for nearest preferable dog poo. Stink rays.)

Grouchy Mrs Stores (Old lady outside her shop. On her knees scrubbing her step. Cartoon soap suds and bubbles rise. Window display of boxes, bottles and jars meticulously rendered. Product names stencilled on. Brasso. Dreft. Lifebuoy. Jif.)

The Broody Moos (a field of bloated cows, pregnancy indicated by swell lines. Moo they go. Moo.)

Dolly Teardrop (a single teardrop shaped like a drooping petal. "Hi I'm Dolly. Join me in my teardrop adventures. Let's see what's making me sad today.")

Terence Teasel (Finely detailed flower head with Little Weed face and spikes for hair. "Ha-ha. Let's see if we can find Dolly Teardrop and make her cry by stabbing her repeatedly with my head.")

Gas Hat (Second World War gas mask man with coiled appendage arms and legs, wearing a toff's top hat. "Wot-ho" he goes.)

This is where he went to distract him from the boredom of school lessons. Double Misery stretched out endlessly through the afternoon. More than one doodle book was confiscated and never seen again. This is what he did while taking his art foundation course at Tech, as eager well-informed teachers droned on about the Bauhaus and the Golden Section. This is what he continued to do even when he first arrived in London. Even when he joined the band. Their first proper recording session documented in cartoon scrawls and a refusal to take any of it too seriously. In time, he came to see it all as a cartoon, with everyone ascribed their own regimented role in the greater Hanna-Barbera scheme of things. Diverting thought into his own imagined Kate Greenaway fairy tale flick book. Or the illustration pages he gazed at in Lewis Carroll or Hilaire Belloc or AA Milne or Kenneth Grahame and all the other *Dream Days* fables that he would much rather inhabit and for some whole days he did.

The fair came once or twice a year. To the Midsummer Fayre and sometimes to Jesus Green. Syd's earliest memories were of the stalls and rides laid out in neatly arranged rows like a formal exhibition hall or flower show marquee full of trestle tables and display stands. He loved to gaze along each row all the way to where the helter-skelter and the ferris wheel rose like architectural monuments. By the time he reached his mid-teens the rides arranged themselves in a more random piecemeal array, as pitches arrived at different times and the evolution of the site developed organically according to space and needs. Syd loved to watch the procession unfurl and assume the shapes that a fairground makes. Haulage lorries full of dodgem cars, Jollity Farm beasts, rifle range ducks, gaudily painted partition blocks, coconut shy cups, hook-a-prize sticks, wires, lights, generators. All unloaded and ready to spark into life.

He remembered the older rides that disappeared over the years. The Cakewalk. The Electric Dragon. The Octopus. The Swirler. The Waltzer. The Speedway. He walked around the entire site the moment everything was up and functioning, breathing in the scent of the rain-sodden grass during a dismal summer, the parched carpet of straw in hot years.

Best of all was the penny arcade, a canvased world within a

world of child adults and boy men all drawn to the hypnotic lure of the apples and oranges spinning in rows. He loved it in there. The soft patter of rain on the bowed roof, the trapped heat clam of undeodorised sweat. The tell-your-fortune machine that for a few small coins suggested that you would be lucky in love. His painterly eye took in the one-armed bandits with their pop art graphics. Black on bright yellow. Yellow on red. The tarnished silver shimmer of the pay-out slots. Las Vegas. WINS. Ambassador. Jubilee. Circus. Snake Eyes. TEN TEN TEN Liberty SIX SIX SIX Cherry Smash. GO. Machines shaped like monsters come to steal all the spare change from your pockets. Machines shaped like robots that might run amok through the town and spread terror like in a cheap sci-fi paperback. Machines shaped like gas pumps. Machines chromed like jukeboxes. All bloated and shark-finned and imported from the nickel and dime dreamland across the ocean.

He liked to hang about by the dodgems, too. Another stop-go world. Spinning around and around in a car with the blurry glare of red and yellow lights flashing very fast. That's where the music sounded best. The Everly Brothers and Del Shannon. Johnny & the Hurricanes and the Shadows. Dick and Dee Dee. 'Kaw-Liga' and 'Goodbye Cruel World', amplified and distorted by the thuggish bass throb of the speakers, bigger and more pulverising than any he'd seen at the social functions or dinner and dances he was dragged along to.

He would watch the fairground guys, all flick knife quiffs and grins, hanging off the back of the cars, taking cash, dispensing change, lingering a little extra with the girls, then relay baton switching to the next passing vehicle and the promise of a date, the lure of a grope. He'd watch them moonwalking against the motion of the Jollity Farm, rising and falling with the ride, stepping dangerously close to the exposed mechanism of the pivot before balletically skipping up onto the central ramp. The choreography of the whole place fascinated him, the sounds, sights and sensations of a child's first immersive environment, the diesel odour and the candy floss scent. The hint of menace and danger when it got really late and the local boys, aggrieved at the attention their hotsies were getting, started to circle. Jemmies and car jacks concealed inside jackets. Blades passed surreptitiously from hand to hand. Give us your stilettos, Brenda. Obliging Brenda wriggling out of her shoes in the long damp grass behind The Waltzer.

Not all of his school mates were allowed to go to the fair. He noticed that. Some who did attend were, to their eternal shame, accompanied by wary protective parents. Meeker kids only came on the cheap ride afternoons, feeling safer in daylight. There were murmurs about the history of the place. The red light caravan where you formed an orderly queue. The unwashed urchins who roamed the perimeter, trying every car door. The hand jobs in dark recesses behind the tarpaulin rows. All this simply made it more thrilling to Syd but he was not unaware of the friends, even school friends, who were allowed to camp under stars with the scout troop, but were banished from within a mile of the common in midsummer when the wild boys gathered.

For his own part, Syd found many of the rides a tad tame. The dodgem goes never lasted long enough. The ferris wheel never whirled speedily enough. He wished sometimes that a ride would come lose from its moorings and just fly off into space like a badly pinned catherine wheel on firework night. Preferably with him on it. Wouldn't that be good? Urging it on, faster faster through the go fastersphere. Hurtling across the starlit skies like that. Long comet trail arcing into pipet-sprayed vapour on a pop art canvas as big as this pop art life. Whooosh!

ONE OF THESE THINGS FIRST

Nicolaus Drake. Actor. Journal Entries. Various 1969–73

Sunday April 13th 1969

Family gathering for *Caesar* on the telly. "Nicolaus Drake is a member of the Royal Shakespeare Company." That received a warm murmur of approval from the room when Betty said it. I tried to explain to her that it doesn't quite work like that and this wasn't a Royal Shakespeare Company production anyway. "Robert Stephens is a National Theatre Player" received that accolade. He was an excellent Mark Antony. When my name did roll by there was a huge cheer from all. Mother dabbed a discrete hanky. You'd have thought I'd played Caesar himself rather than the murdered poet Cinna. After all, I only have about ten lines before I'm slaughtered by the plebs and carried off. "Tear him for his bad verses. Tear him for his bad verses." Family and friends are of course your most loyal and faithful audience. If anyone noticed me dislodge the scenery when I was stabbed they were far too polite to mention it. I've never done that once in the stage production, but put me under the glare of those television spotlights and no polystyrene column is safe.

I told Betty that she will probably have to wait until I'm in something a shade more prestigious before my name is afforded the courtesy of a voiceover. Father said wasn't it a shame that the moment was not to be recorded for posterity. I had to tell him that tape is very expensive and that the Corporation has to preserve its resources for far more important events like the Trooping of the Colour and *The Rolf Harris Show.*

It was strangely reassuring to sleep in my old bed. Everything left as it was the last time I was here. Lulled off to sleep by the gentle sound of Gay next door practising her guitar. All in all a wonderful homecoming but I was glad to get back to the flat and Christopher.

What is my name? Whither am I going?
Where do I dwell? Am I a married man or a bachelor?
Then to answer every man directly and briefly,
wisely and truly: wisely I say, I am a bachelor.

Sunday April 20th 1969

I'm very intrigued by the poet Cinna, both his mythical life and real one, if there is such a thing as a real one. The scholars don't agree on his identity. There's a vast discrepancy in dates regarding when he was supposed to have lived. Shakespeare as unreliable as ever of course when it comes to historical accuracy. There's no trace of the epic poems that made him famous and his lineage seems a tad blurry too. Virgil contradicts all the available evidence and his dates don't tally either. Ovid also mentions him and that's about it. Apparently, he was big on metamorphosis as a theme which makes him even more alluring. I'm very attracted to the idea of transformed identity, it goes with being an actor I suppose. I must investigate further. I feel there is an idea that could be pursued here. A play about a marginal character who is incidental to the main action but comments on it from the sidelines.

I shall store all this information away for when the eager school children come to our workshops and thus enlightened they will go away and pass their A-levels. Like what I did.

Thursday May 22nd 1969

To the BBC for the penultimate day of *Doctor Who* filming. Only one more episode of being a brainwashed soldier and I'm done with this tosh. And so is Patrick Troughton it seems. Making way in the Tardis for, so I'm told, Jon Pertwee in the next series. Mother tells me she appeared with JP in *Murder At The Windmill* and *Miss Pilgrim's Progress* back in the dark ages. I shall miss the subsidised lunches in the BBC canteen. Can't beat it for decent cheap grub if you're an impoverished actor.

Friday May 23rd 1969

Met your actual Kenneth Williams in the BBC canteen. Heard him before I saw him (well of course!) in the queue, loudly proclaiming AT THESE PRICES? In THAT voice. Geoffrey insisted on introducing me. Oh yes, I think I've seen your Coriolanus he said. He hasn't of course. He just wanted to roll that on his tongue. And anyway, I was only a lowly serving man in Cori, one of my several spear carrier roles that has brought me to the dizzying heights of running down BBC corridors with a cardboard ray gun in *Dr Who*. You're tarnishing your gifts dear KW said when I told him what I was working on. I asked him what his plans were now there is to be no more Jules and Sandy. Talks about a TV series apparently but he was very huffy about Bill Cotton not showing any interest in the ideas he's come up with. He's just finishing a radio series. Did you catch it, he enquired? I couldn't lie. No, well nor did the audience for the most part, he said. It didn't sound much cop from the way he described it. You haven't been doing that Hamlet at the Roundhouse have you he asked. He meant the Tony Richardson production I presume. No, I escaped that, I truthed. "Well done you, complete madhouse from what I hear". He's also been filming another *Carry On*. *Carry On Again Doctor*. (The dead weight of that *Again!*) He had an extended moan about it to Geoffrey before he had to dash off to the Paris Theatre. It doesn't seem to occur to him that he could always stop doing them. He was wit and charisma personified but it must surely get tiresome having to be that on all the time. After my brush with the immortal Kenneth it was a bit of an anti-climax to go back to being a brainwashed soldier.

Sunday 21st December 1969

Watched the first episode of *The Owl Service* on ITV. More than a little miffed as I read for Gwyn but "wasn't quite what they were looking for". Too old apparently. And not sufficiently priggish looking for the part of Roger either. Watched it through envious eyes hoping it would be terrible but it was mesmerising. A very brave thing to put on children's television on a Sunday teatime I thought. The lovely Gillian Hills from *Blow-Up* as Alison with her period pains in the opening sequence and all the darkly druid mythological stuff. Gay read the book and urged me to do the same before I attended the audition, and perhaps I should have done. More her kind of thing than mine and I can see where she gets the ideas for some of her songs now. All that folksy-wokesy flowers and owls stuff and the spirits and sprites that inhabit the rocks and the trees. Not really me I'm afraid.

Saturday March 6th 1970

Awful agency photo of me in the back of *The Stage*. Geoffrey's idea. I look very stiff and wooden. G says the aim is to widen my profile as the Shakespearian big parts continue to elude me. Doesn't seem to have made any difference so far. The offers still dribble in for banquet attendees and spear carriers. The irony is of course that I'm still just getting the same low-key roles in films as on the stage. Man chatting at bar in the Officers' Mess. Foppish dreamboat on a passing Cambridge punt, incidental to the main action naturally, just scenic candy. Then there was that totally unconvincing rock drummer in *Take Three Girls*. Two lines of dialogue. "Yeah man," and a half-hearted drum roll was the sum of it. Despite this I like to convince myself that my charisma smouldered throughout. "Look at my charisma smouldering," I said to Christopher as we both watched it through our fingers. "That will be my socks drying in the Flatley," he replied.

Tuesday September 29th 1970

I am to be a hippie in *Crossroads*. "Right up your street," said

Geoffrey when he delivered the glad tidings. "You won't even need to act." Something I will have in common with almost the entire cast I fear. The exterior shots are filmed in Tanworth, so I'm surprised I haven't already strayed into shot at some point as an unpaid extra while walking through the village. "Passer by – Nicolaus Drake". Met most of the cast at the read through. Filming tomorrow, no messing about. It won't take up too much of my time. Only three weeks. I turn up in chalet five as a bit of a mystery man. Rarely leave my room other than to spout what I can only assume is the writer's idea of hippie dialogue at a bewildered Amy Turtle on Reception. After a week of this nonsense I start having all my meals delivered to the chalet and strike up a bit of an understanding with the lovely Diane. Things will deteriorate when it is discovered that I am taking drugs (drug not specified as yet) and then as far as I can ascertain I vanish without trace. As indeed will my career. "I feel you've let the side down terribly," sighed mother uncharitably. The cast are lovely though. A real siege mentality feeling of we're all in this together so come on let's make the best of it. Dame Noele OBE DFC insisted on making everyone beans on toast after the read through. Burnt the pan.

Wednesday October 7th 1970

A day off from recording at the *Crossroads* motel. Slept in my home bed and woke to a glorious golden autumn morning. As I sat in bed nursing a couple of tea Gay amazed me by sheepishly entering my bedroom and throwing an LP record on the bed. Here, I've made this she mumbled. Cover photo of her gazing wistfully out of the window of an upstairs room. I had no idea she was making a record but she's been up in London recording all her songs. Mother confides to me later that she financed it. No one is to tell Dad in case he starts using words like "squandered" and "inheritance". The whole affair seems tantamount to vanity publishing to me but if it makes Gay happy. The thing is, having listened to the record, it's actually quite good. She has a very beguiling breathy quality to her voice and although some of the songs meander on a bit they are impressively constructed. I didn't even know you could finance a recording in such a way. It can't have been cheap but I didn't pursue the ins and outs of it. I jokingly said to G that she should have used one of those recording machines on railway stations that Pinky uses in *Brighton Rock*. This didn't go down well. Do they even still have those machines? I haven't seen one in years. Presumably having put out the record herself means that she won't get the all-important exposure, reviews and suchlike but she's sent some to the pop papers anyway and one or two to people we know at the BBC. I said I'd do what I can to help. The overall impression I get is that she just seems happy to have made a record at all. But that's never enough it is?

Sunday April 11th 1971

Found Mother a bit forlorn and faraway, sifting through old mementos and effects. She perked up a bit when I came in and seemed eager to show me her ancient scrapbooks full of clippings. There was also a stack of old copies of *Plays And Players* retrieved from the cellar, with fusty damp pages and rust stained staples in the centre folds. What a treasure trove though. Yellowing photo of her in her very first stage production. *Oedipus* at the Old Vic the year after the war, although you can hardly tell which one is her among the Theban chorus all comported about. Lovely photo of M taking her long-haired collie Copper for a gambol across Hampstead Heath when she was still quite the thing. Another from 1954 on a boat captioned "in gay holiday mood Molly gets up early in the morning to cruise down the Thames" (!) Lovely framed and autographed publicity still of her as Lady Thiang in *The King And I* in a beautiful oriental outfit. Gilbert Harding snored through the entire opening night, she told me. Also, a photo of her hoofing in a dreadful costume through some awful review she couldn't remember the name of. "I sang a song called Bognor Regis choo-choo", she laughed. Thinks it was the Lyric in Hammersmith. Of her Katherina in *Taming Of The Shrew* the newspaper clipping says "Molly Drake bursts onto the scene as the most untameable of shrews. Anger blazing forth from her every tone and gesture. The other characters are colourless in comparison." Benzedrine? I suggest. "Acting Nicolaus. Acting," she says, going all grand dame on me. A lovely review of her in an adaptation of Andre Gide's novel *The Immoralist* at the Arts Theatre. Homo theme. Lavender marriage. Torn allegiances etc. "Very brave for its time," she tells me.

She then shows me a beautiful photo I've never seen before of the two of us emerging from Anello & Davide's in the Charing Cross Road. Mother in feathery pillbox hat and her lovely mustard coat with favourite broach, clutching bulging bags. I resplendent in school uniform, shiny shoes, shorts, rain mac and all, all the current shades of grey on display in grey old 1950s England. We went to Piccadilly and Fortnum & Mason's after that I remember. I also remembered the shop girls in A&D and the flamboyant boys. "Oh,

they all adored you," says Mother. "You were in your element there."
She said. Giving me a look.

From July 1954 there's a newspaper clipping commemorating
our first TV appearance as a family, Mother playing Aziza in
Special Providence. (Beautiful photograph of her in pearl necklace
and earrings. Long slender fingers. Hands cupped thoughtfully.
Immaculate nails.) Next to that a much smaller photo of a reluctant
little Gay and eager I cast as her children. I remember that day
so well. The hot lights, all the trailing wires that one tried not to
trip over. Playing snakes and ladders with a lovely makeup girl
backstage. I can still smell the grease paint remover just thinking
about it.

Mother, as she is over fond of reminding us, was there at the
very birth of live theatre on TV. Technical breakdowns, fluffed lines,
actors drying in sheer panic, the lot, all at the mercy of fate as the
cameras continued to roll. She recalled a dreadful Ibsen with Peter
Ustinov. "*Peer Gynt.* He hadn't even bothered to learn all his lines.
Hopeless actor. He could only ever play himself."

There she is mentioned in best performers of the year in
1954 alongside Gielgud, Peggy Ashcroft, Dorothy Tutin etc. What
happened? I remember all her enthusiasm seemed to drain from her
as time went on and we children grew older. Perhaps the two are
connected.

I indulge her for half an hour or so before she grows tired.
Can't help thinking there's a kind of sadness underpinning all this.

I get the impression of a life unfulfilled. Perhaps that's why she still lives her old life vicariously through me. I must seem a great disappointment as I shuffle from bit part to bit part. My big break still to come presumably. No "anger blazing forth from every tone or gesture" for me I fear.

Friday May 28th 1971

Gay feeling very sorry for herself as – surprise surprise – no one took the slightest bit of notice of her record. I'm not sure what she expected. You can't just release an LP (a privately pressed one at that) and expect people to flock to you, especially if you do nothing to publicise it. You can't just sit in your room moping. You have to mix and mingle. She's had all the advantages of a comfortable life and there are plenty of times when she could have made the most of family connections in furthering her career but she seems to resist any attempt to help her or suggest ways of getting out of her rut. Won't really listen to advice. Just drifts about the place or goes and sits in the summer house to smoke her exotic cigarettes. She's still writing and playing all the time though. I admire her for that. I hope against hope that her inner resolve will get her through – but is that ever enough, I ask myself? She's obviously quite talented but then so are a lot of people. The difference is they all go out there and make themselves available. I realise this all appears somewhat harsh when set down in a diary like this, but someone needs to tell her. She seems to slip into ever darker and darker moods and I feel sometimes that none of us can reach her. I'll be glad to get back to the bright lights and giddy rush of London.

Monday October 30th 1972

I am writing this while sitting in my caravan overlooking some godforsaken lake or loch as we say up here. There's a kind of misty damp in the air which has permeated my mobile lodgings but the fog seems to be lifting now and the trees on the other side of the water are no longer a shroud. We had the wrap party last night and my head has been split asunder by double cask whisky from the local distillery. I had the technicalities of double cask explained in great detail to me by a lovely young man called Murray. Filming has been a very odd experience I have to say. First my part was written out, then it was written back in again. And I'm still not sure if it will survive the cutting room. The film is meant to be set in springtime so they've had to glue fake leaves and blossom to the trees. I revelled in the whole artifice of the thing. There have been constant budget problems so it's all being done on the cheap – and it's none the worse for it I have to say. It's a very inventive film. I'm involved in some of the dancing and prancing so at least there's a chance of a five second glimpse or two for the family as the camera catches my good side in the light of a seedy tavern. I thought the folky element of the film was going to be all fol-de-rol nonsense but it's much murkier than that, involving human sacrifice of some poor unsuspecting puritan policeman who comes looking for a lost child. The divine Miss Ekland graced us with her presence at the party last night and had none of the Scandinavian haughtiness she sometimes displayed on set. One of the crew told me they are going to use a stand in for one of the more saucy scenes as Miss Ekland refuses to display her derrière. One for the show reel that – Miss Ekland's stunt bum. Perhaps that's the ladies' specialism – stand in buttocks to the stars.

I'd love to see her ad in the back of *The Stage*.

Late on, very drunk, one of the crew staggered over and said "I've been watching you all through the film. You haven't got a fucking clue how it works have you? How to get to your marks, what camera you're on." Before I was able to say how dare you and damn your impertinence he said "and that will be your strength sunshine. Learn to let the camera come to you. You'll never be out of work with that pretty face." He gave my knee a little squeeze and off he staggered again into the merry throng. Later on, I overheard him discussing the Ballet Rambert with Lindsay Kemp. You meet all sorts in this world. The trick is to never look surprised or take anything to heart.

Friday November 10th 1972

Phoned Gay to tell her they are looking for music for "the Scottish film" and that I thought some of her songs might be right up their street, being a bit witchy and sorcerous. She thought I was being sarcastic and dismissed the very idea. I told her to sleep on it. Sleep is all I ever do she said. Poor Mother, having to put up with this all the time. G then tells me she has done a song for a children's education record. Or was it four songs? Oh, that should pay well I said. Get in on the music for schools racket and you're got it made. Oh no she said. There's no money. It's for a charitable trust. Something to do with local council literacy initiatives. All sounds very worthy and noble but it won't pay any bills will it? She sounded half asleep when she talked. Must be the medication she's on. I resisted the temptation to offer her advice. She never listens anyway.

Sunday September 30th 1973

At a loss for something to do this weekend I was flicking through the film listings in *Time Out* and was struck by the preponderance of soft pornography on display even in most legit cinemas. *Get Thee To A Nunnery* and *The Sex Shop* at the Berkeley on Tottenham Court Road. *Naked And Violent* and *Sex Explosion* at the Biograph in grubby Victoria. *Penelope* and *The Bitches* (that's two films although it wouldn't have surprised me had it been one) at the Centa in the Dilly. *Super Dick* and *Extremes* (if you please!) at the Classic on the Charing Cross Road. And who could ignore *Love Play Swedish Style* and *The Loves of A French Pussycat* at The Classic on Great Windmill Street? Something to unite the nations there. Wandering through Leicester Square and into Chinatown the other day I was struck by how ubiquitous the filthy flics are. They are everywhere. Perhaps that's the way to go. I should audition to be a eunuch when they make the sequel to *The Porn Brokers* or *Not Tonight Darling* (50 mins cut from 89 the latter listing said). Now showing at The Jacey in Charing X.

We ended up going to see something called *Wonderwall* at the Camden Film Festival.

Complete tosh. Colourful tosh though and it did have her royal highness Irene Handl in it. Mentioned this to Mother on the phone. "Oh, I worked with Irene," she said. "Some awful pimples and pores thing at the Garrick about a working class family who win the pools." Says Irene was wonderful and can do all the accents. "I played a tart," she added gleefully.

Monday December 31st 1973

I'm completely bushed. I've been so busy. Plenty lined up for next year. I auditioned for the lead part in *Mahler* but Ken Russell said I wasn't rock starry enough so they went for the rugged Mr Daltrey instead. Ken is going to bear me in mind for his next film though which is a musical version of the Who record *Tommy* (oh lordy!). I'm also going to grace the nation's flea pits in a delightful piece of nonsense called *Frightmare*, where I play the butch leader of a motor cycle gang. Had to learn to ride a 500cc Triumph for that, which I regard as my most notable achievement to date. A leading role continues to elude me alas but I live in hope. Who knows what 1974 will bring? At this rate you're going to end up as a bit of a cult said Christopher. Or at least I think that's what he said. It was a terrible line.

IN BLUE WORLD

The spires are rumbling in Notting Hill Gate. Syd Barrett and Steve Took are attempting to form a band. We sent Pearly Spencer to have a gander. What gives man? What gives?

I arrive at my Harrow Road basement studio location at the appointed unearthly hour – apparently there is such a thing as 11am – to find no one home. Vietgrove is all abed at this time of day which begs the question, why was I summonsed? What's the mad rush? Hearing shutters going up a street away I seek out the one caff that caters for the morning crowd. I am served scalding hot tea by a surly matriarch and am sitting by the window, considering whether I should burn my lips by attempting a second sip, when the bustling figure of Tony Secunda goes walking by, furious expression on his face, fists thrust angrily into overcoat pockets. He doesn't look like a man to be tussled with. I risk a hopeful wave. He executes a body swerve which would have done a sober George Best proud. "What are you doing in here?" he bellows. "Aren't they rehearsing yet?" They soon will be.

Secunda doesn't seem in an especially good mood. "Fucking

groups," he says. "You can't take your eyes off them for a second." As we track back towards the rehearsal room he tells me about a certain semi-famous rock band he's been looking after recently, and about how they've just been upstaged by a certain almost as famous support band, managed by someone who is presumably no longer on Secunda's Christmas card list. Said support band kept missing their soundcheck and performance slot when they regularly showed up late, leaving the local promoter no choice but to send the headliner on first. When this happened three nights in a row Secunda and his charges became suspicious. "I sent a crew to have a scout around," he says. Tony has an ominous way of saying "crew". "Found them sitting in a side street in their transit having a smoke. Much as I suspected." Said transit was rocked on its sides till said support band spilled out. Said support band haven't pulled a similar stunt since.

Secunda may seem an odd choice to be managing a pair of miscreants who haven't even properly settled on a name yet but then, as he is quick to remind me, he managed Tyrannosaurus Rex for a while and rocket launched their leader off into the glittery heights of Bolanmania. He remains fiercely loyal to Marc's former sidekick, the man he affectionately calls Tooky. He used to see Syd Barrett and his old band regularly at UFO when he was managing the Move. "Phenomenal with the lights and all the special effects," he says. He reckons he can get Barrett back on track. "All he needs is the right vehicle."

The vehicle at the moment appears to be called In Blue World, although that may change. "Steve wants to change the name of the band to Soul System because he thinks it's more commercial and they'll get more chicks. I told him to cut it out," says Secunda.

Currently, In Blue World is Barrett on guitar, Steve Took on drums and bongos, and an ever-changing array of bass players and rhythm guitarists. In the past few weeks everyone from members of the Pink Fairies to David O'List and Blinky Davison have dropped by to sit in and jam. "Last Thursday I was halfway towards reforming the Nice," says Secunda. On the day I watch them rehearse the auxiliaries are ex-Junior's Eyes and 'Space Oddity' guitarist Mick Wayne and occasional Pink Fairy and Social Deviant Duncan Sanderson on bass. "I've sunk a fair bit of money into this," Secunda says. "I've got a lot of faith in these boys."

Once the band has been summoned from their slumbers I spend a pleasantly mellow afternoon drinking the band's tea, smoking their somewhat harsh Nigerian bush, and watching them rehearse. I also snatch the odd moment with Syd and Steve to formulate what I will loosely refer to as an interview.

"Do you like the bush?" asks Took, as ebullient and cheery as always. "It comes in through the Embassy. Diplomatic bags. What do you think of the band name? It was one of Syd's phrases. He's a fountain of ideas. I wanted to call it Juniper Suction just to wind Marc up".

There's a fair bit of jamming before things settle down into anything like a proper rehearsal. "It sounds a bit like Creedence at the moment," Steve suggests. "They do the best choogle, don't you agree?" Syd looks noncommittal. "It should change as we go on," he says distantly, as if to himself. "Things are liable to move at full speed once we get going. It takes a while. Not like it used to."

Syd has that in absentia thing going on when he speaks. Staring at you through faraway eyes and answering a question you might have asked five minutes ago or maybe didn't ask at all. He reminds me of Beefheart in this respect. So what material are you going to do, I ask, having not heard anything I recognise yet. "We're going to do some of Steve's songs and things I have. That I kept. It's a bit moody so far. I suppose there should be some happy songs. Something that might get in the charts."

The vibe is very W11 informal. A Hawkwind or two drop by, to borrow or bring back gear. "You want to get one of them Mellotrons," shouts Dave Brock from the back of the hall. "Be more like the Moody Blues." This raises a smile from Syd.

The chug-a-lug-choogle eventually eases into something more distinctive. Mick Wayne in particular sounds inspired, taking the weight off Syd and pulling things into shape when the imprecise timing of Took (not the world's most metronomic drummer) and Syd's Telecaster meanderings appear to be going nowhere. "I want to put Mick on the same retainer as the others," says Secunda, "but I don't know if he wants to commit. I need to have a talk with him." Syd going full throttle is still a sight to see, though. The inspired moments only come in short bursts while I'm there, but he retains the ability to wield an echo pedal like a paintbrush and can still peel off an exquisite psychedelic solo as in days of yore.

Can you see this band making records? "I don't see why not," says Syd. "We could do a tour as well. Tony's wife has been working with David Bowie and we might be asked to do some gigs with them." I ask Syd what he thinks of the new glam rock look that's in fashion. "The bands are wearing lipstick. That style seems to be coming back," he agrees. Does he take any credit for it, given that he used to wear make-up and androgynous clothing on stage? "Well everyone was doing it. Arthur Brown was first I think." I mention that I was there at the Roundhouse the night Arthur's head caught alight. "I wouldn't recommend that," says Syd with the merest hint of a twinkle.

At one point a journalist arrives from the underground press. A bit star struck, he tries to engage Syd in conversation. Syd meets his adoring gaze with a noncommittal stare and a string of non-sequiturs about what he had for breakfast. "I'm sorry, I don't speak French," he says, bringing the conversation to an end.

The extent to which Syd is compos mentis has been debatable for some time. Close up he seems to delight in putting people on and hiding behind incomprehension when it suits him. He is perfectly polite to me, and seemingly conscientious about his general role in the scheme of things.

"I hadn't realised how much I'd missed playing," he says. "The thing before in Cambridge [he means the ill-fated Stars venture] was just something to do with friends. I don't know if people thought it was going to be more. I shouldn't have thought so. We only rehearsed a few old songs. I would have done more perhaps. You have to keep busy somehow."

When everybody else goes off for a break Syd and Steve sit alone doodling and jamming. Steve sings a plaintive self-composition, picking out a tentative melody on acoustic guitar while Syd accompanies him on bongos. Then they swap for a lovely version of "Dominoes". You would have put money in the hat if you'd heard them busking it in Portobello Road.

"There you go. Deboraarobed," says Took with a smile. "See what Tyrannosaurus Rex could have been if Marc hadn't disappeared up his own arse," says Secunda.

"People think I spend my time melting into space but I don't," Syd says shortly before I leave. "I live a mundane life really." I detect a certain hesitance in his manner at the end of the rehearsal. For a moment he seems a little lost, standing there in his pop star clothes, still looking the part but not I suspect fully engaged with the task at hand. I ask him how committed he is to the new venture. "It should be possible to see the merit in everything," he says vaguely. "It's just a question of adjusting to your circumstances. It's like looking at a different sun."

Just as I'm leaving, Steve Took bounds over, tripping over a chair that someone has placed thoughtlessly in the middle of the room within clear sight of him. "I've decided we're going to be called Juniper Junction," he calls out. "It will look good on the posters."

The world holds its breath and waits.

Pearly Spencer, *NME* December 9th 1972

THE SCREAMING AB DABS

"What are you driving these days, Nick?" The Major peered at him through bleary bloodshot eyes.

"Midget for town and the A40 Farina for longer hauls," said Nick.

"Just the job," said the Major. "Just the job. Refill?"

"No thanks," said Nick. "I'm probably over the limit already. I'll head home along the back way. Just to be safe."

"Of course," said the Major. "I say, have you heard about this splendid stuff called Alco-Kill? Don't know how it works but some of the chaps in the clubhouse were talking about it. Worth looking into," he said tapping his nose. And with that he staggered off into the gathering. Adrian seized his opportunity and sidled over.

"Ah Nick, just the chap. I've been meaning to catch up with you. Haven't seen you since Henley. Or was it Cowes?"

"Yes, it's been some time hasn't it?" smiled Nick accommodatingly. "Must have been Henley. We didn't make it down to Cowes this year. What with the baby and everything."

"Emma coping okay?"

"Oh, she's been an absolute brick," said Nick. "Of course, Nanny Brick helps."

"Where would we be without them?" said Adrian.

"Quite," said Nick.

"Refill?" asked Adrian, seizing a bottle from a passing pretty girl in a pinny.

"No, I'm driving," said Nick. "I suspect I'm already one over the proverbial."

"Bloody Barbara Castle and her breathalyser," said Adrian. "I say, have you heard about this device called Alco—"

In his diary, Nick's father Rodney mentioned that during August 1972 his son would spend a lot of time in his room listening to his radio and that on the 4th of that month, a Friday, he had "got the horrors" and was too frightened to turn the radio off. Let us delve. On that particular day, at 11:30 in the morning, Radio 4 broadcast the fifth and final extract of Alan Garner's *Elidor*. Read by Geoffrey Banks, part five, "Findhorn", concluded the story of four children who enter the sunlight deprived mythical land of Elidor through a portal in a derelict Manchester church. In the bleak, unsettling wastelands of this world of blighted crops and ruination the children encounter a man who tells them of the Four Treasures that must be retrieved if normal life is to be restored. Once back in Manchester each child (one of whom is called Nicholas) tries to come to terms with the desolate world they have visited. They do so with differing degrees of conviction and resolve. One boy, Roland, hides the treasures they have been entrusted with, firstly in their recently vacated house and then deep in the soil of their new garden.

Strange things immediately start to happen. When Roland first goes to retrieve the treasures, the old house, indeed the entire street, appears charged with static electricity. Ethereal apparitions manifest themselves as floating shadows which Roland at first tries to shrug off as optical illusions. Back home the TV howls with extraterrestrial interference. Electrical gadgets come to life without being plugged in. Nicholas's transistor radio fills with atmospheric crackle that drowns out the programmes. Sinister unseen figures move about noisily in the hall. In a seemingly innocent seance at a children's party, Roland receives messages from the other side. He experiences mentally destabilising episodes as a result, seeing ominous portents in the cheap plastic toys the children are gifted with when they pull crackers at Christmas. And on it goes, as unleashed dark forces slip through a parallel Earth portal and stalk the slum clearance landscape of post-war England. Garner's tale serves as a powerful disavowal of Arcadian innocence, an anti-Narnia. The book's denouement is brutal and bloody. The uncomfortable moral of *Elidor* is that Paradise is lost, never to be regained, not even in childhood.

Later that same day at 6:30pm on Radio 3, *Study On Three* examined "Why ghosts are frightening and how story writers succeed in making fictional ghosts horrific." The programme, hosted by Jonathan Miller, featured as its illustrative text *Lost Hearts* by the writer MR James. Salient extracts from the book were read by Bernard Cribbins. Let us suppose that Nick listened to both of these programmes and was spooked. Let us assume that they infiltrated his psyche and tainted his dreams. Let us continue.

"Who are those children in the bushes?" asked Nick, suddenly amused by the sight of a little boy and a girl standing outside in the rain and waving from the formal arrangement of dwarf conifers and rose bushes that bordered the gravel drive.

"Oh, that will be Phoebe and Giovanni I expect," said Adrian. "You know, Delia and Perry's little perishers."

At that moment Phoebe and Giovanni emerged from a side door and went over to their father who was in a corner holding court on stocks and bonds. Nick was perplexed at the rapidity with which they had covered the ground to the house, more so by the fact that they appeared to be both bone dry and better dressed than they appeared when waving from the bushes. The disparity he put down to drink and gently placed his empty wine glass on a glass-topped table by the window. Adrian continued to badger him about cars.

"I was just wondering, I heard you talking to the Major, and I hope you don't mind me asking but what's the insurance on the Midget? Pretty expensive I'd imagine".

"Oh, not at all," said Nick, politely tolerant as always of small talk. "Fully comprehensive £120. That's with no-claims of course. Would have been far more if I'd taken the policy out in town. That's with Midland Northern and Scottish. Seems a very fair service."

"Oh, I've never considered them," said Adrian. "Are they good?"

"Excellent," said Nick. "Great for business policies, too. Covers you for towing accidents as well. You know Emma and her prangs. She does insist on taking the caravan up to the Lakes during half term."

"Has she still got the soft top?" asked Adrian.

"Oh God that old banger. Yes. Dame Jalopy she calls it. Somewhat grand name for a decrepit pile of rust wouldn't you say?"

"Hello mister," said Giovanni skittering through the crowd. "Did you arrive in that stagecoach?" And off he went again into the throng. Nick pondered the anomaly of the utterance and the strangeness of Giovanni's gait. The way he shimmied and swayed from side to side as he swerved around the various garrulous groupings of adults. Nick also noticed little Phoebe leaning against a wall, surveying the booze-fuelled jamboree with some disdain. She wagged an admonishing finger at her brother as if to say, stop showing off, and then returned to looking sulkily into the middle distance. Father Perry, alert to the dangers of a cascading child rampant among glassware and bone china, swept into the melee and lifted Giovanni high and good naturedly above his head. With one deft move he plonked him against the wall next to his sister and quietly told him to behave. Bribed with tray offerings from a pretty serving girl the two children assumed sullen silence and concentrated on their shortbreads.

"Foxy little minx isn't she?" Nick overheard someone say from an adjacent conversation. Two men laughed leerily at this and purred approvingly into their glasses.

"I heard about the Minx," said Adrian. "Bad luck old chap."

"Oh yes, terrible business," said Nick regaining his conversational bearings. "I see what you mean yes. The Hillman Minx. That was weeks ago".

"What happened?" asked Perry.

"A platoon of cider-happy skinheads took it from the drive and diced it madly through the streets all the way down to the athletics stadium," said Nick. "Then they... torched it, I believe is the popular expression."

"Something needs doing," tutted Adrian.

"Birch the lot of them," said the Major returning to the conversation.

From a far corner, Phoebe made whipping gestures with her right hand. Her face went puce with mock anger. Giovanni let out a little shriek and bared his teeth. The gathering chatted on in high spirits, oblivious to the children's curious antics.

"So, which one's yours?" asked Adrian surveying the parked cars in the drive.

"Mine are at home," said Nick perplexed. "I told you, Emily—"

"No, I mean which MG silly," said Adrian. "Is it the lilac one?"

"To match my shirt, yes," said Nick. "I like to accessorise." This immediately struck him as an odd thing to have uttered because his car was in fact the maroon one. Seeing that Adrian was looking dumbstruck he tried to correct himself. As he did so his mouth went dry and he began to feel lightheaded. "No, mine's the maroon one and I'm parked over by the verge," he managed to say with some difficulty.

"Oh, next to the stagecoach," said Adrian. "I was wondering about that."

"I gather it's to do with the historical pageant in the village," said Perry. "Some of the chaps from the Rotary Club are involved."

"£1500," persisted Adrian.

"I beg your—"

"The outlay. £1500. For your car."

"Oh, I see," said Nick, by now beginning to feel distinctly peculiar. "No, £1400 I believe. My accountant dealt with the paperwork. It's all deductible."

He suddenly felt as if the words emerging from his mouth didn't belong to him.

"Why are the children digging up the driveway?" he said.

No one responded to this. There was a sudden loud crash from the kitchen and all the men cheered in that boorish way men do in the clubhouse or saloon bar when a butter fingered lacky drops a tray of empty glasses.

"Two litre?" said Adrian.

"Sounded like a soup tureen," said Nick. "Oh I see, the infernal car, yes. The not lilac coloured car. That doesn't match my shirt. Yes. Two litre."

"And spares shouldn't be a problem," persisted Adrian.

"I'm sorry," said Nick. "Would you excuse me for a moment?"

"Carpeted boot I'd imagine," Adrian shouted after him as he made off a little woozily towards the hallway. Having waded through swamp-like shagpile for what seemed like some time, he eventually reached a spacious lobby. It was not as he remembered it from previous visits to the house. For a start, it now appeared to have a glass-domed ceiling which he had never encountered before. He was pretty sure he would have noticed the extra light it let in. He gazed upwards with some bemusement and saw that the glass was now decorated in cherubims and seraphims. The peak of the dome was dominated by an angel fresco featuring two children whose faces strongly resembled those of Perry's Phoebe and Giovanni.

He wasn't sure what happened next. Gemma told him later that he passed out in the hall and the children came running into the room where the guests were gathered and shouted for help. Someone offered to call an ambulance. "No need for that," said the Major briskly. "Just give him some air. Walk him about in the garden.

He'll be fine."

"That's it. Do as the Major says. Up we come," said Perry, helping Nick to his feet.

"I'm so sorry," said Nick. "I think it must have been the heat. And when the children... I was looking up and admiring the dome and..." He looked up at the angel fresco for reassurance but the hallway had resumed its normal proportion and there was no glass above.

"That's odd," he said, as he took a sip of water. A couple approached him. "Have you met the wife?" said Bertrand. "Driven by gin she is." "Indebted to gin," his wife agreed, swaying drunkenly on his arm. "Deborah," she slurred. "I've heard so much about you." There was an uncertain pause.

"You're supposed to say, not all of it bad I hope," prompted Bertrand.

"Yes. Go on, say it," said Deborah as well as she could manage.

Nick complied. "Not all of it bad I hope."

"That's it. That wasn't so difficult was it?" Deborah purred in a manner she presumed seductive. Bertrand lit two Pall Malls and gave one to his wife.

"Quiet little thing isn't he?" said Deborah, blowing smoke extravagantly into the air then leaning in theatrically. "You should spend a little time with us. We'll soon liven you up."

"It's difficult at the moment, entertaining I mean," said Nick apologetically. "What with the baby and—"

"Oh, I don't mean with your wife silly," said Deborah. "I mean just the three of us." She attempted a cheeky wink but, half-cut as she was, it manifested itself as an unfortunate facial tic.

"Take no notice of her. She's always like this after half a bottle.

Did I tell you she likes gin? She delights in gin."

"I'm delirious with gin, darling," said Deborah, baring her teeth and shaping to make a snappy little bite.

"Hideously tolerable, isn't she?" said Bertrand.

"Yes," said Nick uncertainly.

"Are you sure we can't tempt you upstairs into something a little more wapacious?" said Deborah going all girly. "Come on pwease Nicky darling," she implored, tugging playfully at his jacket. "Oh, I like this. Velvet is it?"

Just then a crowd rushed out past them in the hall. "Oh blast, it's not a fire is it?" said Deborah.

"No darling, not even your breath is that toxic," responded Bertrand for which he received a playful slap. "It's the stagecoach. I did mention it. Come on."

"Isn't he domineering?" yelled Deborah over her shoulder as she was yanked away. "Come on Nicky," she shouted. "Let's go and see the silly old stagecoach."

Out on the drive a small crowd was admiring the coach and four that stood rather grandly among the Jags and Bentleys. Everyone marvelled at the attention to detail, the plush seated interior, the polished oak beam panelling, the gleaming leather harnesses on the immaculately groomed bay horses. A group of men gathered in a semi-circle and began to loudly articulate the kind of bluffer's knowledge they would normally reserve for wine tastings and the Twickenham Sevens. Adrian stepped forward and tapped one of the huge rear wheels with his knuckles as if in search of defects. "See this? Spring suspension," he said to a couple of uninterested ladies. "Made all the difference to your comfort that did in the 18th century. Elliptical coil that is. Sounds like some kind of elaborate contraceptive device doesn't it?" he added for good measure. The ladies regarded him as if he was contemptable and resumed their conversation about soufflé and extra-marital affairs.

"Didn't expect to see you here Dad," said Nick, surprised to see his father up on the raised gantry, dressed in a coachman's cape.

"You should get out more," said Rodney. "Come and muck in. The chaps from the Rotary would love to see you. Always room for one more on top," he said, patting the plush seating.

"Always room for one more on top," repeated Deborah, leering into Nick's peripheral vision and playfully patting his bottom.

"Your dad's right though," said Macer from the local stud farm. "It's the big thing now, stagecoach racing. We all get dressed up in period costume and have a bit of a grand prix around the village. Some of the locals don't like it of course. It involves closing off the main thoroughfare. But it is Sunday after all."

"I knew nothing about any of this," said Nick, shaking his head in amazement.

"Presumably you're not really up with the jousting either," said Macer.

"Excuse me?"

"The jousting," repeated Macer.

"Jousting as in...?"

"Yes. Every last Sunday of the month we recreate at huge expense a mock-up of the 11th century French tournament complete with authentic pavilions, marquees and pageantry displays. It started off as a bit of a sideshow at the fête but it was such a roaring success the Duke now regularly sets aside one of the larger meadows and leaves us to it".

"I... I really had no idea," said Nick.

"Oh yes. Participants are kitted out in armour, much of it donated from the Duke's private collection of heraldic artifacts. Him off the telly does a turn and gives expert advice on how to forcibly dislodge your opponent from his respective steer. It's tremendous fun. Why don't you come along in three weeks when we next meet?"

"I will," said Nick.

"Splendid," said Macer. "And if you don't like anything from the Duke's collection you can always get kitted out from one of the traditional armorial suppliers up in town, like Fitzwilliam of St James and Edmunds of Pall Mall. All the well-heeled young blades are flocking to these armory boutiques I can tell you. I wouldn't be at all surprised if it turns into a bit of a craze. Tell you what I'll do, why don't I introduce you to some of the jousting in-crowd? We tend to gather at one of the private members clubs. Charlemagnes and El Cidz are the current favourites. I hear there's a new one starting up called Templars. They've got a music license too, so that could be fun. What do you say Nick?"

"I've never heard of any of these places," said Nick utterly dumbfounded.

"That's cos they don't exist, you daft cunt," said Macer. "None of it does. I was pulling your leg. God you're gullible."

With that Macer did a sort of mock equestrian trot over to a corner where Nick recognised some of the stable lads and apprentices from the local yard. From time to time one of them would look over and jeer. "Fitzwilliam of St James," someone would say in a mock posh accent and a roar of raucous laughter would go up.

"Trabb's Boys. It's the cross we must bear," said the Major staggering past and holding up an empty glass in search of replenishment.

A brazier was wheeled over from an outhouse. Chestnuts were roasted. Glasses of hot punch were handed round by the girls in pinnies who by this time had changed into risqué red basques with bunny tails and now seemed to vastly outnumber the guests. The children came out dressed in the same rags that Nick saw when he first spotted them in the bushes and their father proudly announced that they would now perform a series of madrigals and gavottes. Giovanni played a weird kind of contraption like an electric hurdy-gurdy but Nick couldn't see a lead or jack plug or any evidence of the power supply that was apparently amplifying the instrument so well. Phoebe accompanied her brother with a medley of plaintive songs sung in a keening high voice. The madrigals and gavottes gave way to a lengthy saga that told of spurned love and sunken continents and hearts ripped asunder by betrayal. After several verses without the guidance of any form of explanatory introduction the narrative became increasingly hard to follow, slipping first into Franglais then Old Norse. It seemed a strange song to sing before such a boisterous gathering but everyone stood in reverent contemplation as Phoebe's little voice rose gallantly in an effort to be heard above her brother's increasingly violent plucking of the strings. The trees which initially appeared to be full of leaf when Nick had arrived earlier that afternoon now looked stark and bare in the evening sun. A chill wind got up and everyone drifted back indoors, many of them displaying the childlike swaying gait that Giovanni had choreographed when he first weaved through the crowd. Nick began to feel strange again.

After a little more inconsequential chit-chat in the hallway Nick managed to extricate himself from Adrian who had launched with renewed passion into a discourse about the perils of buying a secondhand car. "Check to see if it's been lozenged," he advised. 'It's car dealer's parlance for if the vehicle's obviously been shunted." There seemed to be a moment where Nick could have sworn Adrian said "I bet your wife's been shunted, eh? Eh?" Or perhaps it came from the nearby group of stable lads. "I must away," said Nick eventually.

"Why are you talking like that?" asked Adrian, offended that Nick was looking at his watch. "Why say, I must away? Why not just say, I have to be going?" Adrian sounded genuinely aggrieved, not aggressively so, just wounded. "Oh, it's what we must do," Nick whispered as if to himself. "It's an act. They're all in on it," he said gesturing conspiratorially to the departing gathering as stoles were slipped onto strapless shoulders by obliging chaperones. Nick turned and faced his inquisitor one last time. "We all have many faces as you well know, Adrian. This is just one of mine. The one I use in a social gathering. I'm conditioned to it I'm afraid. Don't let the mask slip Adrian. Never let the mask slip." And with that Nick made off towards his car, pleased with himself that he had delivered a crushing home truth to the boorish automobile-obsessed Adrian. "My own wife has no faces at all," he shouted back with one last triumphant flourish. "None of us do," shouted Macer from the stud farm. "None of us do."

Nick slumped into his car with considerable relief and felt immediately reassured by the comfort of the driver's seat. "What a day it's been," he said to himself. "What a day it's been." He checked the shape of the steering wheel, a tell-tale sign that a car has lozenged according to Adrian, and was pleased to see that it was still rectangular and not diamond shaped. He wound down the driver's side window to get some air. Other guests were drifting out onto the drive. Deborah made rude suggestive hand gestures as she passed. "Have you met my wife, my dream wife?" said Bertrand. "Addicted to gin. Poleaxed by gin." "Made drowsy by gin," slurred Deborah. "Sweet dreams, you innocent little boy." "Don't forget what I said about Alco-Kill," said the Major as he grappled with a huge golfing umbrella in the gathering wind.

Nick started the engine and drove slowly down the floodlit drive and out towards the road. Phoebe and Giovanni waved mysteriously from an ornamental bird bath on the lawn. He made his way steadily along the dark country lane, disappointed that there was no moon to illuminate his route. As the hedgerows gave way to an expanse of fields and open road he increased his speed steadily. His head cleared of party fog and he felt reassured by the cat's eyes glowing on the glistening wet tarmac. He dipped down low over a narrow packhorse bridge and negotiated a shallow brook, testing his brakes as the sign requested. On into the Faery Forest he drove. He was so mesmerised by the way the intertwining branches formed an arc across the road that he only noticed at the last minute the 17th century stagecoach hurtling at great speed towards him, his father resplendent on the gantry making a whiplash of the reins and urging the horses onwards.

He began to scream as he assumed the brace position. He was

still screaming on impact, a dry, parched gasp of a scream. The kind of scream you let out, or think you let out, when awakening from a terrifying dream.

"Nicky. Is everything okay?"

The call came from the master bedroom further along the landing. A mother's worried cry, faraway, distressed and sleep awakened. From a tree perch somewhere in the nearby woods Nick heard the high melancholy call of a barn owl, a lone tremulous note under sombre motionless stars.

PRETEND YOU ARE A POTATO WITH EYELASHES AND... EXIST

"Is anyone getting anything off these madeleines? I'm just getting flashes of previous madeleines."

There was knowing laughter among the gathering as they bit into their delicacies. The previous week there had been a Happening. Or rather an attempt by English college boys and girls to emulate what they understood a Happening to be from what they had heard and read. Everything was based on received information and instinct. And for what they received they were truly thankful.

The conversation revolved around that event. Validation keenly sought despite the veneer of cool indifference. Indulgent wit compulsory. The college mag reviews were cursory, written by people who tolerated eccentricity with withering put downs, who kept that sort of thing at arm's length, who carefully weighed their critiques in levels of sarcastic riposte and spoke archly about anything that wreaked of the continental. The gathering spoke like that too, just a different version of it, coming at the lingua franca from more sympathetic and informed angles. Everyone applied a certain modish embouchure to their licks, shaping disdain and cultivated approval in equal measure.

"What did you think?"

"I was transported—"

The comment was left dangling dryly for the briefest moment. Comic timing.

"—out of the theatre and into the street."

"Quite the junior Ken Tynan aren't you?"

An interjection from elsewhere in the room. All can play this game.

"Really? Kenneth Tynan? It put me more in mind of Dorothy Parker."

The voice seemed to come from underneath the kitchen table. It doesn't matter who said it. Most of them adopt that tone. It's partly a defence mechanism. The dialogue and actors are interchangeable. Boy's dorm argot. Not the females though. They are Verlaine's "pure girls with luminous skin and grave eyes" and they have different ways of stepping into the light. A bottle is passed. There is brief discourse on Dorothy Parker. A reclusive alcoholic now. It is said. Her best work behind her. Not like us. Not like this gathering. The best (and worst) still lies up ahead.

Syd allowed himself a smile at the madeleine comment. He was always generous with his approval. He was the kind of person that if you arrived somewhere, a party, a gig, a riverside gathering and saw him, you instinctively went "Oh good, Syd's here." A tonic for the troops. A good man to go into the trenches with. Waspish wit and verbal dexterity. Word games that adhered to their own playful logic.

He did have a habit of leaving without warning, though. Quite the mercurial mystery boy. He might return later – without any explanation as to where he had been – or he might be gone for good till the next time.

Andrew remembered him from the first Happening they put on. He turned up at the door and said "may I pay you in Danegeld?" "There's no need to pay, an open mind is its own currency," said Andrew, ushering him inside. Later, when the tape loops, lights and recitations were in full free-form flow Syd appeared through the flickering strobes looking spectral. Andrew remembered that. How good he looked in the illumination, like he belonged there, like he was made to merge with the light. He declined an offer to participate, preferring instead just to dolly drift around, being Beat boy enigmatic, taking it all in. All filters open. All modes of expression absorbed. The environment coming at you from every angle. Voices. Snatches of music. Montage. Manipulation. Immersion.

"write your number and pick up sticks". A sudden squall of feedback. A cough. Honky-tonk tape loop. A sax riff. A drum pedal kick. Pick up sticks. *"and you burn"*. *"you had five six sixty scale the heights"*. Piano innards plucked. *"nine legion nine burn it"*. Tape slows to a slur. Heavy sub-sonics tear at the gut. A quarter-inch reel winds backwards. Pinky and Perky babble chat. Mantovani ballroom ghost shuffle. *"sickness addiction senses"*. Stock market share prices

read with dry derision. *"pastel Japanese play boy"*. Musical saws and more Mantovani. *"I love you button girl"*. *"love the impermanent"*. All meaning submerged under a wall of white noise. *"pink matinee marrow"*. The opening riff of Ray Charles's "Busted" looped and fed into more feedback. *"no more percent it goes on this way"*. tom-tom jungle drum. *"Para Handy Para Handy"* Snatch of a children's song *"to sea sea sea to see what he could see see see"*. Cultivated sonorous voice drones in mock profundity *"people receiving words the universe is yourself"*. Ray Charles fades. *"four more years of leak death leech night"*. *"Mouth music. Mmm mmm mmm mmm"*. Roar of an airplane taking off. *"imagine make up imagine about it"*. *"test fucking a fucking test track"*. *"ton up boys going for a burn up old ladies at breakfast"* gentile tea dance music/swing jazz juxtaposition. *"green black still frame"*. *"Oh Rodney! You are SOOPAH!"* *"In Vogue many years you are Estella"*. Sleevenotes ponderously read. *"Until Coltrane Parker..."* Genealogy fed into word sped no sense. Fast as a Parker solo. *"stop winding man!"* *"Opium. Ether"* *"Definite clarinet solo a mask full of liberty"*. *"You are shrinking Abe. Your time is getting short"*. *"For cigarette love phone this number"*. Detuned brass elephants in the tape slow jungle. Slack strings scrapping. *"More Goddess. More machine. Machine Buddha. Stop. Stop I"*. *"In the future you will learn the xylophone"* Lionel Hampton glissando. Glass rim. Theremin. *"In the future you will learn the xylophone and enter the geography florist"*. *"it's already done"*. Snatch of David Frost's dry declamatory drone. *"Can I save?"* *"Stop"* *"Can I save it?"* *"Anyone here?"* The soft shoe shuffle of more ghost ballroom. Medium wave atmospherics. Desert wind. Snatch of *Round The Horne*. A Kenneth Williams cackle. *"Yes, well we've all got your number haven't we ducky?"* Trumpet fanfare. Cacophony of babble voices. *"Alright Kevin?"* *"A mind pecked death. Desert vultures marching to the rhythm of reverse. There's a bit more just after the end. Just after the end had ended. Just after the end of the end. Just after."* Sound of tape reel spooling onwards and offwards.

These were the offspring of a previous generation's radicalism, the beneficiaries of handed down intelligence and outlook. This one the son of a renowned father who is an expert on Nietzsche and an equally renowned mother who writes about Proust. That one the great grandson of an under-secretary of state for the Colonies. Another the son of a lecturer in Zoology. This one comes from a family of Dons. That one expelled from Oundle, and already making his pact with the Beats. His eye on the London salon prize life. That one distantly related to Charles Darwin ("We all are," says some waggish wit, always eager to respond with an affectionate put down, again the defence mechanism thing). That one the child of refugees who arrived pennilessly exiled from Franco's fascist Spain. That one in the corner, the son of a Fellow at Christ's who writes critical appraisals of DH Lawrence which appear on every undergraduate reading list. This one at Magdalene. That one down for St Johns. Those two, eyeing up the talent, aiming to get fresh and in no danger of falling into education's grip at all, who specialise in job avoidance and claiming National Assistance, who graduated in fairground studies and snooker hall moves. The net cast near and wide. The accumulation of free thinking gathered in.

There is an absence of fathers (a common theme). This one died in the war, that one divorced and gone. Syd's father more recently deceased. Never spoken of (nobody did the open grief thing then), instead the pain resides deep down, to come out later, couch-coaxed by therapy, cathartically contorted by primal scream, or by whatever method is currently in vogue. Best ignored for now. Youth permits itself the luxury of avoidance. They pile round whichever tolerant house will have them. Parents who turn a blind eye, or cast an approving one. In such an accommodating setting, permissive proclivities thrive. Bombs that must be banned. Love that must be free (never easy to enact, that one). Many of their parents are or were politically aligned and active. All manifestations of anarchic left and liberalism assimilated. These are the children born of stability, school milk and welfare state provision, heirs to privilege they are barely aware of. Comfortable in their skins, they believe that mainstream politics must be dismantled entirely or simply ignored. The establishment game is a total bore. "A drag" they drawl with one voice as they draw on cigarettes and expound sanguinely on the utopian possibilities of the new world. They willingly forgo the party line, the straight world inconvenience of composite motions and mandates and anything that wreaks of an election manifesto. They shun the clipboard carriers and leaflet deliverers and door knockers on campaign days. They sidestep all this spade work and shoe work and grass root slow endeavour in order to seek out the new Albion that shimmers in mirage form before them. Some of them, who would not be seen dead placing a cross on a ballot form – even if they were 21 and old enough to do so – will place their faith in more esoteric influences and take their instruction from the Tarot or the I Ching. Free to choose from the new spiritual options, of which there are many. These come with an array of no-rules rules regarding commitment, wealth sharing and celibacy. There is theological instruction galore for the initiate to absorb. Those who resist, or overtly distrust the lure of Eastern intrigue will seek salvation, or a different kind of entrapment, in psychoanalysis. There are false gods everywhere and the pitfalls are many. Everyone is pursuing their personal nirvana, their lamp genie, or going gung-ho for chemical oblivion. Many of them will fetch up in London soon enough and regroup there. They will move from rented room to rented room, always retaining close proximity to the scene until eventually they are the scene. Presently they are content to be their own epicentre. And that's enough. Cambridge breeds its own rarefied brand of elevated provincialism. Remote enough to be off the cultural radar, near enough to the capital to click and connect.

This evening they are at Ella's, a woman who has worked her way along the esoterica counter from Transcendentalists to Theosophists to Palmists. Her eldest son currently endures an on-off relationship with formal education and has written an Artaud quote on the kitchen wall. "I have a small mind and I intend to use it." Everyone interprets this in their own way. The madman as genius thing is attractive to some of them. Those who have actually read Artaud, rather than merely absorbed his kitchen wall homilies, offer further salient quotes to be pondered and passed on. Shared wisdom is met with the no strings commitment of the meaningful nod. Everyone is seduced by the fashionable force of Artaud's words. The knowledgeable among them riff on his best one-liners, the ones that would also look good on a hip kitchen wall. "I am myself an absolute abyss," says someone. "Absolutely pissed you mean," says one of the fairground boys who can more than hold their own. More laughter, then it's back to dissecting the Happening night, and planning future poetry and jazz nights, and all the other arts club nights and upstairs room above a pub nights they will put on for door takings and a percentage of the soft drinks sold. It all merges into one huge energised lifeforce of possibilities and put downs. Someone reads from the latest review. "A crowd of about 200 poetry and jazz fans drinking vaguely and dancing even more vaguely." "How do you dance vaguely?" asks someone. Lucy Lea, one of the more overtly exhibitionist Beat chic girls, gets up and demonstrates silently. Everyone laughs madly at her immaculate moody mime. She does it badly well, accurate to the letter. Lucy has more than a little of the blank-eyed Eleanor Bron about her. Second only to the allure of Juliette Gréco in the go-to game. "They always put 'with it' in inverted commas, don't they?" she says. "Perhaps we're all just living our lives in inverted commas," says someone else. "Have you ever thought of that?" The room divides into those who wish to sneer at the pretentiousness of the utterance and those who quietly make wow shapes with their lips and glance around the room to see who else is making the wow shape.

Lucy coins the term "the Bleatniks" to describe those who have little to offer but derision and scorn. She is vivacious and full of life. Syd watches her every move. The way she commands attention without ever fully realising she is doing so, which just makes her all the more attractive. He watched her last week at the local record hop. She wore a shift dress in blue and green hoops over prune tights. The disc jockey put on 'Loop De Loop' by Johnny Thunder and she executed an immaculately cool little mod step dance of her own devising, holding her arms down rigid by her side then raising and drooping her shoulders slightly in time with the music while doing these snappy little stiff-wristed finger clicks that seemed to give her electric shocks. Syd looked at her dancing and thought she was an utter whizz. And he still thinks she is the bees right now as the *Varsity* mag review is parsed for every last detail and the Bleatniks are torn to shreds. This one recognises herself as the girl in the red dress among all the existentialist black. Another rues the fact that he wasn't mentioned by name even though he co-organised the event. And everyone is adamant that the line of free verse quoted, "pretend you are a potato with eyelashes... and EXIST" was uttered by no one or is at best a misquote.

"My father told me that the *Daily Mirror* said worse about Kurt Schwitters in the 1930s," utters another with horse's mouth erudition passed down the generations from Dada to son of Dada. There are further impassioned exchanges about the continued relevance of Kurt Schwitters and Hugo Ball among those who like to hold court, while others draw meaningfully on ciggies, drain beer bottles to the dregs, and just sit soaking it all in. Silence is always a hassle-free option. "We should do something based on the Cabaret Voltaire," says someone. "I thought we already were," says someone else, mock hurt and authentically aggrieved.

Some bad poetry will be read out but will not be judged as bad. Everyone starts somewhere and somewhere might as well be in an empathetic kitchen full of benign tolerance and angular jazz.

Moth eaten minds and mothballed lives. Put away like war medals and forgotten. Sour milk and ration books. Leave them to their daily death. Let the mad glad gods flourish among us. Let the disenchanted dance themselves into a frenzied whirl of crazed dazed love. Let us be the best we will ever be. Now.

All of them set on dethroning the iambic crown wearers with their fledgling attempts at Vers Libre. One of the Juliette Gréco girls gets up and recites with a golly-gosh parody of gaucheness, her own come-hither ode to blank eyed unavailability.

Thirsty dazed and December
April June and Miranda
All the rest are flirty ones
Especially February who is a dirty one. She sends you a filthy valentine
every leap year that sets your heart aflutter and asks you to join her in
the gutter. All the better for seeing the stars my dear.

There is applause. She WILL go far. "Outlandishly lustful," says an arty Artaudian approvingly. "I never knew you could read like that," whispers her boyfriend for now but not much longer. Had Dorothy Parker been there she would have found it all intolerably twee. "Reader, I fwowed up," she might have said. But these are the children of Albion not Algonquin and they are in their element.

It is a gathering that draws succour from hedonistic inclinations, always a work in progress. Always soaking up something new. Whatever the subtle variations in their backgrounds they have somehow all detoured via Bohemia. This is the disposition which bonds them, gives credence to their utterances, as each of them tries on fresh disguises in order to see which one fits.

Some of these allegiances hark back to rock-a-bye babyhood, adjacent prams airing in the post-war sun, hanging obediently from a mother's arms outside a shop, the shared proximity, the locked-eye meeting of infant gazes, each breaching their own private boredom (the first and only frontier to a child) with a sudden mutual understanding, eyeing a back yard trike, a little wooden play hut, a patch of grass they might play on. A spare place at a school desk for the new boy. Budge up. Bonds forged over crayons and playtime games. Saturday morning art class, piano class and any other extra curricula that might tease out talent. Some too shy (or sulky) to speak then. Best buddies now.

Halcyon fade to willow bank dappled sunlight and a punt being lazily navigated downstream, gliding through the Backs, negotiating low bridges and narrow arches, lulled by slow drift and shallow waters towards Grantchester. "There goes Crick," says someone as one of the city's many bicycling eccentrics peddles towards Churchill. Not everyone knows who Crick is. Some assume it's a nickname. "He's the man who knows where all the molecules go," elaborates one of the languorous gathering from his prone position in a barge. Acid up until now has been a form of wit but pretty soon they will all be rearranging the molecules to accommodate the brain scrambling possibilities of the new chemical reality. Steerage will go askew.

It's the best kept secret anyone could ever be in on. Going about their psychedelic business while the world suspects nothing but exuberant antics and the regular irregularities of "that one he's quite a character". The only clue is in the arms, not the eyes, the arms. The eyes give little away in the glaze. The arms lie limp and lifeless, as if Jupiter gravity has zapped them. The arms are the tell-tale signifier to other initiates. Well, that and the dancing for those who venture into kinetic expression, which usually means the girls. The boys are mostly too mannered cool or inhibited to dance. The mod steps get messy in the dance hall. The go-go goes to pieces. The monkey and the hully gully get a little too loosey-goosey and interpretive. Well drilled discotheque moves venture into disarray. Again, all chalked off by oblivious onlookers as teen and twenty high spirits. But Lucy Lea knows and Syd can see that she knows and they soon hook up.

Garden games in May. Parents on sabbatical. Two weeks of absence to enjoy. A sugar cube tinted day. Timeless hours spent staring as water teardrops twinkle like mercury tears from a kitchen tap. Faces elongated in tea spoons. Trees sluggishly waving in the warm southerly breeze, sprinkling cherry blossom bouquets into sun silken hair. All the girls are petal-adorned as they gamine around as gaily as they can go. Diaphanous floaty dresses make swirl patterns in the afterglow. From time to time everything freeze-frames, and everyone is momentarily cast in a randomly assembled stock-still arrangement of youthful perfection. "It will never be as beautiful as this ever again," says one of the gathering. "Until it is," says another. Infinite lifetimes of possibilities pour in. Each is filled in a micro-second. Every gap in the conversation is threaded with the thunderbolt velocity of silent revelation. The eternal wow. Speech is captioned in coloured balloon bubble bursts. Every mind-blown utterance is its own exclamation mark. The grand narrative of the ancients settles like a space ship visitation on the lawn and everyone is convinced by the reality of what they saw. Those who are still transfixed by the kitchen tap have it explained to them later in stuttery gulps and gasps and come-down sorrow that they too didn't bear witness to the splendour of this collective vision that has already shed its essence in the telling and retelling.

"A good shine for every mind," says Syd as he holds court under the apple tree, waiting for Newtonian laws to be disproved and the fruits to fly upwards. "Are you being Buddha?" asks Paul the wise one who is already on his own path to satori. "Yes," said Syd. "Why? Would you like a go?" "Yes, I would," says Paul. "Shove up." And that's how it goes. The wisdom passed along an invisible force field line that sporadically crackles and splutters as someone forgets it's their turn and the moment is lost.

"Who is minding the tap?" asked Paul. "Leave it to its own devices," responds Syd, and they both laugh belly-up at this for some time. "But we can't leave it unattended for too long," cautions Paul. "In case we miss the drip."

Later Syd find a sketch pad and a 2B pencil in an upstairs room and fills pages with impromptu scribbly abstraction. This one called *The Cloudiverse*. That one called *Ground Shake Tree*. A fire engine goes past, bell frantically clanging. Syd is in the moment and executes a series of rhythmic squiggle shapes, hard edged zig-zag lightning bolts, like a Vorticist apparition. Underneath he etches "FLASH SIREN FIRE" in shaky block capitals.

As it's Sunday some decide to go to evensong just down the road, but when they get there they chicken out, the force field around the church just too strong to psychically penetrate, and anyway they are as a congregation far too giggly, peak time profundity having given way to the all-revealing fumbling stumbling absurdity of things. So instead, they sit on the red brick wall outside the church and listen to the sombre low murmur of hymns. Others go to the pub, order fizzy gaseous beer and stare at the specks of oily spillage on the mosaic-tiled tables. They venerate the way the early evening light filters in through armorial stained glass window panels that aren't actually stained at all.

It begins to rain, gently at first but steadily persistent by the time they leave the tavern. The day looks like an ordinary day again and it's as if none of this ever happened. All that remains is the shattered remnant of some perfect other life that can only be recalled when they go to that place in their head where reverie dwells and the dreams reside.

Under his Buddha tree, Syd's sketch pad still lays open, the wind lifts the pages and the rain-soaked squiggles run to smeary smudge.

KEEPSAKE

[Unsent letter, date unknown]

My dearest Francoise,

Here I am, as rashly promised weeks ago, finally writing to you. I'm sorry for the inexcusable absence. And indeed, for my hasty departure the last time we met. Paris is a beautiful city and I should still like to experience the best of it. I enjoyed looking at all the Sunday painters by the embankment and next time would very much like to go and rummage among the markets that you mentioned. If I can overcome certain phobias I think it might be a pleasurable way to while away an hour or three. When it came to making a commitment to my craft, alas, I was found, as so often, wanting. This is, I realise, something I must overcome. I am sorry if I wasted anyone's time or if I didn't present myself in the best possible light. I will make amends.

In many ways I had the perfect circumstances in which to give a good account of myself. No demands were made and the only pressure in evidence was the undue pressure I so often put upon myself. I should have submitted more willingly to the pleasures of the city. One is fully aware that one's governing perception of Paris is overly romantic and predominantly drawn from an almost overbearing awareness of all that bohemian history, coupled with an equally overwhelming sense of all the great artists and writers who have walked those boulevards. In a strange sort of way it was curiously reassuring to see that the buildings are every bit as grubby as I remember them from previous visits and that the pissoirs still pong to high heaven. (Sorry for the crudeness. I shall now attempt to appear more elevated than I currently feel.)

I have constant thoughts about the deeper aspects of my life that I find very difficult to express. Not just things that trouble me, things that bring me great joy, too. Sometimes it's as if I have an emotional circuit too few that doesn't permit me to bridge that gap between ideas and words adequate to the expression of these ideas. I don't want to burden you too much with these thoughts, however, my apologies in advance as they will inevitably intrude onto the page.

By the way, I wrote you a letter a couple of weeks ago and then promptly lost it. It's probably somewhere in the clutter of the house or perhaps mouldering in some country lane where it possibly dropped out of my pocket. Anyway, apologies if I rehash some old thoughts or express them not half as well as I did in the original letter.

I have been listening to the records you gave me. There are some beautiful arrangements. They complement your voice wonderfully. I see clear similarities in what we do and I must ask you about certain elements of composition when we next meet. I know you are keen to collaborate and I am grateful for that, despite my usual trepidation. Perhaps I should attempt to write chanson. The discipline might do me good. It's funny to think, when I started out there was a suggestion that I might write for other people, with publishing the main emphasis rather than performing. That may have been the wiser option, thinking about it. It might have got me away from the obligation to 'self-expression' which seems increasingly a dead end, to me at least. 'Message Personnel' is my favourite of yours from what I've played so far, a beautiful song and I related very strongly to the sentiment. You seem to unburden yourself of so much in that lyric. I doubt if I would ever dare be that direct – not in that way anyway, and yet you have ways of being able to cloak your sentiments in a certain, I don't know what to call it. Charisma? Mystery? It's bewitching to listen to. I am in awe of how you do that. Not just on 'Message Personnel' but other songs too.

How do you cope with the promotional aspect of things? I mean, in terms of publicising the records. Interviews and suchlike. I consented to one once and didn't enjoy the experience at all. The chap who interviewed me was very nice though, I have to say. It's something I've never been able to come to terms with. It seems to me that people are obliged to make more of themselves than they really are in these encounters. The ridiculous way in which the music industry refers to their artists in promotional literature – it seems so overblown to me, as if they are gods bringing the sermon from the mount. They seem to hold them in such high esteem which no musician can possibly live up to.

Thank you so much for the copy of *The Myth Of Sisyphus*. I have delved deeply into it and I find myself annotating the margins and underlining meaningful sentences as if I were an undergraduate again. Camus has so many fine phrases and ideas. I underlined "the flight from light", and the bit about Schopenhauer praising suicide "while seated at a well-set table". And that whole idea of there being some greater scheme or purpose of life which has somehow eluded us. That was very meaningful to me. So much to ponder regarding the human condition!

I realise, as Camus says of Proust, that I am a collector of anxieties. In relation to this, the bit where Camus talks about there being honour in enduring absurdity. I find that difficult, I have to admit. I have enough burdens to shoulder as it is. I know people who can endure absurdity but I have little capacity for it. I seem to lack the necessary faculty. What little honour I possess can't really be surrendered to absurdity, otherwise there will be nothing left. Then again it all depends on what you mean by absurdity I suppose. Overall though I find enough in *Sisyphus* to validate what I do. It inspires in me the hope that whatever thought and philosophy I have put into my work is somehow sufficient and worthwhile and will enable me to endure all the battles ahead. Suffer the slings and arrows and all that.

Philosophy is at the root of everything really isn't it? The search for meaning. I can't say I've made many inroads yet. One feels so futile when one's own shallow thoughts are set against the ruminations of the good and the great. One's turgid scribbles don't really add up to a lot when compared with some of Camus's phrases. "Those waterless deserts where thought reaches its confines" or "that odd state of soul in which the void becomes eloquent". Splendour and futility, he talks about. I know all about that.

Your gift made a timely arrival in my life. I seem to be full of the French influence at the moment. The BBC has been repeating its adaptation of Sartre's *The Roads To Freedom*. It was originally on a couple of years ago but I managed to miss almost every episode then as I was attempting to launch what I shall laughingly refer to as my recording career. Anyway, I have been able to enjoy it to the full this time, although I'm not sure enjoy is the appropriate word. I have fond memories of discussions at school about Sartre and Balzac. Walking the cloisters and the playing fields having these intense debates about what we thought these writers meant when they talked about love and death and commitment. I mention this because I remember you mentioned love as a subject in its many guises when we spoke and it occurs to me how rarely I have used the word itself in my songs. There's the avoidance of love and love almost as a flippant choice and love presented as one option among many and there's all sorts of ways of talking about love indirectly but there's no explicit love in my songs, is there? My songs always make a certain kind of sense when I write them but I don't know how well they translate into everyday thought. I envy writers who have the common touch, the way they can put across complex emotions in simple ways. It seems to be something I lack. My songs are somewhat intangible at times. I need to simplify the whole process. But then what would one be left with? Some fearful element of stark truth I suppose. Or half-truth. But would anybody really want to know about my life, my actual inner life, what I feel and experience at my lowest points?

I've underlined the bit where Camus says that there is no mystery in creation (of a work of art) and that it's only death that brings creation to an end. I find that strangely consoling. I still haven't worked out whether all these thoughts give one justification for carrying on or just simply giving up. One has to maintain the will to carry on, I suppose, but first I must overcome my demons and one of the demons is as you mention love.

Love holds only the certainty of disaster I fear and I freely admit (here boldly in a letter!) that I shrink from the kind of intimacy required to make that leap from a certain kind of kinship to something deeper, if there is anything deeper. In this respect my thoughts and my artistic expression (ha ha! such grand words) are as one.

I remember you talking about detachment and absence, and how you think the French should love my songs more than they do and I've given this some thought, too. I sometimes feel that I'm acting out an impression of someone who writes songs, adopting the mannerisms that I think are appropriate to the task. Certain flourishes that I am prone to, ludicrous in their way I suppose, don't really invite the kind of popular appeal that others in my field enjoy. Should I be more direct, do you think? In my songs I construct this preposterous edifice to shield me, but in many ways it just shields me from me. I'm not sure if any of it truly fulfils the listener. I feel I'm getting into a rut and need to change my ways but I can't see any way of discarding old habits. The songs I've been writing recently are mere trifles really. I throw most of them away.

When I was watching *The Roads To Freedom* I found myself

scribbling down phrases and snatches of dialogue. I'm not sure why, possibly as an aide memoire for future ideas. It's the sort of thing I used to fill exercise books with all the time when I was at school, although not when I went up to Cambridge, which was in retrospect a mistake (the going up to Cambridge I mean, not the failing to scribble things down – I did very little of that at Fitzwilliam.) "Freedom is a mere running away – a myth." That was one that I remember from Sartre. I can't remember if that was in the book or the adaptation, or how faithful the adaptation was to the books. I'm not sure it matters really, does it? Anyway, the TV series has recently finished and it has furnished me with much to think about. But maybe I only have a superficial grasp of what is going on. Perhaps I shall develop a better understanding of these great works as I grow older and read them again, assuming I do find time to read them again, and assuming of course that I do grow older. The message I am getting from *The Myth Of Sisyphus*, if there is one, is that it is better to be than not to be. We soldier on as my father would say.

I continue to read Verlaine and Baudelaire and Mallarmé when I can bring myself to concentrate. Things might be better if I'd open up myself fully to all these influences – their poetic gifts are so grand – instead of saddling myself with all this English reserve.

Rien n'egale en longueur les boituseses journées
Quand sous les lourds flocons des neigeuses années
L'ennui, fruit de la morne incuriosite
Prend le proportions de l'immortalité[1]

---

1   Nothing is longer than the limping days/When under heavy snowflakes of the years/Ennui, the fruit of dulling lassitude/Takes on the size of immortality. CHARLES BAUDELAIRE Spleen (II)

That's the measure of it. Write and tell me about lovely things, or even phone if you feel so inclined. I promise I shall answer. Yours, Nick. X

WAYFARERS ALL

"There is a troubling preponderance of reality don't you think?" said Nigel, a salonista. "Of late I mean."

His fellow salonistas gave this due consideration.

"The Brigadiers are rattling... whatever it is that Brigadiers rattle. And the Mr Whatsits are out in force."

"We must repel all boarders," urged David, a theatrical.

"There's a landlady joke in there somewhere," said Steve, a jester.

"There's a good physics one too," said David. He left it hanging but no one asked him to elaborate so he didn't.

"Have you seen this *Time* feature about the London that now swings?" asked Peter, an Arts Lab dabbler. He held up a magazine for all to see. Exhibit A.

"Look, it's official. It's all in here. The walls of the discotheques are made of caviar. And drinks are served by mermaids. It's all happening, man."

Nigel, seated against the wall, parodically clicked his fingers hipster-style and pulled his peaked cap down low over his eyes as if to hide from the horror of seeing his world reflected back at him from the news stand glossies by some second-rate Paul Revere. What with that and the Brigadiers and the Mr Whatsits and the preponderance of reality thing, Nigel was having something of an intolerable day.

The article was passed round. Salient extracts were read out, studied indifference was punctuated by dismissive snorts and sighs. Secretly though, almost everyone in the room was thrilled to see their in-set selves as others must now see them. "The hair-do's and the hair don'ts" laughed Syd. "I like that very much."

"I preferred it when it was our little secret," sulked Suzi, an It Girl. "Now everyone will know about us."

"I see they mention that silly Antonioni film," said John, a poet.

"I've been asked to be in that," said Phoebe, an ingenue.

"You should," said Michael, an illustrator of no fixed income.

"Oh, don't be a drag darling. I'm hardly going to audition to be a walk on part in someone else's creation, am I?"

"No dear," mocked Jennifer Gentle, a witch. "That would never do. That would never do at all."

Everyone laughed the affectionate empathy laugh.

"Look. A good advert for the group," said Syd, pointing to the *Time* cover shot of a red London bus with "Join The Tea Set" emblazoned along the side.

"It's not an inspiring name though, is it?" ventured Nigel. "You might want to consider changing it".

"I like the name," said Syd. "It has levels."

"I've never liked it either," said another Jennifer, not so gently. "It makes you sound like, I don't know, a bit of a gimmick group."

"It was Rick's suggestion," said Syd. "It's hep. Knowingly hep."

"It's also a get you sued by Ty-Phoo name," suggested Paula, an artist's model.

"Who's backing that whole campaign anyway?" asked another David, a film student. "I mean, I see these commercials on the telly. Drink tea. Join the tea set. Who's behind it?"

"Communists," deadpanned John the poet in his best Peter Cook voice. "Chinese communists. The Yellow Peril."

"When Louis Armstrong comes over to England he immediately sends someone out to buy his tea. His knowingly hip tea," said Don, a busker, stealing a sly look at Syd who was still skim reading the article. "Ronnie Scott told me that."

"Is anyone going to the Aubrey Beardsley at the V&A?" asked Belinda, who was currently sort of being an artist.

"I'll come with you," said Don, eager to further his acquaintance with Belinda, who, being willowy and somewhat gullible, was just his type.

"It says here that Victorianism was only a temporary aberration in the British character," said Syd, quoting the article.

"They've got that so wrong," said Michael. "I mean just look around you. We're practically Pre-Raphaelites."

"What's a Practical Pre-Raphaelite?" asked Jennifer Gentle.

Once again a punchline was not forthcoming, although the occasion and the collective wit of the room demanded one.

"This is all your fault Nigel," said Fred, for the time being, a van driver for a fashionable boutique.

"Yes," chorused everyone.

"If you will go gathering the tribes," said Don.

"I strenuously deny the charge," drawled Nigel. "Well okay, perhaps not strenuously. I languidly deny the charge."

"Smoke the charge more like," said Elvin, a sardonic disbeliever.

"Still, we filled the Albert Hall with poets, didn't we?" said Nigel. And indeed they did. That glorious night a year ago when the exotically dressed gathering first recognised itself as a tribe. Verlaine's raggedy "Po-wets, verse mongering unwashed letter louts," the bane of Nigel's Mr Whatsit and all the Mr Whatsits to come.

Everyone smiled at the memory and the day went back to being beatific.

Another London lies outside those salon windows. A city stitched and mended, tarnished by developers, ring fenced with temporary hoardings. The elderly have pre-NHS faces, last of the few, death embers, old teeth and bones. Pauper lives left to rot among the smouldering ruins of bulldozed Londinium. Midnight braziers, bed boxes, Meth breath and bonfire gatherings. The St Mungo's nocturnal soup run. They go about in this, the beautiful people. The double-barrelled sons of cast-off uniformity and spurned privilege and the errant daughters of clergy and colonels (and the occasional equally errant bluestocking mother.) They make the small hours spark. They peel back time's tidal layers on their acid trips. They see fossils molluscs frankincense and myrrh ground down to calcium dust between the tectonic plates. They seek out north side moss in neglected church yards. Feral cats and kittens multiplying on vacant lots. Hallucinatory searchlight haze rays locate lockets and broaches in bombsite rubble. Raking through the slumland avalanche, half a house here, a rotten buried borough there all the way out to the estuary reaches where the marshland settles and the gases glow.

You didn't see that did you mister swinging London feature man?

Gear change. Same room. Different day.

"How are you today Syd?" asked Nigel, as Syd stood limp-armed and looking a little lost in the doorway.

"I'm oscillating," said Syd. "Sorry, I mean ossifying."

"Sounds like a busy day," said Nigel.

"It is," agreed Syd. "And it's changing by the minute."

"Terms *and* conditions?" said Elvin looking up from a contract. "Terms I'm okay with. Conditions seem somewhat iffy to me."

"What is it?" purred Lucy Lea, by now a model, as she draped herself over Syd's somewhat frail form on the chaise longues.

"It's the college careers people, Lou. They sent me for this commercial artist job and, look, there's a contract and everything."

"How terribly draggy," drawled Phoebe, all trust funded-up and still blocked from last night.

"Ah, Phoebe, my favourite debauchee," said Don, arriving with a battered acoustic guitar and a sheaf of unfinished songs with no commercial potential.

Phoebe got up to make seven coffees, three with sugar, feeling that was her role.

"Where is the job, Elvin?" asked David the film student.

"Berwick Street," Elvin muttered distractedly.

"Take the job till twelve," suggested David. "And if you don't like it just pop round a few offices in your lunch break and see what else is on offer."

This was a period of full employment. Three jobs in a day was not unheard of. Pick and choose. It was the same with religion.

"Is anyone coming to see the Master next week?" asked Nigel.

This was a full year before the Beatles found their Maharishi, and long before Pete Townshend's eyes alighted on his Meher Baba, the same Meher Baba who Syd's Camberwell Robert had taken to see Laurel and Hardy films in the 1930s. A line of saffron robes and shaven heads did not yet weave its way down Oxford Street chanting hare-rama-hare-hare. The Cambridge crowd, as so often, as with light shows, as with DIY chemistry labs, were well ahead of the game. Paul C, he of the lysergic garden rain romp with Syd, had done the overland trail to India, again long before there was a trail to tread, and having found the source of the white light in a tiny village full of converts, came back sun burned, soul burnished, well fed and all divined up. And now he was eager for everyone to share in the initiation.

Many were the branches on the tree of knowledge as would-be devotees sought out alternatives to the drab pieties of traditional Western faith. Belief systems flourished. Their roots entwined and twisted. Buddhists, Hindus, Sikhs and Sufis. Esotericists, Transcendentalists, Tantrics and Tai Chi-ists. Gurus and Swamis. Baha'is and Brahmins. All lined up on an endless pick-a-mystic counter display of competing cosmologies. An A to Zee of good and bad faith, replenished almost on a weekly basis. In this instance, in this specific room on this particular day, attention alighted upon the Master, Hazur Maharaj Charan Singh Ji, the spiritual head of Radha Soami Satsang Beas, Sat Sanghis as his followers became widely known. Up until the mid-1960s those diasporic seers and sages who had uprooted from Calcutta or Armenia to London (sometimes via Paris or New York) made do with temporary ashrams in semi-detached houses in Hendon or Rayners Park, sellotaping their availability above doorbells next to the migrant violin tutors, the seance ladies and the ectoplasm bluffers, or meeting in hired halls and rented rooms to whirl and chant and keep the noise down after 9pm. Rural retreats and country estates were still some way off, as were the chubby little reincarnations with their Rolls Royces and their renouncing of your worldly goods for the good of the godhead, but soon enough there would be yoga circles in Leamington Spa and zithers and ouds in folk clubs, all thanks in part to those like Paul C who sniffed the jasmine scent on the breeze and put faith and trust in their esoteric instincts.

And now, here was the Master, he of the audible light stream, as Paul's literature put it, giving a talk in London. It was the calling that many had been waiting for. But not all. Some remained agnostic. David the theatrical and Elvin, the reluctant form filler, were the out and out sceptics of the group. Nigel though, along with several others among the Cambridge crowd, were drawn to the simplicity of the Satsang teachings, the lack of ceremony and ritual. The idea that divinity resided in us all appealed to them. All that was required was a dedication to the daily practice of meditation and an acknowledgment that there is only one supreme being and that we are all an expression of his love. Abstinence from permissiveness, alcohol, tobacco and recreational drugs was encouraged. Life at this point began to separate into new polarities of secular and sacred.

Syd for the longest time had a foot in both camps. His hedonistic side immersed itself in Orange Sunshine and freshly dipped sugar cubes. His deep and far away side embraced the spirit realm. He dug the epic cartography of *The Lord Of The Rings* and the pantheism of

The Wind In The Willows. He took instruction from the Tarot cards and the I Ching coins. He parsed the implications of a recently thrown 24th Hexagram (Fu Returning) for the guidance it might bring him.

Thunder within the Earth. Return to connect with your true path. Action regains great good fortune. Improvement, in whatever you do. Progress marked by a slow return to original sincerity. This improvement will come in the rhythm of natural chaos. You are experiencing change without will, without plan or arrangement. It occurs on its own, in its own time, in its own quiet way. Your yin lines are receptive. Your yang lines meet no resistance. You sense this change, regeneration. Move within it freely and naturally.

On the day of the winter solstice, Syd summonsed some long-forgotten melody, born of the English hymnal and cross bred with gnostic modalities, and proceeded to write a song commemorating all that he had processed. At the same time he agonised over his decision to abandon his art studies. He recognised in the 24th Hexagram both positives and portents.

Do not accelerate this change, the reading said. *It will develop in its own slow way. Let the waves move in their own time. If you plunge in haste you will find yourself thrashing helplessly about.*

The third line of the Hexagram seemed to foretell prophecy.

You have a tendency to interrupt the flow and turn away negatively. When circumstances have slipped back far enough you reverse yourself and purposefully attempt to regain what you let go. This is fear of completion, fear of attainment. This impulse harms no one but yourself. The sixth line raises the issue of confusion over the returning. If you go astray your defeat will be far reaching. The effect will be felt for years. There will be guilt. Calamities. This turn for the better will have come and gone. You will let it pass you by. You cannot deny the flow of change in the universe. It is a force which will carry you along, not buoyant, you will tumble headlong untethered. But having tumbled you will have to wait patiently for events to resolve themselves again. This might not happen for many years.

All this was thrown into sharp relief when the Master refused to initiate Syd. Some suggested this was because he lacked spiritual maturity. Some sensed that the Master suspected that Syd had made an emotional choice, reached through sudden impulse not thoughtful consideration. Others suspected that the Master detected something more troubling in Syd, some part of his psyche that might unravel should he pursue the wrong path.

For Syd, the troubled waters ran deep. The dichotomy was between serenity and turbulence. On the serenity side lay genetic disposition. His parents were Quakers, they had a no fuss, no frills Quaker wedding, absent of ceremony and the who sits where rigmarole of the reception. The Quaker faith, like many others, celebrated the god within, but did so without rapture or scripture. It placed trust in the positivity of reflection. LSD did this too, of course, but LSD also unleashed psychic tumult. As expressions of revelatory faith went, acid was just as valid as any other catalyst, even though the route map kept changing scale and the contours contracted and expanded seemingly at will. Finding the necessary coordinates to trace the way back to base camp could be tricky at the best of times. Sometimes it was easier to just go with the inner and outer flow of the thing. Look at the sky. Look at the river and reflect that both were good. But it wasn't always that tranquil. LSD also brought on swirling storm-tossed torrents of mind warping turbulence at the flick of a molecular lever.

And thus it was that the Master, picking up perhaps more on the turbulence than the tranquillity, said no. Syd confided his disappointment to Nigel, to Paul, to a receptive audience of sympathetic others. The NO was like a big pop art illuminated road sign and its prohibition hit him hard. "Then you will have to find other signs that say YES," said Nigel. Said Paul. Said everyone in their own way. Assuring Syd. Smoothing things over, for now. And for a while the refusal was forgotten about and dimmed to a memory, buried deep down like everything else. Just another aspect of a complex character make-up, left to settle among the baggage of contradiction that Syd carried everywhere. The expansive introvert. The figurative abstractionist. The nursery rhyme Beat poet. The versatile versifier with his charming ditties and screeds of unfathomable freeform. The permissive harem loner. The unclubbable salonista. The youngest of four brothers and the youngest in his band, the doted upon mummy's boy. The fatherless brooder. The child man who bounced on his heels with a restless energy when he walked, sprinting through his dream days, because when he stopped moving he could lose himself in silence, stares and stasis.

Gear change. Different room. Different day.

"What do you call a drummer without a girlfriend?"

"I have absolutely no idea, Syd. What do you call a drummer without a girlfriend?"

"Oh, that's a shame. I was hoping you could tell me. Now that I'm in a group I need to get fully up to speed with musician humour and I feel somewhat deficient."

The room warms with giggles at the predicament.

"Good news Syd. I've read the tea leaves." Puddle Town Tom, a wind-up merchant and nobody's fool, stared into the bottom of his cup.

"What does it say?"

"It says Congratulations. You've won second prize in a beauty contest. Collect £10 from each player".

"What does my horoscope say?".

Una, an errant daughter, adjusted her glasses and consulted the Oracle, Marie Simone, in her magazine.

"What sign are you Syd?"

"Capricorn."

"Capricorn. Your key word for success is Endeavour. Ooh."

"Is that what it says? Endeavour. Ooh."

"No, that's just me trying to build up a sense of expectation. It says, a quiet day but possibly a message or caller in the afternoon or evening with a really exciting idea for – ooh again – a really exciting idea for a recreational or social activity in later years."

"Then I shall prepare myself," said Syd. "Marie Simone is clever and French and she has her finger on the pulse of all the housewives who read that magazine."

"Let equine companions remain undisturbed. Four seven three six," pondered Elvin.

"I beg your pardon," said Lucy Lea, lazily.

"Four across. Let equine companions remain undisturbed. Four seven three six," repeated Elvin.

"Let sleeping dogs lie," said Syd looking up from the Go board.

"That doesn't fit, does it?" said Elvin huffily.

"Make it fit," said Syd.

"Don't frighten the horses."

"Thank you, Tom."

"I don't get crosswords," said Lucy Lea. "I mean, why do they write the clues like that?"

"I don't do them either," said Syd, placing a sympathetic hand on Lucy's knee.

"I thought you'd like cryptic clues," said Tom.

"No," said Syd. "Why make it hard for yourself?"

"Crypt tick," said Elvin.

"Clipped trick," went Syd.

They riffed on this for a bit and then resumed their game of Go. Go was the cool game. Another strategy option like the Tarot spread and the I Ching's random arrangements. Go was mind sport for those who had long ceased to pick up a racquet or throw an egg-shaped ball. Cribbage for hip cats. Dominoes for lateral thinkers. A hypnotically compelling way to while away a stoned afternoon. 19 by 19 grid lines on a board. Black and white stone pieces. Stalactite progress. The game could end through resignation or when neither player wished to make a further move. "This game singularly fails to live up to its promise of going," said Puddletown Tom, a dissenter. "Go just means board," said Syd. "That's B-O-A-R-D. Not bored." "Which I am," said Tom. The simple slow layering and rearranging of the stones appealed to Syd. It stemmed his momentum, restored equanimity to his metabolism. Coming and going without effort. Sitting there in that room, curtains lifting in the breeze. The West End busily going about its business outside. Police siren wailing from open window left to open window right and away off up the Charing Cross Road. Syd thought of Go's grid assemblage as impermanent paint, slowly shifting like a monochrome light show. He'd sometimes reach for a pad and lazily sketch the lay of the pieces. Impressionist smears or pointillist dabs. Slapdash or meticulous depending on his pharmaceutical intake.

That evening the phone rang. It was Andrew, he of the Cambridge Happenings and Beat shows. "I knew you would phone," said Syd.

"Did the Tarot cards foretell it?" asked Andrew.

"No," said Syd. "Marie Simone in Una's magazine."

"Fancy doing me some art?" asked Andrew. "Anything you like. It's for something I'm putting together. A group participation thing. Feel free to send me anything you want. Or nothing".

Anything or nothing was Syd's kind of brief. He gathered up a random array of found objects scattered around the flat. RD Laing's *The Divided Self*. A promotional pamphlet for the Post Office Tower. *A Pocket Guide To Wild Flowers*. A botany textbook. Beatrix Potter's *The Tale Of Mr Jeremy Fisher*. Bob Cobbing's concrete poetry anthology *ABC In Sound*. Kate Greenaway's *Mother Goose* anthology. The March 1966 issue of *Playboy* magazine. The *Playboy* he had bought for the lengthy Bob Dylan interview, not the nudes ("Three Fresh European Sex Sirens" teased the cover tantalisingly) and certainly not for the exclusive serialisation of Ian

Fleming's latest novella *Octopussy*. "Hentoff" it said on the front page, naming the writer. Dylan not even mentioned, but it was the stream of consciousness flow of Dylan's responses, rather than Nat Hentoff's questions, that fascinated Syd. "What made you go the rock 'n' roll route?" asked Hentoff at one point. Dylan's digression takes in a job in a dime store, an encounter with a high school teacher – "Who's built a special kind of refrigerator that can turn newspaper into lettuce" – and a succession of adversaries who keep burning his house down. "And that's how you became a rock 'n' roll singer?" asks Hentoff when the narrative runs out of steam. "No, that's how I got tuberculosis," says Dylan. Syd devoured the entire surrealist romp in one sitting and vowed that in the unlikely event of him becoming a pop star, this is how he would wish to approach his interviews. Then he turned his attention to the "Three Fresh European Sex Sirens". Scrawling a series of toilet wall daubs on one (speech balloons reading "Fuk Suk and Lik" and "Nipl") he revelled in the sheer childish glee of drawing an arrowed cock and balls in the topless model's cleavage and a spider web emerging from her armpit. He used Bob Cobbing typographics to sculpt wordplay punning in the shape of a penis. A stick figure on a bike climbs the left breast.

One page done.

Setting aside adolescent instincts he constructed a Divided Self cut up ("Disconnected Disjointed Disjoined") and pasted it above a Rauschenberg oval of newspaper picture transfers.

Another page.

A cut up from "The Book Of Proverbs" ("Whoso diggeth a pit shall fall") and other Biblical phrases, Catch-22 ("knobby slabs of white stone") and pages torn from fashion magazines and the pop press. Tom Jones and his manager Tony Cartwright get a mention. More Rauschenberg drip and drag.

Another page.

More Cobbing. ADD a mArk. Red and black squiggles and sickle shapes. Two pages of Kate Greenaway cut ups and stencils, plus characters lifted from his old exercise book jottings. More typographic jumble, muddle and splat. Paint forced through mesh. The Post Office Tower guidebook cut, pasted and rearranged *LIGHT ALL COCKTAIL FREQUENCY EXTREMELY A FREQUENCY EXTREMELY*. Burroughs inspired alpha-beta. Kindergarten images. Paintbox colours.

Another page.

Methodology indebted to the pop artists. Paper cuts, folds and shading. A fondly remembered Rauschenberg quote: "There is no reason not to consider the world as one gigantic painting." All Camberwell teachings absorbed and applicable.

Topical....Typical...Mr Heath.....Mr Wilson....Typical...Topical... Tip Up....Political.

Might turn that into a song at a later date. Meanwhile. Topical Trypical. The nearest Syd's thought processes ever get to political satire. Jo Grimond, leader of the Liberal party, renamed Joke Grimace. They'll never get that. All bases covered. All trace elements erased.

Another page.

More storybook elves and flowerpots, crescent moons and broody moo-cows, toadstools and stamens, jumpy dogs and bubble fish. Jeremy Fisher and petals waving in a most peculiar way. Cut up the work. Cut up the world till all fragments cohere into new runic algebra of everyday sources and avant-garde structures and you still feel it in your fingers later that night when the jack plugs crackle and the electricity surges and the music begins to play you.

It all pours out morning fresh and unmediated. Cryptic ideograms. Enigma codes of hieroglyph. Elliptical/allusional montage pages of typography. New syntaxical/syntactile strategies for transcending sense. Preferring to survey an upper and lower case jumble world instead. Knowledge scramble of e.e. cummings and Bob Cobbing and Paul Klee and all those *Ark* magazines poured over in Camberwell Library. Visual concrete and decorative word confetti. Inscriptive/Instructive. Remembering the joy of Letraset when it first came out. The added incentive of pissing off the more fuddy-duddy element of the tech college teaching staff who said it would destroy the craft skill of sign writing and that pretty soon the only place you would see artisan font work was on the rusted old tin billboards outside corner shops or on the ornate mirrors that still decorated the less salubrious public bars. Syd could dig all that as compositional material, but otherwise he thought old tin billboards outside corner shops were as passé as the Craven A cigarettes they endorsed. As for pubs. Who went to pubs anymore?

All that art school learning, the stuff that went in, all poured into an impromptu commission from a friend. No brief. No ties. No rules. Call the whole thing *FART ENJOY* as a piss weak pun on comfort and joy and hand it over to Andrew in person if he comes to the gig on Saturday. He sent Andrew a handbill. "Eight till late" it said in shimmering op art scarlet and emerald. "Liquid agent Storm. WinDmill propellers to power the mind of age. New Wave Art Strings. Delirium Fun Rays."

Andrew came to the gig. He was expecting some art school leftovers maybe, something from the stack that sat at the end of Syd's bed. Or a hastily crayoned A3 page or two perhaps. "These could be the specimen pages for something I'll do next," said Syd as he flicked through his comfort and joy contribution. "I might do a whole book like this. You've given me lots of new ideas." Jabbering above the room noise, explaining away the thinking behind every page. Eyes shining with enthusiasm.

"You'll stay for the party afterwards of course," he said bouncing on his heels. "I'm so glad you came." Happy then in his world full of possibilities. "You have to watch the show. It's different now. It's an event." And with that he bobbed and weaved his way through the gathering crowd. Merging with the colour wheel projections and heading towards the backstage area. Liquid oils played across his moving form. The walls pulsated with swirling, congealing amoebic blobs. Everyone's acid seemed to kick in simultaneously and the room shattered into a billion synesthetic particles of multi-sensory immersion. Andrew thought once more about how good Syd looked in the flicker blam-pow of the light show.

AN OLD FAIRY TALE

The studio is a womb. A warm place. Safe and secure. These days Nick seems to take his only pleasure there. The music has started to come out stark, certainly starker than it used to. But the studio remains a comfort dwelling. Companionable. A reassuring habitat. Somewhere for the muse to flourish and some of the angst to ebb away. Outside is all hustle and haste but in here incense can be lit, throws draped over speaker cabinets. Everything assumes the intimacy of a boudoir. Only the urgent glow of a red bulb indicates that a recording is in progress and that this is a place of work not a chapel or sanctuary. Although in a way it is.

"Sit down. I've got something I want to play you." My host, whose identity I am contractually sworn to conceal, is a leading player in the murky world of bootlegs and other exotic contraband. Let's just call him X. "Put pharmaceutical distribution operative," he laughs when I suggest various non-de-plumage to keep the cops at bay and the lawyers none the wiser.

We are drinking finely blended tea from china cups in a small converted office room in the attic of his house. Again, I am sufficiently fond of my kneecaps not to reveal the lovely park the property overlooks. He chides me for insisting on mixing milk with my bergamot. "You pleb! Did they teach you nothing in reform school?" Eastern fragrancies waft around the room. Hash burns pepper the sleeve of his silk shirt, insignia stripes earned from time served battles with the Hashashin army. A five-skin joint is painstakingly constructed. The hail beats down in tiny ice balls onto a slanted narrow window above us. A bracketed wall shelf contains a long row of alphabetised tape boxes. "DYLAN" is boldly etched on about three quarters of them. "WHO" reads the last one. "Live at Hull. The night after Leeds. A much better gig," says mien host. "When l told Townshend I'd bootlegged him he said 'about fucking time'. He took it well." Not all of X's clients are as appreciative. He gives me a long list of those who disapprove, including two prominent acts he claims have contracts out on him. "One thing you have to understand is the music industry is full of villains and sharks. It's just that some are more villainous than others."

After these cautionary pleasantries we get down to discussing the business at hand. The various demos and unfinished recordings that should have constituted singer-songwriter Nick Drake's fourth album, had recent events not conspired and legal mechanisms not been activated. "With a typical Dylan, say, I'll initially do a run of 2000–2500," says X, outlining the economics of the thing. "With the Drake I'll probably just do 100, mainly for friends and kindred spirits like yourself."

Drake is a pet project, shall we say? Once X got word that the record company was unwilling to release these latest efforts, variously claiming they are "unfinished" and "sub-standard" he got straight on the case. Tapes were purloined from "friends in low places," studio chat and all, and he got to work on restoring the project according to Drake's original intended track listing – "plus a couple of bonus items". He's even penned the sleevenotes, of which the opening paragraph of this article is just a sample. Entitled *An Old Fairy Tale* after one of the album's most enticing tracks, X is all ready to go with an under the counter release. "All I need is the backdoor key to a pressing plant and we should be ready to roll by next spring at the latest." Knowing that I'm a fan and likely to spread the word he invited me round for an exclusive listen. Teacups are put aside. A conical masterpiece of a joint is lit and away we go.

At the end of the opening track, the gently appealing "Rider On The Wheel (Take #1)" we hear Drake's softly spoken hesitant voice. "Perhaps I should leave that as an instrumental. What do you think John? Just leave that opening...uh... [undecipherable mumble]... I'll play it again." On take two he performs it again at a slightly faster tempo, humming snatches of the verses here and there. I tell X I prefer the hummed version. "I think I do," he laughs. "It's a pretty song don't you think? Kind of a continuity song. Carry on sort of thing. This is what I do."

Next up is 'Black Eyed Dog'. From the title I was expecting a harrowing item, full of foreboding and dread, but I hear little of that. What I do hear is someone channelling the late Blind Al Wilson of Canned Heat. Some might say it's a portrait of a man haunted by his debilitating demons. I hear blue label Liberty. Drake's playing is imprecise and tentative, there's fret buzz where there used to be almost clinical perfection, but the brief lyric speaks of recognition and confrontation. I wouldn't say he sounds at ease with his condition. You don't get the impression he's about to pat the dog on the head and take it for walkies, but there's something cathartic about the song, an offloading of psychic burden. I share these thoughts with my host. "It's tortured artist syndrome innit? The blues myth," he laughs, exhaling a lungful. "They love a bit of suffering, the critics." "They've done it with Syd Barrett too," I reply, referring to Syd's still unreleased masterpiece 'Vegetable Man'. "Hello. I'm Syd the vegetable. I'm a complete nutter." "Exactly," X snarls. "Who the fuck do these people think they are?" "Why do record companies do that?" I ask. "Why do they act as censors?" "It's because they don't understand artistry," X replies as hail turns to snowflakes on the attic window. "They always equate the art with anguish rather than respite from it. Same with Van Gogh. He doesn't twist up a chair because he's twisted inside. He does that because that's how he paints fucking chairs. That's not illness. It's energy. It's vision."

'Hanging On A Star' is next up. Sung in Nick's higher register, the melody and chord patterns evoke both 'Road' and 'Which Will', and like several of the tracks X plays me, reveal clear continuity with the sparer new direction first unveiled on Pink Moon. It's a dismissive shrug of a song, resigned rather than desperate. Some might suggest that it's aimed at the music industry, a bit of a bleat about his manager perhaps. It could even be about a woman. "Yeah, I can see where you're at," says X emerging from a vast plume of smoke. "No one ever thinks of Nick in terms of thwarted love, do they?" I venture. "I don't think most people think of Nick in terms of anything," says X. "He goes over the head of the average punter.

But no, I know what you're saying. You can't imagine him doing an 18 minute song about getting his end away, like Al Stewart can you? But you can only de-sex someone so far. He's not a eunuch is he? Little castrato choir boy Nick. Gives him a whole different dimension if you sew his member back on."

We hear Nick's quietly enquiring voice again after 'Voice From The Mountain'. "Robert could write an arrangement, don't you think?" he says. There is the sound of a tape spooling back and then "I'm not certain about that third verse. I suppose we could lose that" … a pause then a muttered "or re-write it".

"I left the studio chat on deliberately," says X. "Shows he's self-critical about his lyrics." I find that Drake can be a devilishly inconsistent lyric writer. The grace notes don't always land where you expect them to. And they can sometimes be followed by some annoyingly graceless ones. Almost like schoolboy poetry. But frequently Drake's music is so flawless you don't notice the occasional weak lyric. Syd Barrett's the same – albeit in a less cultured and more free-flowing way. There's an inner logic to each man's work that doesn't readily reveal itself.

"Yeah, with Nick, it's kinda Keatsian," says X. "It's a Grecian Urn deal. 'The spirit ditties of no tone', y'know. 'Foster child of silence and slow time' and all that. The figures on the urn, frozen in antiquity, fated never to meet." He winks at me. "You see that's what a public school education does for you Spencer." Then he checks himself. "Of course, it might not be that at all. It might all just be a defence mechanism. A way of not revealing."

There's more studio chat after 'Toe The Line'. John the Engineer. "It's somewhat reminiscent of 'City Clock' don't you think?". "Yes," says Nick slowly. "I was aware of that so I rocked it up in the refrain. Well I say rocked it up." "And refrain," says John. There is warm laughter from both men. "I feel I'm starting to repeat myself. That's the trouble," says Nick. "The trouble," echoes John, deadpan. Okay, it's not exactly Derek & Clive, but it's great to hear such playful interaction between songs. "Come and listen to what we've done so far," says John, and that's the end of side one.

My impression thus far is that there is an urgency to the tracks on the first side, like Drake is genuinely reaching out and trying to make a connection. "And not just content to hide behind the floating gauze. Yeah, I know what you mean," says X. "There's less enigma. That's a good thing."

As if to emphasise the informality, side two commences with Nick's dryly spoken "this is my hit single," before launching into the peeling chords of 'Saw You On A Starship'. Musically it's very similar to 'Fruit Tree', derivatively so in places, while the chorus refrain is lifted directly from 'Parasite'. Lyrically it's quite acidy, opiated even, as overtly druggy as anything he's done since the unreleased 'Been Smoking Too Long' or the man in the shed who spends most of his days out of his head. The reference to the dragon X tells me is heroin. I'm not so sure. "Confessional" I write in my notes, and quite clearly not chart-bound at all.

The title track 'Old Fairytale' owes a certain something to 'Poor Boy' in the melody but the self-mockery of that song is tempered by a certain detachment here. Nick hovering over it all, a benign presence, observing. This seems to be a prevalent mood on side two of the album. 'Fairytale' is a very ambivalent song, ostensibly full of enchantment and wonder, but with Nick the narrator absenting himself from the action. As so often we're ultimately left floating on solid air. Nick's voice cuts in again. "When I played that to my mother she said—" But we never do find out what mother said because the tape runs out.

Talking of Solid Air, we come to what is personally for me the highlight of side two. 'Even Now' is a duet collaboration between Nick and his good friend John Martyn who joins him on narcoleptic layers of overdubbed electric guitar. The lyric is wilfully obscure and puzzling and much of it is drowned in echo as Drake slurs his words and offers a prolonged howl of the title line in what it presumably an affectionate pastiche of his colleague's singing style. Martyn joins him on the ascending chorus with that bear growl of a voice. The result is a joy to behold. The one track that makes the hairs on your neck stand on end. It's the nearest Nick has ever come to funky. "I'm sure if Nick has such a thing as purist fans they'll hate this track," suggests X not unreasonably.

After the intensity of 'Even Now', 'On This Day' is a bit of a comedown. A somewhat tired and uninspired lyric accompanied by perfunctory blues riffs. It's depressing to hear someone as gifted as Drake just recycling old 12-bar clichés with little evident enthusiasm. Essentially a throwaway and easily the weakest cut on the album.

'Paid Brain' is one of two successive tracks X has inserted that apparently weren't part of the original intended running order. For the first four lines the song utilises a similar melody to 'Rider On The Wheel' before seamlessly easing into the 'Poor Boy' chorus melody – the second time Nick references the song on the album and most charmingly effective it is too. You can virtually hear Ray Warleigh's alto rising up in the instrumental break before Drake sings the whole thing again. Of all the tracks on the album this is the one that begs a full band arrangement. At barely two minutes it short changes the listener and I could have stood to hear the full 'Poor Boy' augmentation of this, funky female singers and all.

The penultimate track, 'Sing A Song', is also a little on the short side, which is a pity as it's the nearest I've ever heard to a conventional love serenade from Nick. "I thought I might give that to Francoise," he says at the end. "She could translate it into French. I thought I could remedy—" But the voice trails off into nothingness and we never do discover what could be remedied.

A long slow languorous blues confessional ends the album. 'Long Way To Town' is vaguely reminiscent of 'Know' from *Pink Moon* with its percussive low notes effect. "He sounds a bit like Richie Havens," I suggest. "I've never heard him sound so husky and deep." "Deeper than the deepest blue," says X, eyes closed, swaying and vibing on the riff. "Do you know Lowell Fulson's 'Tollin' Bells'?" he asks. I don't. "In that case I should dig that out. I think he's been listening to Lowell Fulson here." The final slap on the guitar sounds like it's done with genuine anger.

"So, what do you think?" Says X. My initial reaction is that I'm surprised just how much continuity there is with the mood and pared down structures of *Pink Moon*, especially as it's been nearly two and a half years since that record was released. X gives that judgement qualified approval but thinks there are signs that Nick is moving on. "He's getting more like John Martyn," he claims. "Earthier in a way. I'd hoped he would collaborate more. I told Nick to go out and do some gigs with John but you know how it is. Adamant he wouldn't tour."

X suggests we have a listen to *Pink Moon* before I go. To compare and contrast. "I used to think this record was so empty," he says, as the title track kicks in. "Now it seems to fill a mansion room." Another joint is rolled. Another wince as I head to the kitchenette to add milk to my Earl Grey. "There's the Blind Al Wilson voice you mentioned," shouts X as 'Know' sends a primal delta yell out into the late afternoon. ""Know I'm not there". See he's erasing himself already. Always erasing himself."

We remain spellbound by the bitterness and bile of 'Parasite', agreeing that it's our favourite track on the LP. Any sense that Drake is this ethereal whimsy-woo folk singer is wiped out by this song. "If this had turned up for the first time just now people would be projecting all kinds of despair onto it, like they will with 'Black Eyed Dog'," says X. "As it is, it's quite an old song. He always had those feelings lurking." I suggest that he does seem to be working through feelings of utter worthlessness on 'Parasite'. "He was more influenced by that soul-baring Lennon album that people realise. In a way 'Parasite' is his 'Cold Turkey'," says X. "Silver spoon. That's smack that is". I shoot him a quizzical look." Don't ask me how I know that," he says seizing on my visible scepticism at these assertions. "There's more than one way in this life that a man can cover his tracks. Pun fully intended."

I've always been intrigued by the way that the album is bookended by foreboding and prophecy with the title track and 'Things Behind The Sun'. "The whole album casts spells doesn't it? It's a sorcery album," says X. I scribble down a list of descriptions as we listen. It reads back like an I Ching hexagram.

'Place To Be' – acceptance admission want reconciliation
'Road' – retreat avoidance strategy survival
'Which Will' – choice commitment allegiance
'Things Behind The Sun' – forewarning penance prophecy visitation

X casts a stoned eye over my notes. "You could construct a pentagram with *Pink Moon* at the centre of it all. The five points of radiation from the energy force on that record. This shit goes deep with me, Spencer. Here let me show you something before you go." And it's at this point that X lets me read the introductory portion of his intended sleevenotes for the Fairytale bootleg.

I step out into the pale sunshine of a winter's afternoon. Slap bang into the London rush of aimless people going nowhere. Buses and cars all snarled up, bumper to bumper. Weary commuters shuffling through the slush. I feel rejuvenated. I feel like I've experienced a visitation to another world. How much longer can it be before people turn on to Nick Drake's music? In a way it's probably already too late, then again it might be just the beginning.

Pearly Spencer, *Wooden Ships* October 1974

ASHES TO ASHES, SAND TO SAND

Syd surveyed the view from his ninth floor window. The city stacked up like a Rothko. The midway horizon marked off in a red/brown cloudbank blur of heat haze and pollution fumes. Above it, a filtered blue radiance of sky. Below, unfathomable depths of inky blackness. The weatherman on the radio forecast a rainy morrow and the chance of scattershot showers. Respite.

Up there on the ninth floor he embraced the mundanity of his strangeness. He felt enabled and unreachable. He would potter about nocturnally, the TV left on after close down, transmitting ghost static even when he slept. In the daytime he took to keeping the radio on at a low volume, transmissions barely registering, so that everything was reduced to an acceptable level of inaudibility. He accommodated himself willingly to this unobtrusive ambience, content to inhabit a world that posed no semblance of articulation. Erudite talk programmes on Radio 4 were condensed to mumbled inconsequentiality. Pop songs emitted a faint trebly twitter, like fledgling birds who spoke in mini Morse. 'When Will I See You Again' by the Three Degrees and 'Feel Like Makin' Love' by Roberta

Flack were stripped of their yearning beauty and emitted squeaks of sentiment that barely reached the walls.

On his tack board a selection of crudely torn magazine articles and newspaper clippings were arranged haphazardly, overlapping in a messy collage. An old *Radio Times* front cover that had been there since the day he moved in. Photo of David Frost in black and white striped tie. Headline: "Hold The Frost Page!" A business card for Gentle Ghost removals. Menus for nearby Chinese takeaways and Italian bistros. A WH Smith's office planner page remained empty of entries. A hand scrawled note next to it reminded him that he had to be at EMI Studio 3. 12? 1? Question mark.

He squeezed himself into pop star apparel and tried to feel the part. The velvet chord trousers pinched more than they used to. The battered snakeskin boots had seen better days. He gazed at himself in the bathroom mirror. Eyes like knives. A shaving nick on five-day dark stubble. He brushed his teeth rigorously. Swigging toothpaste-tainted water from a dirty mug brought on a coughing fit. Smokers phlegm dotted the basin.

Down in reception Sammy asked him if his TV was still on the blink. "It's okay. I like it like that," said Syd. He'd never cared much for any of the desk staff before Sammy started. They were all too brisk and busily efficient. One woman, Elsa, Portuguese he heard her say, regarded him warily and asked him not to flick his cigarette ash on the floor when he sat on the leather sofa by the window, reading the foyer magazines. Sammy was okay though, relaxed, chatty, happy to indulge Syd when he asked about the taxi

ASHES TO ASHES, SAND TO SAND

life and doing The Knowledge. Knowledgeable himself on account of his brother Harry being in the trade. He was a little too keen to talk about the mixed fortunes of Chelsea Football Club for Syd's liking but generally nothing was too much trouble for him. He'd give Syd his copy of *The Sun* at the end of his shift, which Syd thought exceedingly kind, even though he only used it for the TV guide. And he would point out attractive women, as they stood with well-dressed businessmen by the lifts, lowering his voice to point out which ones weren't paying guests "if you get my drift". Syd didn't always get his drift but was happy to nod along and listen to the high and low points of Sammy's day. "We must go for a jar sometime," Sammy said on more than once occasion, but the offer had yet to be reciprocated.

"Off to play?" he said as he spotted Syd totting a guitar case towards the exit. "Sometime," said Syd, as the stifling air outside greeted him like an oven door left open. Syd turned right and right again, heading for his favourite newsagents on the Kings Road where he bought 20 Virginia Slims. "For my pretty young wife who plays tennis," he told the old woman behind the counter who, having the measure of his other worldliness, often short-changed him. He never questioned or counted the shortfall of coins.

He couldn't remember if they were sending a car for him so he took the tube from Sloane Square to St Johns Wood and walked to Abbey Road. "You've just missed him," said Sammy as the cab driver asked at front desk for a Mister Barrett.

The woman at Abbey Road reception was warm and friendly.

"Just sign in and go on through," she said with a smile. "RK Barrett" he scribbled in shaky left slanting script. "Oh, I'm sorry. I thought they said you were a regular," the receptionist said, as RK Barrett stood there, rooted to the spot. "I'll phone studio three and somebody will come through and fetch you." "Yes, that would be nice," said Syd politely. "I did come here before," he said. "Down that corridor," he added helpfully. An engineer was sent for.

"Rolling Syd."

An open string strum. A loud violent stab at a C shape. Fingers reminding themselves how to form a chord. Another loud C then silence.

"Rolling Syd."

After some fumbling adjustments of tone and volume a tune finally emerges. A Bo Diddley scrub. A reversion to basics. The two-chord shuffle. "Shave and a haircut. Two bits." It goes on for a bit then stops.

At the controls, PJ debates with his assistant whether to keep it, ask for another take, or wipe and start again. He will go on doing this all day. The sessions for the last album began with a formless blues jam just to get Syd in shape and that jam turned into 'Maisie', a piece not without merit if only for the lyrics which seemed to come from nowhere once Syd emerged from his Mandrax haze. *"Maisie... bmm"*. Dry mouthed percussion. Lips working involuntary. Illuminous grin. Inanimate until activated. Moving stiffly about the studio. Estranged from purpose or passion. No magic. Just the dull blues thud of 'Maisie'. Bmm. It closed side one. That was four years ago.

PJ assumed that words would emerge. Give it time, he assured himself. We've got the studio booked for the week. Give it time, agreed his assistant, secretly alarmed at the shambling apparition through the glass who seemed to be taking detachment to startling new levels.

And so it goes on. Another broken blues shuffle. Then three minutes of cautious negotiation with an echo pedal. Syd looking down vacantly as if a painting is taking shape which is none of his doing. These three minutes of abstract colouration give PJ hope. Give him something to grasp at. We can use that bit. Do that bit again, Syd. But you could never ask Syd that. It never came out the same again. You might just as well ask the clouds if they wouldn't mind going back to how they were yesterday lunchtime.

Next, a sudden over-amplified lurch, as if the control room request had derailed him and he'd lost all semblance of muscle memory and motor skill. Then an angry stab at a hard rock riff. Could be anyone. Could be the Groundhogs. Could be Slade or Stray. A brief flurry of chord changes played as if on autopilot. There's a mounting desolate emptiness to it all. Like watching a soundcheck for a performance that will never take place. Next, a tuneful lyrical blues with semi-focus and potential but again it goes nowhere, a train running off the rails. More threadbare hints of melodies that grope towards substance but never quite arrive. Foot on the entropy pedal.

At one point, PJ has to leave the room and choke back tears. He keeps getting the briefest glimpse of Syd trying in there, distractedly attempting what's expected of him. Half understanding the brief. What's happened to the third album that he told *Melody Maker* about in 1971? "12 singles. And jolly good singles." And where are the words? There's a moment where Syd says "I'm going to sing now," but he goes to the toilet instead. When he comes back he starts to turn the volume down on his guitar, slowly at first, so they compensate in the control room by upping the levels on the desk, but then Syd turns it down to micro-audibility that only the studio carpet dust mites can detect. Reverting to Chelsea Cloisters tendencies, sufficiently in possession of his faculties to suspect that this will be regarded as a Have You Got It Yet art prank when what he is really seeking is a new lo-fi ambience, a fresh sonic habitat he might feel more comfortable in. Erasing expectation, fret by fret, notch by notch, tuning peg by tuning peg until there's nothing left to cling to. He often felt like that in the band. Drowned in the blizzard of lights, blitzed on acid, never knowing the next note till it came. Just a flickering shadow. Morse tones. Pickup clicks that grow fainter until they disappear altogether.

Back in the cold light of now there are fragments of half-remembered blues patterns, learned in the school common room and tech college refectory with Fred. The grant-assisted carefree apprenticeship. Resolution was never an issue then. No pressure. And now? Now, pressure is seemingly all there is. Pressure and malfunction and blank beats. The ocean tide long since stemmed. Now only stagnant waters. An involuntary impulse and barely that. An old Blind Boy Fuller tune he used to doodle. Can't remember the name any more. It had a lyric, *"ashes to ashes/sand to sand"*, he liked that bit. A Juke Boy Bonner tune too. What was that? One of

Duggie's. Duggie had all those Folkways anthologies. A treasure trove of crackly old recordings in dog-eared battered sleeves. And so it went on, a fluffed riff, a fumbled melody, a disjointed bit of 12-bar train to nowhere.

And yet when you forage on through the scrambled matrix, a dot to dot pattern slowly begins to form, albeit one that only Syd can detect. He's worked out a new arrangement of 'Beechwoods', stripped the original of its staccato 'Taxman' rhythm and its decrescendo glide and replaced it with something more thoughtful and folky. "I'm so glad you're here," he'd told Mick Rock when he turned up on behalf of *Rolling Stone* magazine three autumns earlier. Played him a new arrangement of 'Love You'. Going back over old ground even then, trying to get it right. And still trying in episodic glimpses, as if restoring order to the chaotic past might just work, might just give him reason to carry on. There's a handful of tunes in his head. And there are words. Despite what PJ suspects there are scraps of rhyme and unreason in pocket strips of crumpled paper. Stuff he's been working on in rare moments of creative spark. Words and phrases that might still be versified yet, even at this late juncture. He looked at them in the toilet, just to see if they were adequate. A bundle of them in his right trouser pocket. Torn into strips. Cut ups that still cohered. Something akin to 'Word Song'. He still scribbled them occasionally. Therapy to temper the voices and focus the inner jabber and babble. Suspecting that the articulation of more meaningful truths now lay way beyond him, had done since the Master rejected him, but this might do for now. Might do instead. Might have to. Semantic parlour games.

Truth monger chin rest route flower gell nozzle carapace flat beg oak shovel and shot dog nose nuzzle flammable lord eyes aqua Caesar seizure steam press iron Orion Aragorn

Cleopatra patchwork laughing next thing listen singing bells hells quick march drive by kit bag tie dye loose items

"What's that one called?" Syd mutters to himself as he takes a piss. "Call it 'B Side'," he responds. Call them all 'B Side'. Call the third album *B side*. Less expectations that way.

In the left pocket was a peach of a song. A reminder of better days. He hardly ever thought like that anymore. Only ever went there in his dream sleep but the occasional lyric still came out like that when reverie sang to him as if from an earlier more hopeful life.

This little girl in a country lane/till the echoes come/she stays the same/ till
The echo came/Cos our little world went all the way/
In the world that you're coming from

Some time ago in your garden
Stark in her moonbeams
Her earth empty arms
In the world that you're somewhere from

To rest a head on her scent wetted shoulders
To be/just to be
Pot full of weeds still grow in the garden

Herbs and shed/pleasant wed
In the place that you're sometimes from

This little girl in a country lane/till the echoes come/she stays the same/
till
The echo came/Cos our little world went all the way round and back
again/
In the world that you're coming from

Back in the studio his hand hovered above his left pocket. He was about to pull that one out when he noticed the red light was off and an EMI technician was in the booth repatching the desk.

He turned left and went to the canteen, had a quiet smoke, listened to the chit-chat of orchestral musicians recording a Sibelius symphony in Studio One, looked out of the window, watched a squirrel busying itself on the flagstones outside beside a spreading horse chestnut tree. Eager for autumn's drop. A police car sounded loudly from the street.

He committed himself for a couple more days. On the third he emptied his pockets of paper strips. Threw them in a corridor bin. Gave up on words. On communication full stop. Started to meet PJ's intercom requests with dark stares and startled eyes. Turned left when he fancied a cup of tea and a bun on an EMI logo-stamped plate. Turned right when he'd had enough for the day. On the fourth day he turned right for the very last time. "Maybe I'll figure something out and come back in a year," he said to the concerned and empathetic young engineer. "Sorry you picked the wrong hero," he said as PJ, oblivious to the significance of the moment, shuffled cue sheets in the studio and looked at a tangle of unusable tape.

Because in the end, all those interstellar overtures, all that stratospheric guitar fire that strafed the domed skies in English municipal halls and old European aircraft hangars, it all came down to this. A recording log sheet full of arbitrary titles, timings, pencilled scribbles and scrawls, hopelessly hopeful suggestions for further use in a future that would never arrive. "More echo". "Very out of tune". "Weird bit". "Useable for overdub". "Basic track". "Fast bit". Circles and arrows indicating what might slot where, should mind-shot Syd turn up again tomorrow or the day after or in a year and do some more slow weird basic out of tune bits.

Back at Chelsea Cloisters he was greeted by Sammy at the reception desk. "There's been a power cut," he said. "It's back on then," said Syd seeing nothing unusual in the brightly lit foyer. "No, but it's blown your fridge. There's blood everywhere." Sammy explained how the maintenance staff had gone round checking plug points once power was restored and found that several faulty appliances had been unable to cope with the surge. The residents on the top floor seemed to have suffered the most. "All them fridges needed replacing anyway," Sammy reasoned. "They've been there since the rooms got converted. Museum pieces most of them." Syd walked towards the lift. "Better not until we've done safety checks," said Sammy. "Walk up. It'll keep you fit." "I'll wait here," said Syd, settling tired-limbed onto the reception area sofa. Sammy gave him a look and turned to deal with a customer checking in.

"Gonna get in some nice new fridges with decent freezers," said Sammy when he came up to the room later with an electrician. "Look at the state of this. All this meat's spoiled. You shouldn't really keep that much without eating it. It's a health hazard. Sorry about the mess. They cleaned up what they could." Blood trails ran from the bottom of the fridge towards the kitchen door, staining the worn lino. Two bottles of Jif sat on a small Formica topped table. A blood-soaked mop rested against the wall. "Blimey, you ain't half got some guitars," said Sammy. "Take one," said Syd. "I don't need that many. Or any."

A FURTHER STRANGE ENCOUNTER

They prescribe grainy pills, shit in a shell. Dirty downers. Nothing that gives you shiny mind, just the stuff that has you staring at the walls brain-numb. Stale breath. A different nausea to the everyday other kind. An urge to retch. Someone who isn't you dribbles thick linctus. One minute you are fine. Placidity restored. Then the medication regime kicks in. Dulling you into submission. Pampering you with an all-over embalming glaze. Lack of appetite. Meals barely touched or unattended. Toying absently with what's on the end of your fork. The *Naked Lunch* that Burroughs said everyone gets to. Wise words in ghost life fading to withered stems and dead petals a long time ago. Ambition and urgency reduced to a scrubland lot, a bombsite, a slum. Clambering through the ruins of your dreams at night. Trying to remember. Depleted days. Lack of detail. Dirty smogadon fog. Word slur. Hazy jive. Faces loom up and out and at 'em atom ant and sometimes you have a hard time tracing that slimy snail trail back to you. Dry mouth. Spit fleck. Cleft palate. Mush mouth. Colours all mixed down and watery. Just the blood rush for music. Mealtime comes around again. Served to you courteously. Slow time passes. Silver salver salivate. Gravy congeals. Plate falls to the floor and everything spills. Leave it sitting there where it landed on the polished parquet floor. Watch it dry and harden. All things fester. Liquid skin. Turning translucent. The absence of thought is deafening. Shake the bottle. Sip of water. Gulp them down again. One house point to you. One gold star. Well played Nicolaus. Jolly good show.

The only trouble is, you have to keep this up every day. No half measures. If you miss a day or two, or more, the imbalance is restored and all the good is undone.

Syd, too, is in the grip of storm-tossed torment unravelling. Coordinates that mesh and spark on good days, overload and short circuit on bad ones. Disorder and dislocation become the norm. Thoughts that fail to sustain the grasp. A brain-splattered palette that no longer makes pretty patterns. Shunning medication. Sinking into the mud and slurry, down into the place of mad twists and people with their heads on backwards. Everything a blank or blur and no idea if yesterday was Tuesday.

When they met for a third (or was it fourth?) time Nick remembered the first encounter but had forgotten the second. All abandoned cars and unpaid parking tickets roll into one after a while. Syd remembered the second but not the first encounter in Kensington Market. He doubted if he'd ever been in Kensington Market. He remembered the Fred Flintstone tie, though. He was collecting the full set. There was in all likelihood a third meeting, possibly by the Serpentine. Blank-eyed strangers gazing at the boating lake. Syd brought stale bread for the ducks. Everyone and everything slowed to dream motion. Or perhaps it was Hampstead Heath. Either way, they tried to convince themselves there was an engagement they kept which featured parkland and water. Another possibility, they agreed, involved both of them gravitating towards a basement squat in Ladbroke Grove, mutually attracted via a common acquaintance with an interest in selling them instant obliteration. Little said. Surrounded by human flotsam and mental debris. Watching others pursue their own chosen degradation. Arc sprays of muddy blood on bare walls. Foil raised to barely parted lips and lit. Silently exhaling in the emptiness of another grey day. Rain dripping from trees. Traffic a dull muted hum. Police sirens and paranoia.

There must have been written correspondence too, they agreed. Or at least a phone call. Otherwise how would they have found themselves here in this airless room.

"You find me in somewhat bad repair I'm afraid," said Nick.

"Not feeling too good myself," said Syd, mimicking the cadence of a rock song and perhaps not according the sentiment the sensitivity it deserved.

"It's not what you think it is," said Nick.

"What isn't?"

"This place," said Nick. "It's not a madhouse. It's a halfway madhouse."

"There's a distinction?' asked Syd.

Nick attempted a smile. More of an audition perhaps rather than an actual smile.

"What would you like?" asked the ever-generous Syd. "The refreshments are on me."

"Warm milk," replied Nick. "Ask them if they can make me a warm milk."

"A warm milk for my friend," said Syd at the serving hatch. "And I will have a soup, please."

"I'll bring them over mate."

At table, more shared silence. This bedraggled Estragon and haunted Vladimir, so alike in their vacancy. Threadbare stage set. Working towards intelligibility then lapsing again. Dialogue in stutters and starts. Time passes. Warm milk and chicken broth arrive.

"Shall I go first?" asked Nick, politeness personified in his quiet despair. Somewhere in an adjacent room music was playing. 'Our House'. Staring at the fire for hours and hours. Further down the corridor some sort of occupational art therapy was taking place. Crayoned evidence dotted the corridor walls. Nick knotted up at the pin board options. Cloudiness smeared his vision. The drive and desire to join in wouldn't come no matter how hard he tried to force it.

"There has been, shall I call it, an incident," said Syd, failing to observe the tenuous protocol that might have allowed more agreeable ways in which communication might be negotiated. Words fish-hooked from some shallow place by the water's edge where fragments gather but sentences refuse to formulate.

"That is to say."

"I met someone."

"Who I hadn't seen for some time. In the street I mean. In the Kings Road".

"It had been a long while I suppose. We were looking in the shop window at clothes. She wore a maxi coat just like the one in the window. And black boots. And I – she came back to the Cloisters. I live at the top. Nine floors in the lift. And I hadn't. I didn't mean—"

"It was meant to be friendly. Sort of a – a bit of a joke, but I realise. The problem is—"

Nick stared straight ahead and then down at the skin forming on his warm milk and then ahead again while Syd continued to assemble the jigsaw pieces of a conversation. Doing the border first and working his way towards the middle. The detail that makes a picture.

"I hadn't seen her in quite a while. She was chatty as people can be. I mean she spoke to me first. I recognised her. She was sometimes there at the flat. The other flat. Used to come to all the gigs".

"So, I went to the kitchen and made a cup of tea. And all the while I suppose I must have been jabbering away. I don't really see anyone. I've forgotten how. But at one point I think. Well I know I did. I sort of regret it now like one regrets a lot of things. And I shouted. You'd better take your clothes off if we're going to do this. And the radio was on. The kitchen radio and the song was – I can't remember the song. Something in the charts I suppose. Sort of funky trucking music. And I shouted, yeah baby. Or something like that. I assumed I was being funny somehow. Almost the joker. And then she was gone. I didn't hear the door. I mean I came out of the kitchen with the tea and she'd gone. I went out to the lift. And it was still there. I shouted down the stairs."

Nick, until this moment, had been absent. Away in his thoughts. Shut down. But something in the way Syd shouted about shouting down the stairs and something about the way he was becoming increasingly, almost violently agitated in his animation brought him to. He looked at what was in front of him. Fixed Syd in his stare. And spoke.

"You did what?"

"I mean she needn't have come back with me. It was only five minutes and she was chatty. But she went away again. People do that. They just fuck off and desert you. Women can be like that. Arousing. I used to get that all the time. Banging at my door when I lived in Earl's Court. It got too much. They fuck with my head too much. The whole situation. I mean, women. They're nothing but cunt trouble. Wasting my time. Stupid bitch. She would have enjoyed sucking my—"

At this Nick was roused to an anger that Syd had never witnessed before. He had barely ever seen him animated, yet alone articulate for any length of time. Normally he was prairie tumbleweed, drifting rootless across arid plains. Now he rose up from his chair and stood tall.

"You shouted at her? You got her in you room and said you were going to—"

"I suppose I scared her, yes."

"And is that how you treat women? You make me wretch, actually physically sick, to listen to such... my friend was like that the last time I saw him. Being all lovey-dovey in the kitchen. Putting his arms around her waist and whispering sweet nothings, and then he takes me to the pub and he's chatting up the barmaid. It's pathetic. All of it. Pathetic. I told her when we got back. Told her everything. He gets on stage and sings tender love songs. And he acts like that. It's all an act. All of it. Performing. Free love. There's nothing free. Everything comes at a cost. I don't know why she stays with him. I don't know why any woman would. It's not the first time. I've seen—"

At that point Nick ran out of breath and made an attempt to compose himself. His heart was racing. He sat down again. The man at the serving hatch was looking at him.

"I mean where is... where is there any love in this life? A reason for going on. People need. If people were. If platonic love were—"

But little else was forthcoming. He'd said his piece and, regretting it already, retired to his reticence.

Syd was taken aback. Alarmed even. A feeling of contrition washed over him. He now wished that he'd never agreed to visit. He wished the day hadn't happened. He wished that he and his cunt trouble hadn't coincided at that shop window. He wished events had not conspired. Should have just said hello and hurried on his way. He would do that from now on.

Nothing was said for some time.

"I'm sorry," said Nick eventually.

"So am I," said Syd.

There was no agreement as to what they were sorry for. They were actually sorry for different reasons, bigger things, issues that ran deeper and darker, but the matter was closed, nothing further was articulated, nothing more was shared.

If anything, Nick's contrition was more severe. More time served and convoluted, and it seemed to pierce him far more profoundly. He put his head in his hands.

"I'm in an awful tangle," he said. He slowly removed the hands from his face and placed them palms down on the tabletop, as if conducting a seance and trying to mediate messages from the afterlife.

Syd observes his hands. His long slender fingers. His filthy bitten nails. "You're shaking," he said.

"Yes, I'm supposed to be taking Stelazine, among other things. But I keep missing the dosage. And stopping. Then starting again."

"Is that how you're trying to get through the tangle?"

"One option."

"But you keep stopping and starting."

"Yes."

"It's probably best to do one thing or another."

"You know about these things, do you?" It came out quietly sarcastic.

"Yes," said Syd. "I suppose you could say I'm pursuing..."

But Syd never said what he was pursuing. Nick waited, but no further information was forthcoming.

"Do you know of a Doctor Laing?" he asked.

"Yes. They tried to get me to see him," said Syd. "At Wimpole Street I think."

Nick detected a hint of paranoia in that "they", neither a general or specific they, a more sinister they, a collective oppressor. It would never have occurred to him that they might refer to Syd's old band mates and concerned friends. People who might be steering him towards someone with the professional acumen to make sense of his incoherence. Who might accord his action, and inaction, meaning and significance.

"What happened?" he asked. "At Wimpole Street."

"I wouldn't get in the car. Or go with them. Or when I was... or when I worked out... anyway I wouldn't go. I'm not on that path. I don't think there's a career in it. I'm more inclined towards..."

The words ran out of road once more.

"Do you know much about Doctor Laing?" Syd asked eventually.

"Only what my father told me. I mean I'd heard of him. I'm aware of his books. My father moves in those circles. My grandfather was a medical man."

"Yes, he's quite fashionable," said Syd. "Good Bad Mad. That's how it goes isn't it? Or it used to. Some of my friends went into all that. Therapy. Anti-psychiatry. I mean the ones who didn't find God. The master rejected me you see. I couldn't go that way. The guru path."

Nick detected a hint of theological regret. "I do sometimes wonder if religion might be the answer," he said. "Would it absolve me?"

The question was rhetorical and just hung there in the early autumn air.

"Laing says it's all tied up with the family," said Syd. "That's what my therapy friends say. I can see how that might be fruitful."

"Yes," considered Nick. "Although unfortunately that just gives me something else to reject. I want something to... somewhere to belong somehow. I don't think I want to peel back layers or go down into my innermost thoughts. It's not a place I wish to dwell for any length of time."

"No?" asked Syd.

"No," said Nick firmly. "Perhaps you are more analytical. You've been a painter. I thought all painters were analytical."

"You'd have thought so," said Syd. "You're better off not knowing anyway," he added abruptly, as if the entire subject had suddenly caused him offence. That seemed to bring that particular avenue of enquiry to an end, but then, after a pause, he said, "I should never have given up my studies, my art degree. I should have stuck with it."

"It's not too late to go back," said Nick.

"It is," said Syd, again with abrupt finality, but each time he seemed to ward off further questioning he then revealed a little more, as if in debate with himself.

"I could do that. Painting. I couldn't do the group thing. I thought I could, but it all got out of hand. I mean they called us a hype on *Juke Box Jury*, and perhaps we were, you know. Compared with everything else. Acid flash in a pan".

Nick smiled at that. For a moment he detected a common spark, not long extinguished.

"I thought about joining the army," he said.

"Oh, no don't do that," said Syd faintly alarmed. Then came a rueful smile. "You've just reminded me. We considered that. When I was at Tech, working my way through to Foundation. A friend and I. We dreamed up a scheme where we were going to visit all the recruitment offices. I can't remember how it worked now. There was a signing on fee they paid you, and we thought we could – I mean we didn't think. It sounds like something students do in rag week. Except we would have probably got shot in Aden or Cyprus. We had more fun then." Syd disappeared into the memory mist once again.

Nick, not having invested a scintilla of levity in the matter, was horrified.

"No, this wasn't a prank. I've seriously thought about joining the army. It might possibly give me a sense of—"

He thought for some time about what joining the army might have given him a sense of, but the more he thought, that too disappeared into his lengthening list of unfeasible schemes.

"My options are finite," he said despairingly. "When it comes to the crunch I just can't seem to—"

"Are you still making music?" asked Syd.

"Yes. I'm supposed to be. I'm going to Paris next month and then when I get back I've promised myself I will make the effort."

"Then you should," said Syd. "If it's in you, do it. Promise me you will. I can't any more. I tried. It was strange. Nothing came out."

"Will you continue to make records?" asked Nick politely. "It's what is expected of you."

"No," said Syd. "I don't think so. No, I think I'm finished with all that. I must be. Otherwise I would have done it by now. I almost made a record on my own in 1967 you know but they lost the tape I made. The demo tape with all the new songs on it. Otherwise I could have started sooner."

"You could have recorded them again, surely. I'm rarely satisfied with anything I record. I always want to do it again."

"It's the art school thing," said Syd. "Never repeat. Anyway, it's getting too late now. I'm getting too old. I'll be 30 in no time. All the bands that start up. I'd need a different haircut for a start. And some new clothes."

He laughed quietly to himself. "I'm turning into myths and fables," he said. "Kevin wrote me a song. I heard it on the radio. It was perfect. Like seeing an old photo of when we were all happy and handsome. Floating and boating. It really was all a dream, he was right. It was just like a dream."

"I've had a song written about me too," said Nick. "He probably thinks I don't know. Old sniff of the barmaid's apron. I shouldn't say that. He's shown me nothing but kindness and hospitality. And Beverley. It cheers me to see them both. Giving me shelter and a bed."

"You should tell them that, not me," said Syd. "You should always thank people for acts of kindness. And tell him you like his song. It might be important for him to know."

"I'm not the sort of person who does," said Nick. "I suspect I'm incapable. But it is a lovely song so I should, next time I see them. I will," he said as if trying to convince himself. "Yes, I certainly will."

"Kevin wanted to form a band with me," said Syd. "I could have done it. He came to see me at the flat. I'd just painted my floorboards."

"Why didn't you?" said Nick. "You'll be full of shipwrecks and regrets sooner that you think."

"Ah, well you see, he found me in somewhat ill repair," said Syd with a smile.

Nick pondered their mutual malady. Elbows on table. Chin cupped in hand. "Perhaps I should move down there by the sea. It might be better than home."

"I never go home," said Syd.

"I frequently go home," said Nick. "When I give up here I shall go home. And give up some more."

"Home is where the art is," said Syd.

"Not in my case," said Nick, although this was far from true.

"No, I was being literal," said Syd. "That's where all my paintings are. And my scribbles for songs. And my diaries."

This wasn't true either. He still had plenty of table scraps stored up in his Chelsea room. Squirrelled away for the harsh winter. Not everything had been destroyed. Yet.

"I'm missing the seasons," said Syd.

"You get seasons in London you know. Haven't you noticed?"

"Not like in Cambridge," said Syd. "You feel the weather there.

You get a different kind of mist. You see the clouds spreading across the Fens."

"After the harvest," said Nick. "The rain. That smell. I like that."

"Yes," said Syd. "Here it's either hot concrete or cold concrete."

Both men took a moment to think about their scent memory. Their common loss.

"I feel I should apologise," said Nick.

"To who?"

"To everyone. For everything. To my friends. To my family. I cause them little but suffering."

There was another significant pause during which entire lifetimes rolled by.

"I damaged my room," said Nick, eyes moistening with tears. "My lovely electric guitar. I smashed it. I did great damage to the piano. To the ornaments."

"Don't smash things up, it's counter-productive," said Syd.

"I know," said Nick, full of remorse.

"I sometimes smash things up," said Syd. "It never works. It said in that piece that they wrote in the *NME* that I smashed my head through the basement ceiling. I mean I'm not sure how I would have done that, but it said it, so myths and fables it is. I damaged the basement ceiling. There's not actually much headroom down there. It's a very cramped cellar. Some allowance could have been for the limited space I feel. Still."

Nick looked at him alarmed. All things being relative he had not yet resorted to smashing up the summer house. Or taking a pneumatic drill to the croquet lawn. He studied Syd's tousled and unwashed hair for signs of ceiling plaster.

"Some of the stuff they've been saying is true though," said Syd. "I mean I did tell the band to get a saxophone player in and some chick singers. And they did. It's on the last record."

"Sometimes I feel I should go back to the saxophone," said Nick, attempting to rekindle a little faith in his own endeavors. "Really let rip. It might be a more agreeable outlet than singing."

"Yes, you'd have the advantage of no words," said Syd. "I'm thinking I should try and find a way back into my art. That voice instead. It's preferable. I mean you can absent yourself from painting in a different way but it's still the better option."

"Preferable to music?" asked Nick.

"Yes, immensely preferable."

"Imagine if music were more like a Titian. Or Rembrandt," Nick mused. "Grander, you know. Better framed. Classical proportion. The Old Masters."

"Or the new ones. Picasso. Any of them," said Syd. "That perspective seemed reachable to me at the time. I met his son you know, Claude. In France".

"France is a good place to meet people," agreed Nick. "I'm going there soon."

"Yes, you said."

"And when I get back I'll record more songs. This milk has gone cold."

"The chicken soup was not up to much, either" said Syd. "Let's not meet here next time."

BLIND DATE, *MELODY MAKER* 19TH AUGUST 1967

Syd Barrett bounced into the *MM* office just ahead of the imminent recording of his solo LP *Boom Tunes* set to be produced by Joe Boyd. "It's really exciting," said Syd. "Apparently there are just a couple of contract things to be sorted out before we go into the studio. But that's all just business stuff. I don't think there will be any problems." A glass of Syd's favourite tipple, Campari and soda, was poured, ashtrays were summonsed and the guitarist settled down to listen to ten of this week's hottest new releases.

The Jimi Hendrix Experience, 'Burning Of The Midnight Lamp'

That introduction on the Cry Baby is beautiful. That's one of best I've heard. It's Jimi Hendrix of course. It's unbelievable, the sound he can get out of a guitar. The drumming is good too. Sort of jazz drumming, not what you'd necessarily expect to hear. Great atmosphere on this. I like to create atmospheres. It's like painting with sound. The light show makes it even better. He's had a few hits already and this will be another hit. This has a different feeling to the previous ones, though. The way it soars like that at the ending is very impressive.

Jon, 'Is It Love?'

I've no idea who this is. It has a nice mood. The backing and everything. There's some echo and handclaps too. He's sort of muffled with his singing, but I like that and the way the beat goes with the voice. I think I might have heard this on Radio London. It's a shame the pop stations are being closed down, don't you think? I used to go to the Big L discotheque when I first moved to London. I prefer the verse to the chorus. Those high voices in the background are good too. We've done that in the group on some songs. I don't expect I'll be doing so much of that on my own though.

Ken Dodd, 'Mine'

Sounds a bit crackly at the start. I'd take it back to the shop if I'd bought it. I can hear this being sung in a club. Or on *Workers' Playtime*. The bit about winter spring or harvest time is good. It's worth mentioning the seasons on a record so people know what time of year it is. I wouldn't be surprised if this is Ken Dodd. I thought it was. I'm glad I guessed correctly. He sings this sort of song very well. You need to be careful making those kind of promises on a record. People aren't always true to what they say. I wouldn't hold this against him. I suppose I'd have to say that lots of people will like it but I could survive if I never heard it again.

Smoke, 'If The Weather's Sunny'

When's it going to get started? That piano isn't really up to the task. I don't know who it is. It sounds like the Moody Blues used to sound. It sounds like it's changing its direction halfway through but then just goes back to rambling along. It's nothing much to write home about and it came as a relief when it ended. Short records are sometimes the best when they sound like this. I can imagine the group standing behind that partition on *Juke Box Jury* and making those faces when the panel says it could be better and they suggest ways of improving it. I don't think it will be a hit.

Bystanders, 'Pattern People'

I think I've heard a version of this by somebody else. Can't remember who though. Is it American? One of those groups in candy stripe blazers? It's a very well put together song. They keep telling you they're pattern people but I expect they'll be telling you something else on the B side. This will probably get played on the radio. It gets boring after a while. I like the tuba though. Is it a tuba? I might use one on my record.

The Dubliners, 'Black Velvet Band'

I know who this is but I can't remember their name. The main singer has a very distinctive voice. They did *"you're drunk you silly old moo"*, a few months ago. They sang it on *Top Of The Pops*. All sorts of music get in the charts. It shows that people aren't narrow-minded. UFO is an Irish club the rest of the week when the underground groups aren't on. There's a big shamrock on the wall. They'll probably play it there. The woman in the song seems very mysterious. Her eyes they shone like diamonds. That's good. It's a very poetic way of looking at things.

Eric Burdon, 'Good Times'

This is very funny. He regrets all the good times he had. He's putting on a jolly good show sort of voice to mimic the straight and narrow people. I don't know if he'll find a better way of life though. It's a more vaudeville style than what he used to do. I assume it's Eric Burdon. Is it? I thought it was. He's changed a lot since 'House Of The Rising Sun'. Change is good as long as you go the right way about it. He's swapped the group round a bit hasn't he? I expect they all wear radar shoes and flower power shirts. They won't always need to dress like that. It will be something else next year.

David Garrick, 'Don't Go Out Into The Rain'

It's another one of those records that tells you all about the weather. Like the one you played before about it being sunny. Is it Davy Jones of the Monkees? I've no idea who it is. Is it that singer who sounds like Anthony Newley? I can't remember his name. The one who did the song about the laughing gnome. The orchestration is similar. Then it must be someone who's already famous I expect but I can't think who. It's a peculiar notion. The idea of melting in the rain. Is she made out of sugar or is sugar her nickname? I used to have a girlfriend called Twig but you can't really put that in a song can you? Unless you disguised it really well I suppose but then what would be the point?

Ivor Cutler, 'A Great Grey Grasshopper'

Oh, this is a splendid song. This is the way to go. It's Ivor Cutler isn't it? I saw him on BBC2. The Beatles really like him. It's a very way out way of doing simple things. I like that. I'd love to do a song like that. Some of the things I've written are a bit like this but I never show them to the group. This is the best record you've played me. This and the Jimi Hendrix one. Imagine them on the same bill. He should have his own TV show. I bet the guests would be great too. I'm so glad you played me this. I'll be in a good mood for the rest of the day now.

Engelbert Humperdinck, 'The Last Waltz'

It's Engelbert isn't it? I thought it was. That voice gives it away. I expect this is going to be number one for the rest of the year. It's a bit desperate. The lyrics I mean. The band sound bored, especially the drummer, so I hope they're getting well paid. Imagine if this was the last song of the night at the church hall discotheque. You'd be better off doing your loving in the bus shelter. Take it off. It's horrible.

ESCALATOR OVER THE HILL

The day had the washed-out pallor of subdued Technicolor as Syd surveyed the city from his ninth floor window. He settled into another static dérive and pondered his disinclination. The room was temporarily becalmed, but all about him was the evidence of atrophy and damage. The guitars that were no longer strummed. The encrusted cups and plates that received only a cursory swill under the taps. Fruit flies hovering in fetid air. A fridge full of inedibles. Curdled milk and mould-coated Blue Band. Cardboard boat cargoes of musty figs and shrivelled pitted dates. Fermenting smoked oysters that resembled laboratory specimens in their cloudy glass jars. Rotting pork chops and pock-marked salami. Blue white cultures on tomatoes in leak dampened brown paper bags. All decaying away like some petri dish art instillation. A modern day Miss Haversham's, reconfigured as Barney's Beanery. Viewing by appointment only. Benign curator going somnambulistically about his business as if viewing the exhibits for the first time. Projects started and abandoned. A coffee table mound of polystyrene cups serrated into thin spaghetti strips like tiny macramé lampshades. Oxfam book purchases scissored into random cut ups and pasted crudely onto cork board. Detritus strewn about the carpet. The trampled ruination of wasted days. Fraying temper and late-night anguish marked in wall stains and cracked glass. Broken crockery foot-swept into corners. An unread notification from the hotel management warning that he was one tolerance away from eviction. The cleaning lady who refused to come in unless he started airing the room. The complaints from adjoining tenants about the banging on the wall when their TV was on at a reasonable volume.

Syd fed all options through his differscope and they all came out nullified and identical. Be silent, be satisfied, he told himself in an attempt at reassurance. A harking back to his parent's calm Quaker temperaments and their shared passivity. A consolation mantra. An effort to convince himself that this malady would pass. But still his thoughts tarnished in torpor and turmoil. He lit a cigarette, which like all the others smoked him. Life dragged down to the butt. Saucer ashtrays full of stubs and stale blue cinders.

Something about this day was different though. He realised he had to be somewhere, but where? He recalled vague promises he had made to himself. Nothing on the calendar. Just birthday prompts for family he rarely saw. A present perhaps? A book token? No not books. Guitars. He thought it might have something to do with guitars. A Guild or Martin maybe. But he didn't have a Guild or Martin among his diminishing stock. Not a model that he ever played. He sifted through the rubble of memory to try and retrieve whatever it was.

On Saturday November 23rd 1974 Nick Drake spent the day with friends. The atmosphere was convivial. Warm welcome. Guests ushered into the glow. Curtains drawn. Rooms that echo with easy laughter. Conversation. Music. Wine. Supper. People come and go as they so often do. Always a next time.

The sunset burned scarlet. The evening sky was tyre tread. Another late autumn show of defiant splendour with winter hovering in the wings, awaiting its cue. A waxing gibbous moon peeking through just as everyone was leaving, illuminating doorstep goodbyes and homeward treks.

By Sunday the drawbridge was up again. The portcullis down. Closed off. Obdurate. Incommunicado. Nick retired early to his room that evening. He listened to Bach's *Brandenburg Concerto No 2* and it reminded him of that glorious night at the Queen Elizabeth Hall and the showcase concert, the string ensemble, the fumbled and gauche intros, but happy then, happy that people seemed to believe in him and were willing to provide the creative and emotional space for him to blossom and shine in the springtime of his life.

After listening to Bach he turned on Radio 3 and was surprised to hear the lingering string crescendo of Barry White's 'Can't Get Enough Of Your Love, Babe'. White's rich baritone purring the paradox and ambiguity of desire. Love overflowing yet love unfulfilled. The commitment fix. The drums metronomic and on it. The presenter Derek Jewell came on afterwards and bestowed high cultural blessing upon the benighted White. Orchestrator supreme. Next, he played two tracks from John Lennon's recent *Walls And Bridges* LP. The first, 'Old Dirt Road', had a dirge-like opening similar to that of 'Jealous Guy'. The sound of Lennon coasting. The words hard to make out, drowned in sumptuous production. A harmony vocalist Nick didn't recognise as Harry Nilsson. He thought back to the rawness of 'Cold Turkey', a track he surprised his friends by raving about. A junk-sick hit single so brutally raw and honest and alive, no frills, no embellishment. It pierced Nick to his very soul and made him fearful that something similar lurked inside his own. 'Old Dirt Road' was a plod in comparison. *"Keep on keeping on"* Lennon urged over the outro. Lukewarm platitudes. Worn out slogans. Jive homilies debased by riches.

Jewell played another track off *Walls And Bridges*, 'Bless You'. Muddy narcoleptic mix. Cocktail lounge slick. Tastefully bland arrangement. All tidied up. Lennon's voice pure and yearning though, the only good thing to emerge from the sludge. Singing like he meant it. Being the jealous guy again. Bruised by loss. Actual loss that listeners could relate to. Thinking of his woman in someone else's arms. A different sweat on the bedding. Bad karma. Not the instant kind. The type that seeps deeper than any sex stain on the sheets. Nick tried to remember the last time he was drunk, or even pleasurably stoned. Or felt the intimacy of a reassuring hug. Even last night, congenial though it was, he still shunned the loving touch.

'Bless You' faded on the radio. Jewell paid lip-service to a rock god. Summonsing Fab Four glories in order to excuse the current lovelorn manifestation of a mislaid muse. Nick contrasted the presenter's homage with what he had just heard. He thought the arrangements pedestrian and complacent. Lennon's charisma worn down by weariness and time. It depressed him that so much music had become this lacklustre. Had Derek Jewell played another track from the album, 'Whatever Gets You Thru The Night', who knows how things might have played out? The directness of the sentiment might have appealed to Nick, might have cleansed a few clogged pores, might have bucked his ideas up. Or perhaps he would have just thought it bland, insultingly platitudinous. Just another preachy trouble cure from a quick fix world. If only getting through the night were that easy.

Jewell then turned his attention to *Escalator Over The Hill*, a triple LP by Carla Bley and Paul Haines. Released three years earlier on the JCOA label, the presenter thought this a very significant album, and dedicated a lengthy proportion of the programme to it. After some explanatory comment about the scope and ambition of the record he played side three in its entirety, followed by a nine and a half minute track from side six called 'End Of Rawalpindi'. Nick struggled to find reference points for it all. The record's intensity panicked him. Side three commenced like German cabaret music in woozy waltz time but the dramatis personae and sheer scale of the offering overwhelmed him. It was all too busy and bustling, like being flattened against a wall by the rush of city crowd commuters. He'd had dreams like that. Walking headlong into the throng and never emerging out the other side.

There seemed to be no let-up. Even when the full ensemble arrangements paused for a reflective interlude he braced himself for the next frantic onslaught of oration, brass and heavy rock guitar. He sat on the edge of his bed, scared to turn the radio off, gripped as so often by some sick spell he was powerless to break. *"It's not what you can say"* intoned a trance like voice doused in echo, *"it's not what you can do"*. Spooked by yet another invocation of spirit voices talking to him through the aether, he took the message as instruction. Things beyond his measure. Omens. There was a brief moment on 'End Of Rawalpindi' that reminded him of a more abrasive *Astral Weeks*, the way the melodies overlapped and intertwined. He thought back to a time, so recent and yet so distant, when all the bold aspirations of jazz, rock, poetry and theatrics merged and everything seemed possible. He could once imagine a time when all this grand ambition still seemed scalable, a rock that could be pushed up the mountain and rolled down the other side but no longer, not now. He listened to Jack Bruce wailing what he thought was *"it's a game"* and took it as confirmation. He listened to Bruce's voice curling around the rhythm, Eastern inflections, raga tones, and thought of all the drive and aspiration he once had. He turned off the radio.

High up in Chelsea Cloisters, Syd too was listening to *Escalator Over The Hill*. He found much of it to his liking. He submitted willingly to the incessant chaos. Bits of 'Businessmen' reminded him of 'Interstellar Overdrive'. If he imagined hard enough there was still sufficient memory that he could restore. Welded arcs of echorec, shards of starsparks sent out into the cold clear night. The lyrics too he found palatable. He correctly identified what Nick heard as *"it's a game"* as *"it's again"*. The tape loop of life. Everything circling endlessly in an Escher illusion. No up. No down. Perspective askew. An abnormality he had grown used to. The words cascaded and whirled in random paper trail fragments. He drifted in and out of the unsense. It seemed a familiar place.

Timeworn and weary Nick consoled himself with a little Camus. He read then reread a couple of densely philosophical paragraphs and felt himself edging a little closer to understanding. Oh, my tiny tiny life he muttered, half remembering a line from the televised *Roads To Freedom*. All the wisdom you ever really need is in here, he said to himself, comfort patting the cover and pressing the open book to his still warm heart. *The Myth Of Sisyphus* portioning out truth particles to him in late night revelatory flashes. That's when the truths often came, bare naked and more sensuous than any flesh. Reminders of the ceaseless toil. The heavy measured steps. "No fate that cannot be surmounted by scorn," Camus said. "No sun without shadow."

Keep going. That's the message. But in the small hours that loom so large Nick's instincts run counter to that, even though Camus assures him that each atom is a world. Every mineral flake of the night-filled mountain is a universe. Blake had already taught him the grain of sand thing. He had the measure of that. Camus offered confirmation and consolation. He thought of every youthful insight he'd ever woven into a song, some earnestly callow, some poetically astute, some vainglorious, some humble, some shrouded in cryptic mystery, some bursting into holy flame before he could even get them down on the page.

And yet, he thought to himself, and yet somehow it's never enough. None of it is. The craft guild applique. The precisely calibrated technique. When words are no longer adequate tools for the telling it all goes awry. It used to be simple. Now it all spirals away before instinct reaches finger touch, and it keeps doing that until in the end exertion is halted and there's only afterthought and leftovers and echoes of images that grow dim in the pale winter light. The talent you can cocoon in isolation, you will find succour and constant renewal there if you have the emotional reserves to fall back on, but what if you no longer have the reserves, if you've drained the tank empty of everything but anguish? If you no longer have sufficient stratagems to combat the unseen marauding armies that gather. What then? What awaits once you relinquish the gifts? You want to cry out in pain but you strain to make a baby fist. You sit in a lonely kitchen at 3am and you ponder your options. What it would be like to be gone. What it would be like to absent yourself permanently from another round of ever-shortening days. You scoop memory dust from the bottom of a cereal bowl and you wonder. You think of that Jackson C Frank song you used to sing before all this. Before the beginning. Before goodly sin and the fall. 'Here Come The Blues'. A bittersweet rendition, an exquisite parody of mannerism. Donning the garb of the sophisticated pasticheur when such garments suited you. Riding the coat tails of the ghosts of mimicry. Here comes lonely. Here come the blues. Here come more portents in the shape of ominous song. No bottle of pills can kill this pain. Would you ever want to put that to the test? To die without knowing if one was adequate to the task of living? Hoping that one day someone, somewhere would have sought out what you were seeking, too. But they would have arrived by now, wouldn't they? If they were coming. Would anyone notice your absence, or ask after you or enquire about your welfare? Haven't seen Nick in a while. Is he okay? Express polite concern and then continue walking the dog down a quiet country lane. Pausing to marvel at the lithesome poetry of the harvest barley swaying lazily in the wind.

You muse on all that as you cradle a cup. You walk to the window to stare at the waxing gibbous moon. You gaze blankly at the star-flung dispersals of the galaxies. You wash down a handful of pills with a swig and a gulp and then another. And then to bed to sleep it off. Or wait for providence to take you in its grasp. Soon you go drowsy and begin your descent. Others in the house are deep in their own sleep, oblivious to the unfathomable depths of your slumber.

Those final sinking seconds. A low wintery mist hangs in the distance, shrouding the trees, dulling the silhouettes of the hedgerows. There is a beckoning glow just beyond that bend in the road where spirits gather and souls depart. And after that, a sort of lurid alluring half-light. Mute the music. No more sound, just a brief occluded flicker and candle tallows extinguished by unseen slender fingers. Existence slips the grip. No more illusion. No more delusion. No more delirium. Dreamless waves. Submerge and drift away. Follow the fading star to the last horizon. Take the escalator over the hill. Gaze into the blue grey vale of the eternal. Then gone.

Syd went in search of absence. He remembered what it was. Nick said he had smashed his electric guitar and Syd promised him he would replace it. "You can have one of mine." An act of kindness to go with all the other acts of kindness that connected him with who he used to be. The kid in the coffee bar and college canteen who would always give you his only coins if you hadn't got the change for a cup of tea. The waning pop star who told his friend Mick that he would still like to be rich so he could put money into his physicals and buy food for all his friends. Thinking of art as 'physical'. An enactment. A doing word. Now that there was no longer any doing, he thought the least that he could do was pass on a surplus guitar to someone who seemed to need it far more than he did. He realised that the act of creation was keeping Nick alive. He suspected it was killing him, too, but didn't Nick tell him also that he was still writing songs, that he was intending to make a new LP. Syd had suggested to him that he write a hit single. "People seem to like them." Nick had just shrugged and laughed a rare laugh at the preposterous thought of it, but you never know, he thought, you never truly know, do you?

And so, on the Monday morning of November 25th Syd selected a cherry red Epiphone Crestwood from his diminishing stock and pledged that he would seek out the man he had spoken to across tea stained tables and would gift him with this guitar. It still had the £185 s/h price tag on it and Syd had never so much as strummed a note on it since he'd brought it home from the shop. He'd bought it chiefly because he liked the name. He thought Epiphone Crestwood sounded like an old Delta bluesman, out of the same mould as someone who might christen their son Thelonious Sphere. Belatedly it occurred to him that he had never once asked Nick his surname and that this might prove problematic. The only Nick he knew was the Nick in his old band. He reasoned though that the music industry was a small place. He imagined London as a rolled-out map, showing all the recording studios and record company offices. He thought of all the times, even after he'd stopped making records, even when blank-eyed and out of it when he had walked into the Speakeasy or some other music industry watering hole and discovered that his membership of an unspoken club still gained him entry and acceptance and that strangely familiar faces were prepared to stand him a drink. Where to begin though? First, he went to Trident Studio in St Anne's Court just off Wardour Street. Neat little reception area. Queen's *Sheer Heart Attack* playing at conversation-friendly volume through state of the art speakers. Everyone acting out their allocated part with the requisite degree of mildly stoned indifference. Rock biz sang-froid. Absence of bustle and hustle. Hip receptionist with frosted orange lips, frankincense scented sheepskin coat draped over her office chair. She casually regards the bedraggled looking visitor, adjusts her big round tinted glasses, and says "can I help you?" in a classless blasé drawl.

Syd's enquiry threw a spanner into the laid-back protocol of the day. Internal switchboard calls were made. Studio engineers were summoned from their coffee break. An A&R man recognised the guitar carrying musician and leaned into the receptionist's ear as Syd stood gazing at a glass framed portrait of David Bowie high kicking in white pants. "What do you think of the sounds, Syd?" he asked as 'Killer Queen' was nudged up in volume. "Is comic opera making a comeback?" came the reply in a vacant whisper.

The visitor's predicament was repeated to the gathering.

"I think I might know the cat you mean. Nic Jones was it?" said a tape operator.

Syd offered an involuntary shrug of the shoulders.

"Folk singer isn't he?" asked the studio manager.

Nick didn't sound like a folk a singer from how little he had described himself to Syd and sometimes you can tell a lot about a person from how they don't describe themselves.

"Well, that's the only one I can think of, Nic Jones," repeated the tape operator when Syd failed to respond. "Very skilful guitar player."

"Yes, he sounds clever," said Syd hesitantly, although for all the clarification this offered he might as well have said, "Yes, he wears a green jacket and blue trousers."

"Go down to Transatlantic," said an electrician. "They'll know, mate. All the folk musicians are on Transatlantic."

"Do you have an address?"

"I'll have a look. I think I have a phone number. I'll give them a call."

"You're very kind," said Syd. "It's awfully good of you to go to this trouble."

"No bother at all mate. I think they're in Hampstead."

"Are you sure Dave? I think they might have moved," said the receptionist. "Excuse me. I have to take this call."

Syd took a taxi to Hampstead. No dice.

The next day he took a taxi to the EMI studios at Abbey Road, but when he walked up the steps towards reception he suddenly froze in fear, remembering his previous fruitless visit three months earlier. Despondently he got on a bus and headed back towards the West End. I'll try some other places tomorrow, he thought. I'll make a list and I'll pretend I'm on The Knowledge. "He might have recorded the new LP by now," he said, causing a fellow passenger to look up from his crossword puzzle and stare at the muttering stranger.

Nick was found in the late morning stillness. Nanny first, then Mother Molly, a portion of her own life draining in an instant.

Everything framed and contained in that moment. The child you bore. The soul bond you hold onto and the rest you let go. No more dishevelled shuffle down village lanes. No more avoidance of greeting. No more anger or anguish. At peace. The necessary arrangements are made. Friends and family gather at the place of worship and go placidly amidst. Branches all bare now, no leaves left, save for the gnarled and twisted church yard yew, evergreen and firmly rooted, resisting the winter wind. All these personable young strangers come to pay respect, threading their remembrance into memory beads. Tales that warm a cold room in the telling. Igniting brief flickering sparks like freshly lit logs that spit from the grate. These people his parents never knew, who once shared their own meaningful or agonising silences with Molly and Rodney Drake's only son. Living in the suspended animation of an Aquarian age they thought might never end, but all things do end. Here they come now with their customary politeness and tired eyes and well elocuted sing-song sad hellos. The shortest days. Holly and star leafed Ivy. Sonorous hymns and occasional sidelong glances at others in the congregation. Everyone surrendering their private compassion to the shared moment, cloaking secular insecurities in tentative god song. The hedgerows laden with blood red berries, the lanes serenaded by the plaintive lamentation chirp of a foraging robin. Brittle blue sky. Ground already frosting. Must be going. Hesitant handshakes, hugs and goodbyes. Off into the dusk light. Waved away and heavy-legged treading back to the absence in the house. Lights going on in distant cottages. Wood smoke and hearth logs and the strangely comforting barren December drabness of it all.

Christmas comes. One for sorrow. One less place at table. One less ribbon-bowed parcel under the tree. Nan, who once changed your nappies, pampered and dabbed your pink wriggling form, takes a forgetful extra clutch of silver service from the drawer. Molly goes to the foot of the stairs as if to ask will you be joining us for supper Nicky before the words catch in her throat and she pads silently past the untouched piano. Sheet music left exactly as it was. Gay finds that unrehearsed lines are sometimes the hardest ones to speak. Rodney polishes a pair of shoes for no reason he can remember.

The winter grave is covered by a thick quilt of fallen leaves, ochre and rust. Grass mound slowly settles. Freshly dug earth merges with other earth dug long ago. A simple headstone engraving gives benefit to doubt.

And now we rise.

Preachers and pulpit dwellers who knew little or nothing of Nick's music assumed that was something biblical and puzzled over the attribution. Ezekiel, someone suggested hopefully. Ecclesiastes, ventured another.

And we are everywhere.

Metaphysics etched into stone and air. The leaves undisturbed where they lay. Turning to pulp and mulch. The snowdrops and crocuses come and go and still hardly anyone outside of family or friends is aware of the absence. And then, come February, that writer guy, the one who talked about tortured Syd and cellar headroom, and turned him into myths and fables, that same writer guy pens another poignant eulogy to doomed and damaged youth. And only then does the wider audience learn of Nick's fate, the kids who buy Bowie and the students who listen to Little Feat and believe in *Pretzel Logic*. Only at this page-turning moment do they find out what had happened to the barely known Nick with his three albums on Island. And even then, how little they really know. Clairvoyance was never in his gift so Nick could not have foreseen that one day the young would embrace his sad and saddening perplexity and find solace in the muse that had ultimately deserted and undone him.

And slow they came at first, the new disciples, the ones who carry their shrine in their head and rite of passage paperbacks in backpacks. Their hesitant inquisitive footfall leads through a creaky gate to an oak shaded grave and then tentatively over the gravel to the house. They build that inner draught-proof place where candles never go out. And eventually they are everywhere just like the headstone said. But not yet. Not for some while. At first there is only the absence, the barely ever there even when he was there. Spectral auras. Ghost imprints. Time's tidal drift. But year on year, more of these willing converts come and sit on the bench in the church porch and bear witness to the passing of the seasons. They watch the slanting spring rain and the summer cloud shadows sweeping the fields and the gossamer webs gleaming on autumn morns and they hold true to the one thing that encompasses them all. The bond that cannot be broken when day is done. They find sustenance in these secular prayer offerings and the glossolalia spoken in a tongue that they intuitively understand. The songs are cast anew in ancient sunlight. They assume a purity that cannot be weathered by age or measured in the simple slow decay of the years. 'Day Is Done' resonates with multiple echoes of the English hymnal. Sabine Baring Gould's *"Now the day is over/Night is drawing nigh"*, written a century earlier in 1867, also contains the line *"When the morning wakens/Then I may arise"*. Robert Murray M'Cheyne's 'How Much I Owe', written in 1837, commences with the lines *"When this passing world is done/When has sunk yon glaring sun"*. The concluding verse of John Ellerton's 'When The Day Of Toil Is Done', written in 1870, commences *"When the breath of life is flown/When the grave must claim its own"*. The penultimate verse begins *"When for vanished days we yearn/Days that never can return"*. Nick's songs plough deeper and richer into the soil of the land than even these young converts know. Their lyrical evocations are spirit-driven and timeless. Their immortality is etched into the ages and will outlast any lichened and storm blasted headstone.

And meanwhile back in London, Syd, oblivious, continues to seek out the absence. Spending his days in futile pursuit. Going from studio to studio to record company office clutching an Epiphone Crestwood then returning footsore and hungry to his Chelsea retreat. Up there on the ninth floor, slipping ever looser the surly bonds of reason. Entire days, weeks, hibernating. Phoning out for food. Going to bad seed up there above and beyond it all and out of reach. Feeling the earth willing him down, down lower than the elevator ever goes. Braving the outside less and less, watching dead leaves skitter in the wind, holding onto his insides some days, clutching tight in case his ulcerating dyspeptic guts spill out onto the pavement. Subject to the gravitational cross-tides of despondency and sloth. Spring heeled no longer. Medicated shuffle and slouch. Just temporary, the doctor said. Get you back on your feet. Stabilise you for a bit. Negotiating the tolerable banalities of everyday life and shunning everything else. And still walking everywhere. Entire A-Z pages covered in his prescription-dazed dérive. Trailing an imaginary tuk-tuk round Chinatown for his own irregular amusement. Going into launderettes and watching other people's washing for a bit. Sitting in the barber's queue, then changing his mind about a haircut. Maintaining his habit of walking into the tobacconists and buying a different brand of cigarettes every time. Disque Bleu one day. Dunhill the next. Doing the pedestrian drift from shop window to shop window. Crazy paving London in his psychogeographic footprint. Disorder slowly sliding into a form of mannered delirium. The guy you gave a wide berth to if you saw him coming. Some weeks better than others.

He divested himself of all fashionable apparel and any remaining trappings of pop stardom. As he began to put on weight he threw out all his satin and silk and began buying beige or blue serge slacks from Marks and Spencer's, short-sleeved shirts with a breast pocket from C&A, hooped T-shirts from Horne Brothers or the Army and Navy Store. Out went the snakeskin boots from the Chelsea Cobbler, the sleeveless orange Afghan from Granny Takes A Trip, discarded along with all the ruffled shirts and chiffon scarves and crushed velvet and paisley. Out went anything that might remind him of a time when the errant doting daughters of brigadiers and clerics used to rouge his lips and kohl his eyes and send him off to *Top Of The Pops* dressed in Petticoat Lane cast-offs and frock coats and furs. He reverted instead to an older benign expressionless uncle version of himself. A walking denial.

On his more agreeable days Syd still liked to seek out former haunts to remind himself of who he could have been. He'd walk to the Tate or National or V&A. He'd sit in the same Bloomsbury café where he and David used to discuss the pop stars and TV personalities they'd seen on the streets when they first arrived giddy-eyed and hopeful in Swinging London. Three points for Petula Clark getting out of a sports car. Two for Hank Marvin and Bruce Welch emerging from a taxi. One for Kenny Lynch outside the Talk of the Town happily signing an autograph. Four for Benny Hill strolling tanned and healthy across Chelsea Bridge.

These were the brighter days, ember remnants of pleasurable memory, brain waves surging with survival strategies. There were still moments that amused him while he was out on his restless travels. London as a versatile character actor will rarely give an under rehearsed performance. There was the man in Hyde Park who shouted "come back here you rag-eared little cunt" at his gleefully off the leash mongrel dog. The kid who jumped into an Arab's unattended Rolls Royce outside the Dorchester Hotel and, unused to the luxury bite of the clutch, stalled the engine immediately. Syd watched him run off down Park Lane, out of condition door staff in fruitless panting pursuit. Some of Sammy's off-colour jokes in the Cloisters reception area amused him too, but he was less enthused when Sammy insisted on showing him the daily antics of Hagar the Horrible, a box panel strip cartoon in *The Sun*. Comedy Vikings were never his thing.

These were the rare moments of episodic relief. On more turmoil-driven days he found himself increasingly in the grasp of some insurmountable malaise, no longer sinking, sunk. He tended to avoid all but the most necessary social contact. It only led to confusion and strife. One early evening he found himself in an upstairs bar in Leicester Square. "Didn't this place used to be the Whisky a Go-Go?" a friendly stranger buying drinks at the bar asked erroneously. "The one on Sunset Strip you mean?" answered Syd, causing the stranger to retreat from the line of fire and back to his table whereupon repeating the exchange a music business colleague told him who he had just been talking to, and thus another cryptic encounter worked its way into the apocrypha.

Eventually the guitar quest was quietly put aside. It had become a burden to him. A fruitless pursuit. His right shoulder ached with all the carrying and if it hadn't been for the courteous taxi drivers who tolerated his incessant questions about The Knowledge he would have given up sooner. One day he slipped into Top Gear in Denmark Street, a favoured location for so many of his compulsive purchases, and surreptitiously propped the Epiphone next to a display rack. He was making his way back towards the Charing Cross Road when a young assistant called out and beckoned him back to the shop. "You accidentally left this," he said. Syd, for once, feigned absent mindedness. It seemed he couldn't even give the thing away. It became an albatross, an unwanted appendage.

Had he only made the connection, the Sound Techniques studio in Old Church Street, where Nick had recorded most of his songs, was a but a ten minute walk away from Chelsea Cloisters. Here Syd might have found resolution and would have learned about his friend's fate. A tape box, all marked up with those final sessions, will have still sat warm upon the shelves. In the not so long ago days of optimism and hope Syd, too, had recorded here. His first sessions with the band before Abbey Road beckoned. Joe made them crackle and come alive. The sound of UFO compressed and condensed into a hit single. But now even the recent past was a blur of ghostly corrosion. As the weeks wore on and the task wore him down his own state of mind deteriorated alarmingly. One day, in his confusion, he even turned up at the BBC in White City in the expectation that Nick would be appearing on that evening's recording of *Top Of The Pops*. And even if he wasn't, he reasoned unreasonably, somebody would know when he had last been on the show. He never got past the wary commissioner on the gate. One bright and breezy April afternoon the instrument was purposefully abandoned in an empty tube carriage on the Hammersmith and City line at Latimer Road. By then Syd's daily sojourns had started to be woven into the narrative of rock lore. A rumour here. A sighting there. Those who had witnessed him on his travels and liked to ascribe motives to every mundane act assumed that Syd must be about to resume his recording career. Others read more fatalistic portends into the gesture. "He wanders round London carrying a guitar, as if to remind him of his former glory," spake the fable makers, saying more about themselves and their romanticising of failure than they ever said about Syd. There was always somebody somewhere writing about the faded glory of the culture – a culture only two decades old that had barely developed a paunch yet. Now Syd became their poster boy for doomed youth. Nick would eventually join him, the two of them finally reunited in unfulfilled legacy, supposition and myth.

On the morning of June 4th 1975, a warm sunny Wednesday, Syd walked into a barber's shop on the Fulham Palace Road and asked if they wouldn't mind awfully shaving his hair down to a number one crop. The barber, although reluctant, was more than grateful for the custom and the £5 tip proffered in advance. It had been a quiet week and there was no one else waiting in the queue. "Going away this year, sir?" he asked routinely. "I have no way of knowing," said Syd. The radio was on, playing the hits of the day, Judy Collins, 'Send In The Clowns', Disco Tex and his Sex-O-Lettes, 'Get Dancing', 10cc, 'I'm Not In Love'. "Time for a revived 45," said the DJ just before the 10.30pm news. 'Penny Lane' played. The sun was ablaze and as blond as butter therefore a fireman did not rush in from the pouring rain. It was mid-summer, much too early for a nurse to be selling poppies from a tray. But otherwise it was still just as if everybody was in a play. Closing scene. The cast ready to take their final bow and curtain calls. "The Beatles there from the bygone days of flower power," said the DJ inanely. "Do you remember flower power? Painted faces, kaftans and love beads and all that? I said Grandad, take it off, you look ridiculous." The barber chuckled to himself. Syd studied his face in the mirror. His puffy pallor, his surprisingly baby faced blank eyed stare. "Could you shave my eyebrows as well?" he asked. "Oh, no I'm not doing that for you," replied the barber, meeting Syd's reflected gaze nervously and hurrying along with his task. "Never mind," said Syd. "I can always do that at home." "I really wouldn't advise it sir," urged the barber, removing a shoulder towel, hastily brushing his customer's bare neck and swiftly swivelling him out of his chair.

"Doing anything exciting today sir?" he asked politely as Syd stood gently patting his newly shorn crop and looking quizzically as if at another person in the mirror.

"Not as such," replied Syd. "Not today. Tomorrow though I'm off to meet my makers."

A WORD ABOUT SOURCES.

Most of this book spilled from my own creative imagination. Where I have allowed reality to intervene I bounced ideas off my primary research for *Syd Barrett : A Very Irregular Head* (Faber and Faber 2010) and the Drake estate's anthology *Nick Drake : Remembered For A While* (John Murray. 2014) With regard to the latter, detail from this essential and definitive compendium gives local colour to several chapters, and in the case of chapters ten and fourteen draws specifically upon Rodney Drake's diary entries. Chapter eighteen, *An Old Fairytale* uses as its launchpad the section from *Remembered For A While* entitled *The Fourth Album* written by Peter Paphides. The song titles are Nick Drake's. The melodies, tempos and other embellishments came from my own head and will remain there.

I am also indebted to Robert Medley's autobiography *Drawn From The Life* (Faber and Faber 1983) for shining so much light on the long 1960s – i.e. the 1960s that begins in the 1920s. It also helped me flesh out the intellectual milieu of the Camberwell School of Art that Syd encountered as a student. In the chapter entitled *Wayfarers All* I adapted the reading of Hexagram 24 (Fiu Returning) from Sam

Reifler's *I Ching : A New Interpretation For Modern Times* (Bantam Books 1974.) The Genome Project, which has faithfully reproduced online the entire contents of the *Radio Times* complete with all BBC programme listings, remains the essential internet resource for anyone who wants a little historical actuality to accompany their parallel reality.

The Map Is Not The Territory by Alan Woods and Ralph Rumney (Manchester University Press 2001) introduced me to Rumney's concept of the static dérive and enhanced my painterly perspective no end.

Much of the philosophical underpinning of the Nick Drake portion of this book is informed by *The Myth of Sisyphus and other essays* by Albert Camus (Hamish Hamilton 1955.)

The rest you'll have to work out for yourself. I wish you well on your quest.

Rob Chapman. January 2024.

OTHER BOOKS BY ROB CHAPMAN

Selling The Sixties :
The Pirates and Pop Music Radio
(Routledge. 1992)

Album Covers From The Vinyl Junkyard
(Booth Clibborn Editions. 1997)

Dusk Music
(Flambard Press. 2008)

Syd Barrett : A Very Irregular Head
(Faber and Faber 2010)

Psychedelia and Other Colours
(Faber and Faber 2015)

Ad Lib. Repeat To Fade
(self published 2020)

All I Want Is Out Of Here
(self published 2021)

The Lyrics of Syd Barrett
(Omnibus Press 2021)

www.rob-chapman.com

Printed in Great Britain
by Amazon

46187031R00155